PRAISE

for Preraphaelites in Love by Gay Daly

"This book is a perfect handbook to Victorian times in England . . . Love, sex, style, elegance, wit, adventure—all of that is in these pages."
—Carolyn See, author of *Golden Days*, in the *Los Angeles Times*

"This book resembles a well-structured George Eliot novel, and like George Eliot, Daly has the rare gift of being able to convey the sheer rapturous joy of artists painting at the height of their powers."
—Joseph Olshan, author of *Clara's Heart*, in *Newsday*

"A hypnotic, intelligent, sensational book."
—*Los Angeles Times*

"An often touching, sometimes hilarious, always engrossing portrait of the high-minded Victorian Brotherhood, their romances and their almost incestuous cross-connections . . . amorous biography at its witty, perceptive best."
—*Publishers Weekly*

"Engrossing . . . Though the convolutions of these relationships are quite complex, Daly succeeds in keeping her narrative clear, and is particularly astute in delving into the attitude of the period towards women."
—*Kirkus Reviews*

MORE
From The Sager Group

Seven Men: Memories of an Unconventional Love Life

Lifeboat No. 8: An Untold Tale of Love, Loss and Surviving the Titanic

The Stories We Tell: Classic True Tales by America's Greatest Women Journalists

New Stories We Tell: True Tales by America's Next Generation of Great Women Journalists

Newswomen: Twenty-five Years of Front Page Journalism

Janet's World: The Inside Story of Washington Post Pulitzer Fabulist Janet Cooke

I'll Show You Mine: Everyday People Talk Candidly About Love, Sex and Intimacy.

High Tolerance: A Novel of Sex, Race, Celebrity, Murder. . . and Marijuana.

For more information, please see www. TheSagerGroup.net

A NOVEL BY

GAY DALY

MISS
HAVILLAND

Miss Havilland, A Novel

Copyright © 2020 Gay Daly
All rights reserved.

Cover Designed by Michael J. Walsh and
Siori Kitajima, SF AppWorks LLC

Cover Illustration (detail): A. Giametti,
Waving Tearful Farewell. Date: circa 1915
Copyright © Mary Evans Picture Library 2017

Cataloging-in-Publication data for this book is
available from the Library of Congress
ISBNs:
Paperback
978-1-950154-03-6
1-950154-03-3
eBook
978-1-950154-04-3
1-950154-04-1

Published by The Sager Group LLC
www.TheSagerGroup.net

MISS HAVILLAND

A NOVEL BY

GAY DALY

THE SAGER GROUP

Artifex Te Adiuva

For Jay
For Woo
For Wendy

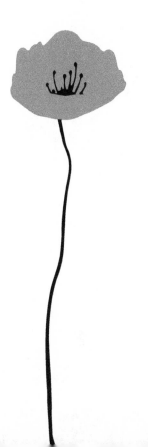

CONTENTS

CHAPTER 1

The old Billy would have been the first passenger to jump off the train. Waiting at the head of the platform, I searched every face, hoping the next would be his, growing more anxious by the minute. He'd telegraphed asking me to meet this train. I'd already spent two weeks in Paris waiting for him after I'd finished my work at General Pershing's headquarters. But many of the wounded at Billy's field hospital hadn't been able to leave after the armistice—they were too weak to travel— and so he had stayed on to nurse them.

Sunlight was streaming through the glass roof of the station. The steam from the engines and the heat of the sun made the platform warm, almost too warm, but after the long, damp winter I was grateful. I knew Billy would be, too, since he'd spent those months sleeping in a drafty canvas tent.

The winter and the misery of his patients had depressed his spirits; he hadn't hidden that in his letters. But I was more concerned about what I'd seen when I'd last visited him at his hospital, especially the hollowed-out grayness of his eyes. By the time the last straggler from the train, a weary-looking woman in a ratty fur coat, passed the barrier, fear had begun to poke its bony fingers into my chest.

I was holding a handkerchief Billy's mother had given me when I was in high school, a lovely thing she'd embroidered with lilies of the valley. Startled by a ripping sound, I looked down and saw I'd been twisting it in my hands without realizing it. Staring at the torn bit of linen, I fought back tears.

Perhaps I'd missed Billy as he left the train, though that seemed unlikely. Taller than most Frenchmen, he would have stood out in the crowd. Thousands of times over the years I'd seen his rangy frame and the lithe grace with which he carried himself, the sea-green eyes. I knew Billy's face better than I knew my own. So I began an increasingly frantic search. I tried the *tabac* in case he'd gone to buy cigarettes or a newspaper, checked the café and went out into the street. Still no Billy.

Running back into the station, I made myself sit down on a bench to try to calm myself as I watched dust motes float on the air. People passed by—amputees with crutches, men with empty sleeves, women dressed in black—all bearing their sorrow with dignity. How could I justify falling apart in front of them? Wherever Billy was, he was alive—after all, he'd sent that telegram—and he had come through the war, miraculously, unhurt.

I finally spotted him leaning against a wall near the board that announced arrivals and departures, smoking a cigarette, and studying a scrawny pigeon strutting at his feet. I almost wept with relief. But then I thought: He asked me to meet him here. Why isn't he searching for me?

Only four years earlier, after the British had taken a beating at Ypres and the Germans were closing in on Paris, Billy had climbed aboard a train at home in California, eager to join the fight, eager to be the daring and honorable man his father would have wanted him to be. As his train left the station in San Jose that morning, despite the grave danger he was heading toward, he'd waved and blown a last few kisses.

The man who dropped his cigarette and crushed it with the toe of his boot was a grim shadow of that boy. Approaching quietly, I touched his arm, hoping that once he saw me his face would light up. Just at that moment, the pigeon flapped its wings, startling both of us, and we watched as it sailed high into the metal fretwork that supported the station's glass roof.

Reaching out to touch my cheek with his fingertips, he traced its curve the way a blind man might, as if to make sure that cheek was really mine. But when I put my arms around him, his body felt stiff, like an iron bar. I whispered in his ear, as a mother would to a frightened child, "It's okay, it's over. I love you. You're tired, we're going home." In a low voice, so soft I almost couldn't hear it, he murmured, "I love you, too."

Smoothing the front of his khaki shirt, he tucked it in, checked his watch, and reached up to ruffle my hair.

"There wasn't a blessed thing to eat on that train. I'm hungry, and you better be, too." That sounded like the old Billy, so I risked teasing him.

"Didn't they feed you at that hospital? You're skinny as a garter snake on a diet."

He shrugged.

Dinner was a series of shrugs. I asked if they'd closed down his hospital.

"Nope, still open."

I asked if the surgeon he'd assisted was still there.

"Um hmm."

I asked if he needed rest; I shared the news from home. What did he want to see in Paris? His short answers led nowhere: Not tired. We could see any sights I wanted to see, he would accompany me. I could choose a play for us to see.

His detachment was unnerving, to put it mildly. The Billy I'd known since we were children had lived vitally, at the heart of things. He'd invented games and made me join him, taking risks I would never have considered if left to myself, leading me into mischief, teaching me to be brave. My father read *A Tale of Two Cities* aloud to us before we were old enough to read it ourselves. For weeks afterward, we'd acted out Dickens' story in our backyard, assigning parts to every kid in the neighborhood. Using odds and ends of old lumber, Billy had built a makeshift guillotine. Needless to say, he always insisted on playing the part of Sydney Carton. At the end of the play, he would climb the steps, declaiming Carton's vision of France reborn, Paris once more a beautiful city, and the French "a brilliant people rising from this abyss . . . in their struggles to be truly free."

Now, no longer young, the two of us had joined in the latest fight to drag France back from the edge of destruction. Paris had been saved, and we were there, in the city, with a chance to glory in its survival. But, sadly, along with everything else, including me, the city seemed to hold no charm for him.

As he sat in silence over the dinner he'd barely touched, I had time, too much time, to study him. His skin was patchy and sallow, his forehead graven with deep lines. In the carefree days before the war, when he was repairing his dilapidated car, his hands had always been covered with cuts, the fingernails black with grease. Now those nails were trimmed and clean, the skin unnaturally white. At the hospital, he'd had to scrub them constantly, to ward off infection. His hands were so dry they looked like they'd been dusted with flour.

After the waiter cleared the table, Billy took out a cigarette and tried to light it, but his hand shook so violently he had trouble striking the match. I had to look away.

As soon as he paid the check, we left the bistro and walked across the Pont Neuf to our modest *pension* in the Rue des Grands-Augustins. It was still early, and the streets were filled with crowds enjoying one of the first pleasant evenings of the year. While waiting for Billy, I had walked along the stone embankment by the Seine in the dark, watching the reflection of the lights dip and gleam on the water, looking forward to the night we would walk along the river together and begin to talk about the years we'd been apart. But on that first evening he didn't have the heart for it, and neither did I.

Later, I lay awake, unable to sleep. At dinner Billy hadn't even seemed present. Did he feel guilty about leaving his patients behind? I hadn't seen him since November, not long after the armistice, when I'd paid him a hurried visit after he'd sent me a worrisome postcard. His handwriting, usually plain as day, had been so jagged I could read only a few words.

When I reached the hospital and found the tent where he was hard at work, I decided to wait by the door. As he moved from bed to bed, I saw him care for his patients, changing dressings, encouraging those who looked distressed, joking with men who needed to laugh—a gifted nurse who would one day become a great doctor. But the longer I watched, the more obvious it became that something was wrong. It felt as if he were someone else, an actor playing the part of Billy, brilliantly, yet slightly off balance. Later that day, when I asked if he was all right, he dismissed my concern, saying that, like everyone else, he was just very tired. Yes, the war was over, but there were still a lot of patients.

In the months since then, I'd convinced myself that getting away from that terminus of horror and death would be his deliverance, but now I saw I had been naïve.

I had no memories of myself without Billy; we were born months apart. While he was my cousin, he might as well have been my brother. He'd been the sun, and I'd basked in his warmth. What would become of me if that light were extinguished? As soon as I'd seen his anguished face at the Gare de l'Est, I should have started to think more about what he needed, instead of being so wrapped up in my wish for him to comfort me. The prickly straw poking through the thin sheet on my mattress felt like a fitting punishment. I lay there, waiting for the church bells to chime. The hours of the night passed slowly; it seemed as if dawn would never come.

What should I have expected? For three years, more than a thousand days, he had patched up the wounded and helped the dying make their peace. How many amputated arms and legs had he carried out of the operating room? How many faces had he seen torn up by shrapnel? How many gallons of blood? How had such a gentle soul borne it all? As a boy, when he caught a mouse in the kitchen, he'd slip the little pest in his shirt pocket and ride his bike out to the orchards to find it a new home.

The next morning I knocked on Billy's door and found him already awake, reading the newspaper, slouched in a wicker armchair so decrepit it looked like it might collapse under him. When I suggested we get breakfast, he feigned enthusiasm. I steered us to a bakery on the Boulevard Saint-Germain. Knowing how much Billy loved chocolate, I ordered *pains au chocolat* and sat us down at a table on the sidewalk. I loved to watch Parisians sauntering along with that casual grace the rest of us envy—and can never copy. But Billy had no eyes for *le chic*. When I finished licking the chocolate off my fingers, I looked over and saw him chewing his pastry mechanically, as if it were dry toast. His eyes looked into the distance, beyond me, beyond the city, to a place I doubted I would be able to travel with him.

It isn't just his body that needs to be fed, I thought. His spirit is hungry. Taking his hand, I pulled him to his feet, and we walked the few blocks to the Sainte-Chapelle. In the weeks I'd waited for him, it had become my refuge, in a way no church at home ever was. This majestic building had survived for seven centuries; even the German planes that rained bombs down on Paris had missed it.

The first time I'd seen light stream through its windows, through the thousands of bits of glass—blue and red, green and gold—I'd felt as if I were inside a kaleidoscope, its patterns shimmering and changing as I walked from one end to the other. The colors bloomed, inducing a kind of rapture, and I remember thinking I hope this is what heaven is like. But when I turned to look at Billy, he appeared so forlorn I reached for his hand, and I was relieved when he held mine tight. To me, he felt so light I was afraid he might float away if I didn't anchor him to the ground.

By late afternoon, we had reached the top of the stairs that led to Sacré-Coeur and stood looking out over the city. I felt triumph in the fact that the Germans had failed to destroy it. But more and more, I felt Billy was marking time, anxious to get away from me and from Paris.

I had to ask what was wrong, but I hesitated, afraid of what I might hear. Dinner that night was awkward, conversation sparse. Afterward we agreed to walk along the river, despite a chill in the air. Finally, I forced myself to say, "Billy, you seem so unhappy. Whatever I do seems to make it worse."

"No, dear, not at all. I appreciate everything you've done, and you have done *everything*: found us a comfortable place to stay, fed me delicious meals and shown me beautiful things. I'm just worn out. Don't worry so much."

"Do you ever have bad dreams?" I asked.

"Nope."

"Really? Never? For me, visiting your hospital was more frightening than any nightmare. None of that creeps into your dreams?"

"No, honey. When I could grab some shut-eye, I'd fall into a dead sleep. Didn't move a muscle till somebody shook me awake for the next shift."

I knew he was lying. The studied casualness with which he'd told his little story had given him away.

I considered backing off, which was clearly what he wanted. But mightn't he feel I was abandoning him? Or was I the one concerned about being abandoned? The next night I said, "Billy, I need to talk about the war. I think it would help to leave some of it behind, here. If we don't—"

"No," he said sharply, cutting me off.

"Please."

"Talking makes it worse," he said. "It's better to forget. If you need to talk about it, talk to somebody else."

Although I was frightened by his vehemence, I pressed. "The more we sweep our demons under the rug, the more insidious they'll become."

"This is my problem. I'll handle it," he said. "I'm not even sure I want to go home."

"You can't be serious. Your mother and sister are living for the day you return."

"I can't stand the thought of going back to a bunch of phony parades and speeches about how we're all a lot of heroes. There was no victory. There's nothing to celebrate. Everyone's chattering about how wonderful it is that the war's over, even you. For the dead, it is not just the war that's over."

"How dare you? Chattering! You really think you're the only one who cares about the dead? That I don't?"

We stood on the cobblestones of the medieval street, not touching, consumed by hurt. Two lovers passed by, heads together, sharing a private joke, and I felt even more alone.

Finally, his voice close to breaking, Billy said, "I'm so sorry. I'm a miserable goddamned son of a bitch. You've done everything but stand on your head to please me. Start home by yourself. Let me make my own way when I'm ready. I'm not going to hurt Mother or little Alice."

Putting my arm around his shoulder and drawing him toward me, I said, "You're not a son of a bitch. No way I'm leaving you here by yourself. Why don't we just go home? Maybe we'll see Paris again someday."

CHAPTER 2

There were few troopships and thousands of Americans eager to leave France. We were stuck in Paris for weeks until we were assigned berths on the USS *Huntington*, an armored cruiser that had been assigned the happier job of taking soldiers home. Because I was a woman, I got a cabin of my own. Billy had only a hammock deep in the hold, in a room filled with dozens of men. The ship had few comforts, and it was packed tight, but nobody minded all that much. We were going home.

The atmosphere on board was one of feverish gaiety, the passengers intent on one last, long party before they had to sober up and go back to work. The trip was a far cry from my journey two years earlier when I had sailed from the United States to France to help with the war effort. Back then, we'd all held our breath, waiting for a German U-boat to sneak up and send us to the bottom of the ocean.

I still had an evening gown with me, a periwinkle-blue lace, once lovely, now frayed and stained. Before dinner I did my best to sponge it off, and tried to wash my hair in the icy water dribbling from the tap in my little sink. A ragtag band had been put together by some passengers, and when they began to play after dinner, I asked Billy to dance. We'd learned to dance together, when were young, practicing in his living room, taking turns cranking the Victrola. But he turned me down and went up on deck, leaving me behind in my bedraggled dress.

After he left, a handsome lieutenant asked if he could interest me in a foxtrot. Moving me around the floor expertly, he asked if I was a nurse, but before I could answer, I spotted Billy framed by the doorway, scanning the crowd. Once he caught sight of me, he barged over, grabbed the lieutenant's shoulder and lit into him.

"Who are you? What do you think you're doing?"

I tried to intervene. "Billy, please. Lieutenant Tucker just asked me for a dance. What's wrong with you?"

"Wrong with me? I should ask you that question! Why are you dancing with a stranger?"

"Was I supposed to sit at our table all night with my hands folded in my lap? Dancing's not a crime."

Leaping in to ease the tension, the lieutenant said he'd meant no harm. Billy glared at him. I realized Billy's voice had risen over the music, and everyone was staring. I thought he might throw a punch. Apologizing hurriedly and grabbing Billy's arm, I hissed into his ear, "Okay, we're settling this somewhere else," and dragged him up to the deck.

The Billy I knew would never have done anything so rude. Nor would he have missed a chance to waltz me around the floor. Instead of shouting at him, which was what I wanted to do, I forced myself to keep my temper and ask why he'd reacted so violently.

"I didn't like the idea of that guy pawing you."

His choice of words was infuriating. "Pawing me? We were dancing. That's all."

"You don't know what he was thinking. Or where he was hoping that dance might lead."

"You're acting like a jealous lover. What is going on?"

He stomped off. Even though it was cold and I had no wrap, I decided to stay on deck. In my tiny cabin I'd feel trapped.

My heart was beating as fast as a hummingbird's. I felt as if I had a fever, despite the wind blowing off the sea. When Billy attacked the lieutenant, it had felt to me as if he thought he had the right to build a fence around us, as if I belonged to him in some way I didn't understand.

Suddenly, I was glad I had not yet told him about Arthur.

CHAPTER 3

I'd met Arthur Bayard in the summer of 1917 when I went to Washington to work for the State Department, shortly after the United States entered the war. One night, walking back to the house where I boarded in Georgetown, I turned up 21st Street toward the P Street Bridge. If I had chosen, say, 22nd Street, I might never have spoken to Arthur, and I would have lived a different life entirely.

As I turned onto P, I saw his familiar figure—we were both cryptographers—emerging from a shop, carrying a brown paper parcel tied with string, which had to be laundry. In the office, when I should have been working, I'd spent a good deal of time studying the symmetry of his face, his sapphire-blue eyes and long dark lashes, the ivory skin and thick black hair. He was slight and not that tall, about five foot nine, a couple of inches shorter than me.

Through the office grapevine, I'd heard that Dr. Bayard, a linguist, was very likely the youngest professor at Harvard. He'd been appointed to an endowed chair two years earlier when he was only thirty. I found him hard to read. At times, he seemed keenly observant; at others, so inwardly focused it was hard to tell if he was seeing anything at all. Almost everything about him seemed neat and contained. No matter how hot the day, he never took off his jacket. Yet there was nothing pompous or stuffy about him. If something struck him funny, he would break out into a musical laugh, a little loud for polite company, and I found that endearing. Nonetheless, he'd remained sufficiently intimidating that I'd never said anything more to him than "Good morning."

But in these circumstances, meeting him in the street, it would have been odd not to speak. "Good evening, Dr. Bayard," I said. "Are you picking up your laundry?" Immediately, I thought how silly that question sounded. Of course, he was picking up his laundry.

He asked why I was out so late, and I said that, after a day hunched over my desk, I needed to walk off the stiffness. He was distressed by the idea of my walking alone in the dark. I said there were still plenty of people out and about. Just because people were walking down the street hardly guaranteed they were good people, he countered, which made me laugh—and him frown.

When I told him I walked all over Washington by myself without giving it a thought, he said, "Miss Havilland, did you grow up in a big city? I think not." I started to take offense; he was treating me like a child. Then I thought: Who am I kidding? I don't know what I'm doing half the time. I admitted I came from a sleepy farm town in California that fancied itself a city.

"I'm from Boston," he said. "I honestly believe you're taking a risk, without realizing it. Would you mind if I saw you to your door? If anything happened to you, I would have that on my conscience." I was touched by his grave politeness.

The next night I looked up from sorting the papers on my desk to find Arthur standing over me.

"Do you plan to walk home alone this evening?"

"Yes. It's perfectly safe."

"I beg to differ."

With that, we fell into a pattern of walking home together every night.

As our workload kept increasing, we often had to stay late. When we left the office so late the streets had emptied, I was grateful for Arthur's protection. Left to myself, I would have been one of very few women walking the streets who wasn't a streetwalker.

In the beginning, we talked about the obvious: cryptography. One evening Arthur asked if we could please talk about something—anything—else. He needed a respite from the pressure. I understood. Sometimes when I was trying to decrypt, my mind would shut down, like an engine that had been running too fast for too long. Until I came to Washington, I'd always loved my work: I was a natural mathematician, and I'd thought cryptography would come easily. Wrong.

When we began to talk about the rest of our lives, Arthur asked me question after question. I told him a great deal about myself, including the beginning of my investigations in the field of number theory, work I had had to put aside for the war effort. At first, Arthur's interest delighted me, but as he continued to deflect my questions about his life, his reticence made me uneasy, and a little sad. I wanted more than a polite friendship.

When I asked what it was like to teach at Harvard, he said, "I expect it's much like teaching at any college."

When I asked about his parents and his brother—he had mentioned an older brother, Nathaniel—he said, "Like all families, we have our problems."

One Sunday when we were walking in Rock Creek Park, out of the blue Arthur said, "I don't quite understand who Billy is. You talk about him almost as if he were a brother, but I know you're an only child."

In truth, I couldn't explain, even to myself, why I was so hesitant to let Arthur know how much I loved Billy. But I could certainly tell him who he was. "Billy is my cousin, but you're right—he is the closest thing I have to a brother. My mother and his mother are sisters, and you can see the back of their house from our kitchen window. When we were little, after breakfast, we'd meet in the yard and play until one mother or the other called us in for lunch."

"I don't know where he is or what he does," Arthur said. "Is he still at college?"

"I wish. He left California for France right after the war started. He's assisting a surgeon in a hospital near the front. I haven't had even a postcard from him in nine weeks. He might be busy. Maybe the ship carrying a letter from him to me was sunk by the Germans. Maybe he's dead. Since there's nothing I can do about it, I try to push it to the back of my mind. But often I fail."

When I saw a strange look on Arthur's face, I pressed. For the first time, he told me what was bothering him.

"I fervently hope Billy is all right. In light of your worries, what I was thinking is going to sound self-indulgent. I envy Billy just as I envy my brother, Nathaniel. When Nat finishes officer training in Georgia, he'll go overseas and command his own platoon. My work here feels like a cheat. The real fighting's going on in France. I have a hard time living with myself: Nat risking his life while I sit at home, safe, playing around with German puzzles."

"No," I said. "You have a great gift for decrypting, something few people have. Even if you never pick up a gun, solving those puzzles may save thousands of lives—there's nothing trivial about that. We all want the war to end. I don't want one more person to be killed, not even a German."

As solemn as the moment was, when Arthur wrapped his arms around me and I felt the warmth of his chest against mine, I was elated.

We began spending more time together. Sundays, our only day off, were saved for each other. Arthur took me to the theatre, to the symphony; he introduced me to chamber music. Until then my knowledge of music had been limited to dance tunes and the hymns we sang in church. But Arthur never made me feel foolish. He enjoyed sharing his world with me, freeing me to ask questions and venture opinions without worrying whether I sounded ignorant.

I was falling in love, hard. But I was not certain what Arthur felt; he remained oddly formal at times. One evening he took me to a musicale where a tenor sang the *Winterreise*, the Schubert song cycle about a rejected lover who struggles with despair until he finally accepts his loneliness. The little crowd of elegantly dressed ladies and gentlemen listened politely but whispered a good deal to each other while I wondered if these songs foretold my future.

Later that night my fears were laid to rest. Instead of saying goodnight to Arthur on the steps, I invited him into the parlor. After I closed the door, he took me in his arms and kissed me, at first tenderly and then with urgency, kisses I returned eagerly. Now such kisses happen on the first date, but then love unfolded more slowly and carefully. Even the use of a first name could be thrilling, a sign of greater intimacy to come. I doubt I'm the only woman who longs for a world in which the first kiss remains precious.

Time alone was hard to come by. Propriety stopped me from inviting Arthur up to my room, nor could he invite me to his. The parlor of either house was no guarantee of privacy because at any moment another boarder might walk in. We spent a lot of Sundays in Rock Creek Park, renting horses from the stable and heading north to the park's deserted upper reaches. While I hadn't been raised like Arthur with riding lessons and English saddles, I could hold my own. When we'd visited our uncle's ranch out in the valley, Billy and I had learned to ride bareback.

Once we found a secluded spot, we'd search for a patch of level ground and spread out a blanket. While we ate our sandwiches and emptied a flask of coffee, we talked about everything—the war, our work, this intense city where we lived now, but most of all about my childhood. Arthur seemed to be interested in every detail of my growing up.

Of course, I told him my mother had taught me her native language—she'd spoken German to me since the day I was born. My happiest memories of her go back to the days before I learned to read, when she'd let me sit on the couch next to her while she read German folk tales aloud. If I didn't understand a word, I would raise a finger and try to say it. She'd tell me what the word meant, and we'd practice pronouncing the word and spelling it. In high school I'd studied German, but my mother still held me to her own high standard. Not trusting the teacher to do her job, she corrected my essays, and she drilled me on verbs while we prepared dinner. What's more, my mother always spoke to her sister Dora in German; consequently, I was highly motivated to learn the spoken language so I could listen in on their conversations.

On another Sunday afternoon, Arthur said, "Tell me about your father." Looking back, I wish I'd been bolder, that I'd insisted he tell me just as much about his father, but I'd begun taking his reticence for granted.

"I wanted to be just like him, loving, funny and smart. An accident put him in a wheelchair before I was born. He can walk, but every step is painful. At night, he drags himself up the stairs to bed. In the morning, he lowers himself back down, one stair at a time. Half of me can't bear to watch; the other half has to, in case he starts to fall. He works at home. After he got hurt, the Southern Pacific Railroad kept him on as a dispatcher by stringing a wire from the depot to our house."

"It must have been hard having a father in a wheelchair," Arthur said.

"Not as hard as you think. When you're a child, the world you're born into is the only world you know. Whatever it is, it feels natural to you. Besides, if he hadn't been in that wheelchair, I wouldn't be sitting here with you. I'd be teaching math at the high school in town."

"I refuse to believe that," Arthur said. "I have wondered how you became the singular woman that you are. Gifted mathematicians are rare: Women mathematicians are just about unheard of."

"The safest place to hide from my mother's wrath was my father's office. So long as I was quiet, he'd let me spend the day curled up on his lumpy green couch, coloring and daydreaming. I spent hours watching his fingers fly over the telegraph key. I begged him to show me how to do it, and eventually he agreed to teach me. It was more fun than any game. Once you get the hang of it, Morse is simple. The patterns you hear when you tap the key have a rhythm, a kind of music. If you know the notes, you can play any tune. Every operator develops his own voice—when my father heard a particular rhythm, he knew exactly who was sending a wire."

"How old were you when he taught you?"

"I think, uh, about four."

"Four?"

"He was the perfect father for me. By then, he'd already taught me my numbers."

I paused to think. I wanted to tell Arthur more but thought I might sound silly. Yet I wanted him to know me in all my strangeness. He had made it abundantly clear he was interested in whatever I had to say, which might be liberating, if I could just allow myself.

"I've never told anyone this before. For me each number was a fairy, with her own magical powers. There was an ancient, knobby pepper tree in our backyard, with a swing hanging from one of its branches. I spent hours there, watching my fairies: some small, iridescent figures, taking to the sky on wings patterned with a delicate tracery of veins like dragonflies; others dusky woodland creatures who hid among the shrubbery and built tiny houses out of dried grass and leaves. Having no enemies, they were free to dance and play and sing. They were my closest friends, never angry, always understanding me."

"That doesn't sound silly to me," Arthur said. "I had a private world of my own when I was a boy, peopled by letters of the alphabet."

"What did they look like?"

"I'll tell you another time. Don't stop."

"My father offered to teach me more games. What kid would say no to that? I didn't know the names of the games were addition, subtraction, multiplication, and division. He taught me to multiply two numbers in my head, then he'd throw out another number, and I had to keep multiplying, then another and another. It was a good discipline, kind of mental gymnastics.

"Like most children, I couldn't wait to start school, but it wasn't long before I hated it. I couldn't spend the day with my father anymore. I quickly saw I was never going to fit in.

"The teachers taught us the same number games, but the pinched looks on their faces told me that for them it was drudgery.

"One morning, watching the second hand creep around the clock, I came up with a scheme to show off that I already knew their games. Writing down one long number and then another longer number, I divided the first into the second and defiantly wrote EVELYN in big block letters at the top of the page. When we filed out for recess, I left the paper on the teacher's desk.

"When we returned to the classroom, she asked who had done that problem for me. When I insisted I'd done it myself, she called me a smart aleck and a liar. I acted like a brat, offering to do a problem while she watched me, even offering to let her pick the numbers. She told me to sit at my desk, put my hands where she could see them, and not say another word for the rest of the day. I started to sass her, but she told me that, if I didn't hush up, she'd send me straight to the principal. Since I knew the principal would telephone my mother, I just about stopped breathing.

"The minute I got home, I ran to my father, poured out my fury, and announced I would never speak to that stupid old woman again. He made me an offer: If I forced myself to be polite in class, he would teach me lots more math at home. There was one condition: I had to promise never to mention at school what we were doing.

"After we made that deal, I could tolerate school, barely. Daddy and I tore through fractions, decimals, and percents. Each one was a new world to me, with its own internal logic and perfection.

"He bought me an algebra textbook. When I saw those mysterious letters and symbols, I was hungry to make sense of them. When the school bell rang, I was the first one out the door. To pacify my mother, I'd drink the glass of milk she left on the kitchen counter even though she knew I found milk revolting. Then, until I had to do chores before dinner, I sat with my textbook balanced on the arm of the old green couch, a pencil in hand and a notebook on my lap.

"I dreaded chores because they meant tangling with my mother and her standards of perfection. In her estimation, no silver spoon I polished was ever shiny enough. The drain board I scrubbed was never as white as white should be.

"My parents didn't argue. My father rarely even contradicted my mother. But one afternoon, she appeared in the doorway of his office and told me I needed to go straight to the ironing board because a mountain of ironing was waiting.

"When my father said the ironing could wait, my mother insisted. Out of nowhere, he started yelling. I froze. 'Hannah, do you really want to stop the child from learning? Most girls would rather play with dolls. If that was what Evelyn wanted to do, it would be fine with me. But she doesn't. I don't care if I ever wear another ironed shirt as long as I live.'

"I was scared Mamma would shout back at him—she certainly didn't hesitate to yell at me. But she just stood there, glaring, until she slammed the door on her way out.

"I was proud my father defended me. But I'd had no idea he could blow up like that. One angry parent was already more than I could handle. I'd always believed he loved Mamma just the same as he loved me, but now I wasn't so sure. He'd never yelled at me, and I hoped he never would. From then on, I was even more obedient. I guess that's why I liked geometry more than algebra."

Arthur broke in. "You just lost me."

"A geometric proof exists for its own sake. It needs no other justification; it's free of messiness and hurt feelings."

"Math was your refuge," Arthur said.

"Yes, and all I wanted was a chance to stay there, undisturbed, with only my father for company. That is why cryptography insults my mind. It's an ungodly waste of time—and the antithesis of mathematical understanding. Codes are strings of symbols, purposefully random. Without logic, charm, or beauty. They exist only to generate violence."

"You're right," Arthur said. "But don't get sidetracked. You're telling me how your mind was born, how it grew, and what it longs for. Right now, that's what is important to me."

God knows I didn't think my intellectual development was more important than the war, but I loved his reply. The intensity of his interest meant everything to me.

"Once I was ready for calculus, we hit a roadblock. My father had never studied it, so we decided to try to learn it together. Understanding functions, derivatives, and integrals was our last big adventure. When my father began to struggle, he said, 'I have to find you another teacher.'

"I begged him not to, but he insisted. 'You're a thoroughbred, and I won't become your donkey. I'll slow you down. It's inevitable.'

"I hated the idea of leaving him behind. I hated the idea of studying with a stranger. He found a teacher at the high school, Miss Koenig, who agreed to tutor me. Once I realized she loved math as much as I did, I began to accept her. Until I graduated, I spent Wednesday afternoons with her after the last bell rang, doing extra, more challenging work. Her expectations were high, but I was never tempted to give up, no matter how hard the work. I craved that feeling of triumph once I did understand. There is no pleasure as great as that which exists in the realm of pure thought."

I'd been looking out into the distance, caught up in my story. When I turned to look at Arthur, I was taken aback. Tears were brimming in his eyes. I had no idea what had made him cry, but I took him in my arms to comfort him.

After that, a lot of our time was spent not talking at all, lying together on our wool blanket. Soon we moved beyond kissing, and it became harder and harder to stop. But Arthur always did. At first I was grateful, but as time passed I no longer wanted to. I'd never known this kind of pure, unfiltered physical bliss. But I couldn't bring myself to talk to Arthur about any of this. Like most "ladies," I had never discussed such intimate things with anyone; I didn't even have the language for them.

And so we drifted on a sea of unsatisfied desire.

CHAPTER 4

On board the USS Huntington
April 1919

Suddenly, the cold snapped me out of my reverie, and I realized I was shivering. As I walked down to my cabin, I wished Arthur was on the ship with me, or that, at least, I'd had the courage to tell Billy about Arthur. But if seeing me dance with Lieutenant Tucker had made him so angry, how would he deal with the news I was going to marry another man?

The next night Billy asked me to take a turn on deck with him. We fell into reminiscing about the days when we were young and carefree. This should have been a relief, but the contrast of that innocent time with our situation on the ship was torment.

My first memory is Billy chasing me in the backyard, the sun shining down on us. He was laughing because he knew it was just a matter of when, not if, he would catch me. Neither of us remembered a time when the other wasn't there. Since our two families lived in houses that backed onto each other, we were always in one house or the other—unless we were playing in the garden, hiding out in the fort we'd built from scraps of wood we'd found in Billy's garage, or tearing around on our bikes. Not long after we learned to ride, we found our way to the orchards on the edge of town where we got to know the pickers, who tossed plums and apricots down to us as they plucked them from the trees.

We gorged on the fruit. The juice got all over our hands and ran down our cheeks. When we'd had enough, we'd strip down to our underwear and jump in the creek to wash off. In no time we'd be splashing each other, yelling and tickling. In the beginning it was a fair fight. Either of us could hold the other under water till they begged for mercy. But by the time we were eight or nine, he was stronger and could pin me down effortlessly. If he kept me under too long, I'd rocket up out of the water, hopping mad. But my anger lasted only until we kissed and made up.

As time passed, we grew too old for splashing. Billy would tow me lazily through the water. We didn't speak, lost in the feeling of floating as one. We never wanted to leave, even after the sun sank low in the sky, signaling it was time to go home.

Our lives flowed on in this quiet groove for many years. School came easily to both of us. Billy's dad was the only doctor in the county. The year Billy was twelve, his father bought a car so it would be easier to make house calls, and he taught Billy to drive. When there was an emergency at night, he'd wake Billy, and they would go speeding off. A lot of operations were done at home back then, and Dr. Greenfield taught his son to assist. Billy helped with many difficult births. He learned to suture deep cuts, and sometimes his father entrusted him with closing up when a surgery was finished.

Three years later, a virulent influenza swept through the valley, and Dr. Greenfield insisted on driving himself to see his patients. Billy begged to go along, but his father made his son stay at home, to keep him safe from contagion. Unfortunately, he neglected himself, working day and night for weeks. None of us was surprised when he came down with the flu, but we weren't scared until he grew too weak to get out of bed. Until then his great strength had carried him through everything. An outside nurse, immune because she had already survived the flu, was hired. Dora, Billy, and Alice were not allowed near him. Despite her dedication, the nurse couldn't save her patient, and he died of respiratory failure.

Our families were devastated. My mother worried most about Dora. Looking back, I think Billy may have been even more deeply hurt. He forced himself to appear calm and steady because he wanted to take his dad's place, caring for his mother and sister. To fight his grief, he studied harder. He was determined to go to medical school, to be worthy of his father's legacy.

A couple of nights before the *Huntington* was scheduled to dock in New York, Billy asked if I'd like to go to the lounge with him for coffee. Once we'd filled our cups from the urn, we settled ourselves on the sofa near a radiator, which gave off a pathetic little trickle of heat.

I was shaking with cold, so after we sat down, I kicked off my shoes and tucked my feet up under my skirt. Billy wrapped his coat around my shoulders, then built a wall of cushions around us to trap our body heat. It reminded me of the two of us hiding out in our fort in the back garden.

Billy asked me a surprising question, surprising because, implicitly, it raised the subject of what the war had done to us.

"Do you ever think about what it's going to be like once we're home again?" I could hear in his voice that this wasn't a casual question. "I can't even remember entirely what home looks like . . . "

"I know what you mean," I said. "I've been gone two years, but it feels like twenty. When we left, we were children."

"Yep. Sometimes I wonder who I am now, whether I can turn myself back into a schoolboy. Going to class, taking tests, truckling to professors who were too old to be drafted and won't have the faintest idea what it was like over there.

"You're not the same person either," he continued, reaching out to take my icy hands in his warm ones. "You're stronger.

Sharper. You know how to take care of yourself. How in the world are you going to live in that house again with your mother?"

"What made you think of that?" I asked.

"I was thinking about how hard she fought to stop you from going away to college."

What had dragged up that ancient history for him? Had he sensed I was planning to go away again, to marry and not return?

"Hard?" I said. "It was, wasn't it? It felt like we were fighting over my freedom . . . I guess we were."

"If she'd had her way, she would have kept you home, in a prison of her own making," Billy said. "But you fought your way out. I was so damned proud of you."

"But if you hadn't threatened to stay home, too, I don't know if I ever would have made it to Stanford. You put everything on the line for me. Everything."

"Nah, you did it yourself, Squirt," he said, using one of his favorite nicknames for me. "Don't give me too much credit." Standing up, he put a hand on my shoulder and leaned down to kiss the top of my head. "Right now, I'm tired enough. I need to go below and get some sleep." Before he turned away, I caught sight of his old lopsided grin, the right side of his mouth turned up a little higher than the left. I guess I should have known better, but a flicker of hope ran through me. He hadn't called me Squirt in years.

CHAPTER 5

Without Billy's encouragement, after high school I might have gritted my teeth, given in and stayed home, forcing myself to play the part of the "good girl." For years I'd dreamed of going to Stanford, but Mamma wouldn't hear of it. She was adamant that after high school I would attend the local Normal School where I could train to be a math teacher.

My rescue came without warning. Senior year, Miss Koenig, my long-time tutor, was also my math teacher. One day, during class, I was staring out the window, paying no attention to what she was writing on the board because I already understood it.

Her voice broke through my daydreaming. I realized she had asked me more than once to go to the board and write out a proof from the problem set we'd been given for homework the night before. So I hustled up to the blackboard and grabbed a stick of chalk.

After I finished, she said, "Miss Havilland, what you have written is correct but, I am afraid, not thorough. Not for the first time your mind has rushed ahead of your fingers and left out a number of steps. Please look at what you have scribbled on the board, and see if you can add those missing steps."

Quickly, I saw the gaps in my logic and tried to fix them by writing between the lines, adding tiny numbers where there wasn't enough room for them. The finished product was a mess, but it was complete. Thoroughly embarrassed, I turned to look at Miss Koenig.

"Thank you for obliging me, Miss Havilland. Please see me after class."

Chagrined, I walked back to my desk. Self-conscious because I was taller than all but two of the boys in the class, I had a tendency to slouch. Worse, I could feel my braids flapping against the back of my dress. Would Mamma ever let me put my hair up? Seventeen, and still in braids, which was mortifying. Vanity gave way to a more pressing matter: What kind of dressing down lay in wait for me after class?

As soon as the other students filed out of the room, the girls gossiping in low tones, the boys elbowing each other, Miss Koenig said, "Evelyn, I apologize for my harshness, but I had a reason. We both know your mind operates so quickly you often see the proof whole and don't bother to record all the steps by which you reach a conclusion. That speed is a great gift, but it will become an Achilles heel. Once you need to prove to your colleagues how you arrived at a conclusion, demonstrating every step of your thinking will be essential. I am determined you will have that chance."

I had no idea where she was going with this.

"Don't worry about your next class," she said. "I'll write you a note. I want to speak to you, about something I've been considering for a long time." Sitting down at her desk, she motioned for me to take a seat at a desk in the front row. The desks were rather small for me, so I had to bend down and lever myself into one of them, which only added to my self-consciousness.

"Unfortunately," she said, "you are, like myself, female. Nonetheless, you *must* go to the university."

It was painful to hear my fondest wish spoken aloud when there was no chance of it coming true.

"Your gifts must not be wasted scrubbing shirts on a wash-board and heating irons on the stove. You are that rare thing: a mathematician. Given the chance, you will do original work."

I didn't know what to say. Eventually, I mumbled something to the effect of "I don't see how you can know that."

"Don't equivocate with me, young lady. You know you are in a class by yourself."

It was true I'd figured out my mastery of mathematics had outstripped Miss Koenig's, but I hadn't wanted her to know I knew that. On the other hand, even if it was painful to leave her behind, it was exciting to venture ahead by myself. She was no fool—she'd seen me travel beyond where she could go. I should have given her more credit.

Getting up from her chair and coming over to stand close to me, she waited for a response.

"I appreciate your faith in me," I said. "You know I would do anything to go to the university. But my mother is absolutely opposed. Since we couldn't afford it, even if she agreed to let me go, it wouldn't make any difference."

"No! You can't let her waste your talent. I *won't* let it happen. I've already spoken to Edmund Howard. We've known each other forever—he grew up on the same street as my family. That cannery of his wasn't always so lucrative, but now he has plenty of money. He's agreed to cover everything: tuition, room, and board. All you have to earn is your pocket money, which you can do, easily, by tutoring."

"Mr. Howard? He hardly knows me."

"But he knows me. His wife was my closest friend. My friendship with Eleanor started in high school when we discovered that, unlike the other girls, we were interested in more than beaux and dress patterns.

"She was a very intelligent woman, who adored her husband. They wanted children badly, but it never happened. She spent too much of her short life embroidering, with little but a basket of brightly colored wools for company.

"After school, I'd stop by and visit her on my way home. Sitting out in the garden, we reveled in the chance to talk about subjects regarded as unsuitable for ladies—politics, suffrage, the theories of Marx and Darwin, the tragedy of Oscar Wilde. She asked if I would teach her the rudiments of calculus. For me, that was happiness, to be able to give her something no one else could. For her, it was a refreshing break in the afternoon, an antidote to the tedium of morning calls where conversation was confined to the weather, who was going to have a baby, and the servant problem.

"When she was thirty-seven, Eleanor died without warning—it was probably a stroke. She'd have wanted you to go to college; she'd have hated the waste of a first-class brain every bit as much as I would. When I asked Edmund if he would be willing to help you, he said, 'Excellent idea. Do something useful with my money. Besides, think how happy it would have made Ellie.' All you need is permission from your parents. Your father will say yes."

"But my mother," I said gloomily, "will not."

Miss Koenig was quiet for a moment. "Tell her why you want to go. If you can't convince her, I will. I will not let you go to the Normal. I did, and I can tell you it is not enough."

I dreaded the evening ahead. I sat in my room that afternoon reliving other occasions on which I'd infuriated my mother. She loved knitting, and, when I was little, I loved to watch her do it, her fingers a blur. Every stitch was perfect. So I asked her to teach me.

I can still picture her, looming over me, a towering figure in stiff black serge. Her hair, a brown so dark it looked black, was parted severely down the middle and pulled back into a tight bun. There wasn't a soft corner or angle anywhere on her body, not that it mattered, since she believed hugging a child bred weakness. I have no memories of climbing into her lap.

Producing a ball of thin, scratchy brown yarn and two long silver metal needles, she cast on a row of stitches, then showed me how to stick the needle into a stitch, wrap the yarn around the needle, and pull the new loop off to create a new stitch. It looked easy. She thrust the needles in my hands and told me to practice while she went downstairs to boil water for laundry. Before long I'd created a tangle of weird-looking loops, which I had no idea how to fix.

When my mother saw what I'd done, she snapped, "How did this happen? I showed you how to do it!"

I nodded, my head bent in shame.

Impatiently, she ripped out my loops and started over. With irritation, she knitted several new stitches, describing what she was doing each time. I tried again, and botched it again.

"No! Don't stick the needle in back of the stitch. The front, the front! Pay attention!"

I was getting more and more nervous as I failed to stick the needle in the right place. "No, no, no! Left to right, not right to left!" I had no idea what she meant. Scared to voice my confusion, I sat there dumbly.

I spent what felt like an eternity in my room twisting yarn around those needles. The square I produced looked like a cobweb woven by a drunken spider. It wouldn't have been much use as a rag, given how full of holes it was, and I felt like I wasn't worth much more myself. If I went back downstairs, my mother would just yell at me again, so I lingered. Finally, when she came upstairs and saw my scrambled effort, she lost all patience. "Absolutely hopeless! An idiot can knit!"

She stomped back down the stairs. I heard her turn the mangle to squeeze water out of the laundry so fast I thought she might break the machine.

I knew I had to tell my parents about Mr. Howard's offer, but as I sat at the dinner table, my stomach roiling, I didn't know how to start. I kept putting it off, waiting till we'd finished eating, rationalizing that riling up my mother when she was hungry would be about as smart as grabbing raw meat from the mouth of a starved lion.

I steeled myself not to back down. I wanted my chance. I didn't want my mother to take it away, though I knew she would try. News of Miss Koenig's plan would inevitably unleash her acid tongue. I vowed not to shed a tear. I would not lose my temper—that would also put me at a disadvantage. There was nothing my mother enjoyed so much as a chance to come out swinging.

When it was time for me to clear the table, I told my parents I had something I needed to tell them first. Mr. Howard had offered to pay my way to Stanford, and Miss Koenig was certain that, if I applied, I would be accepted.

When I finished, Mamma hissed: "Over my dead body."

"Mamma, please. This means the world to me."

"That damned Elsie Koenig, putting high-tone notions in your head about how you're smarter than everybody else."

She gave me a filthy look. In her eyes, pride had been my greatest offense, even as a small child. We both knew she believed I was guilty again—she didn't need to say a word. "I do not think that," I said fiercely. "I know it would be a sin of pride."

After dinner Daddy took refuge in his office, on the pretext of finishing some paperwork. As soon as I'd dried the last dish, Mamma called me into the parlor where she was lying in wait, ready to pounce.

"I'm going over there tomorrow morning to tell Elsie Koenig to keep her nose out of other people's business. The nerve."

"Mamma, Miss Koenig believes in me. She doesn't want me to end up teaching high school."

"Teaching is an honorable profession. Don't ever sneer at the Normal School—or at me."

"That's unfair. I am not sneering. I just want more."

"And you think you're not proud? I wish I could laugh."

"Mamma, you value education as much as I do. I'll have a better chance at a first-class university."

"Your place is here, with your father. If I go first, who's going to take care of him?"

For a moment I was speechless: Using her death as a cudgel to beat me was brutal, even for her. Blind with fury, I lashed out: "Mamma, he's been in that wheelchair since before I was born!"

As if he'd been summoned, the door opened and Daddy wheeled his chair into the room. Mamma and I froze, fearing he'd overheard our foolish, heated words.

"What's up, ladies? Should I beat a hasty retreat?"

"No, Will," Mamma said, "please join us. We'd love your company."

Not taken in by that sugary invitation, he looked right at her, but directed his question to me. "What's all the commotion about, Evelyn?"

"We were talking about Mr. Howard's offer. Mamma hates the idea. She hates me."

Mamma whipped round, and I could feel her eyes boring into me. "*Hates you?* That is an outrage. I spend every minute of every day taking care of you and your father. That isn't love? If you loved me, you wouldn't be so ready to run off."

"Mamma, it's hardly running away. The university is an hour away by train. In four years, I'll be home for good."

Daddy said gently, "Hannah, we'll miss her. But how can we make her say no to such an opportunity? She'd always regret it. You know she can do it."

"If our daughter must have more schooling, she can attend the Normal."

"Mamma, mathematicians at the university are doing important new work. I want to learn about what they're doing. I want to see if I can do it too." Getting up out of the chair, I was so distracted I caught my sleeve on a nail and tore it. My mother glared.

"God in heaven. Leave that dress by my sewing machine, and I'll mend the sleeve in the morning. A clumsy chit of a girl like you thinks she can hop right onto the world stage. How many women mathematicians are there? *None.*"

CHAPTER 6

As soon as I alerted Billy to the fight in progress at our house, he passed the news along to his mother, my Aunt Dora. Later in the week, she arranged to spend a day with Mamma, ostensibly to help her with canning, a tiresome job that went more quickly if you had company. Fruit was cheap that year because the harvest had been bountiful. It was going to rot if the farmers didn't sell it right away, so our kitchen was packed with crates of fruit and vegetables. By early afternoon, they'd put up two dozen jars of jam: apricot and peach, as well as quarts of tomatoes and a batch of sweet pickle. Leaving them to cool, they carried their sewing baskets to the porch, happy to get out of the hot kitchen and off their feet.

Mamma darned socks, and Dora hemmed shirts for Billy. I had spent my share of days on that porch, wrestling with my own basket of mending, listening to Dora muse on how soon "the boy" would outgrow the shirt she was sewing. That autumn "the boy" Billy was seventeen, and she thought he should have finished growing, but that didn't seem to be the case. He towered over her. Until she had a son, she'd never known what it meant to grow into a man's body. Height came first. The slower formation of muscle, sinew, and bones took years longer.

She loved how he took his strength for granted. It was nothing for him to carry a cord of wood that the delivery trucked had dumped at the end of the driveway and stack it all neatly in the shed outside the kitchen door. What took him half an hour would have taken her half a day, after which her muscles would have been screaming. He reminded her of his father, whom she had loved to distraction.

On that afternoon, as the sweat dried on her dress, Dora kept stalling, putting off the moment when she had to confront her sister. I know because I was in the kitchen; the window over the sink was open; and my ear was out on a stalk. I was straining to hear every word. Billy had alerted me that she was coming today with more in mind than jam. Mamma, the elder sister, was in the habit of telling Dora how to live her life. It was not easy for Dora to turn the tables, but she felt she owed it to me, her beloved niece, to speak up.

"Hannah, I've been thinking about Evelyn."

"Hmm."

"Howard's rich. Lord, the man must have rooms in his house where he just stacks the gold bars." Dora laughed, but Mamma did not.

"So what's your point?"

"I think you should let her go. This chance won't come again."

"I've already told her no," Mamma said firmly.

"Is it only your decision?" I watched her smooth out the wrinkles in her skirt, looking down at them so she wouldn't have to look at my mother.

"Yes. I'm her mother. I must protect her father: He would miss her terribly."

Of course, Dora knew my father would miss me. But she wasn't going to let her sister make Will's happiness the ground on which this decision had to be made. "Did he say no?"

"Will lives and breathes for her. He would agree to anything she wanted. But why should she be taken from him?" Mamma said. "How much pleasure does he have in his life?"

"Surely he wants what would make her happy."

"She can be happy here. If she chooses."

"You know she's brilliant, don't you?"

"You think I'm a hopeless old fool? I don't know my own daughter?" Mamma was on fire by then.

"What's she going to do here?" Dora asked.

"Teach mathematics at the high school. An honorable job for any woman."

"But she's not any woman. She'll be wasted here, teaching boys who are only marking time till they can quit and go work in the orchards and girls whose best hope is a husband who owns a store so they don't have to pick prunes. She'll resent you the rest of her life."

"No," Mamma said. "She will not. I've raised her to respect me."

"Hannah, why are you so harsh on that girl? Are you jealous?"

"Jealous? How in God's name could I possibly be jealous of my own daughter?"

"Because she'll have chances you didn't. If that's what's at the bottom of this, it's time you had a reckoning with yourself. I think she has a duty to use her brain, and you have a duty to let her go. Billy's going."

"The university is a place for men," Mamma insisted.

"How unfair and stupid is that? What if you and I had been able to go? We were smart enough, weren't we?"

Mamma cracked a smile. I'm sure she knew Dora was right, but she tacked in a different direction. "I think it will lead to trouble. Too much schooling will make her a wilder mustang than she is already! Nobody will marry her."

"Didn't Will marry you? He hasn't broken you yet."

"Men like Will don't grow on trees," Mamma said. "I was lucky."

"Do you ever tell him that?"

Mamma had no answer for that question. Having closed the hole in the sock she was repairing, she bit off the thread so hard she tore a new hole in it.

"What point is there in her going to that fancy school? She'll end up teaching at the high school anyway."

"You don't know that. The world has to change. One day, we'll vote!" Dora said, bursting into laughter. "I know that's not all that funny, but if I don't laugh, I'll cry. What you refuse to see is that Evelyn could be the kind of woman who breaks through, who clears the way for other women who come after her."

"When Elsie Koenig retires, they'll need to replace her. This town has been good to us. We need to give something back."

"You don't mean that. You just can't bear to let her go," Dora said. "Do you think it's easy for me to let Billy go?"

"I have no intention of losing her."

Risking Mamma's wrath, Dora said, "That is the danger, and you're blind to it. If you insist she stay home, you *will* lose her."

November 1912

For weeks, Mamma and I were at a stalemate, barely speaking.

Soon after Thanksgiving, I resolved to ask Daddy for help. By that point, he was my only hope. One afternoon, after I'd dropped my schoolbooks in my room, I slipped quietly into his office where he was hunched over the telegraph key.

Some days nothing happened. No signalman missed the command to detour onto a siding. No storms, no lightning struck a tree that hit a track that stopped a train and sent everything haywire. But even quiet days were taxing. The effort of listening attentively, hour after hour, was a discipline, and a trust. Tons of steel hurtling down tracks, risks in abeyance but lying in wait.

I walked behind his desk and leaned down to kiss his pale, soft cheek. Turning toward me in his chair, Daddy put his arms around my neck and gave me a hug.

"Can a man get a cup of tea around here?"

I gave him another kiss and went to put the kettle on. While I bent over the sink to draw water, I heard a train whistle blowing wildly, somehow sinister in the wind. When the kettle shrieked, a shudder ran through me: Whatever was menacing out there dwelt inside the house, too.

While I poured the tea, I asked if he was all right, because he seemed a little off-kilter.

"Hell of a day. Milk train from Frisco broke down early this morning, north of Watsonville. Chaos, of course. It took two hours to get the damned train onto a siding, God knows why. I'm tired. Would you send these last couple of wires for me?"

When Daddy was teaching me Morse code, he would pull me up on his lap and let me pretend to tap out messages. We started our lessons with a little ritual I loved. I'd whisper in his ear that I loved him more than the sun, the moon, and the stars. He'd turn me around to face the key, square off my shoulders with his hands and announce with mock gruffness, "Time to get to work." I was more than willing. Wanting to be as powerful as my father, I believed his power was related to what he could do with that key.

By the time I was six, I would sit at the dinner table and tap out my parents' conversations, to improve my speed and rhythm. Once I was proficient, my father let me send signals for him: His trust taught me to take responsibility for my actions. I loved having this capacity other kids didn't have, but I also understood I could never take it for granted. Daddy had drummed into me that the safety of passengers and freight was at stake.

On that afternoon of my senior year, I sat down next to him to send the wires while he drank his tea. Sitting so close made me aware of his strong, well-muscled shoulders: His arms had to do the work his legs couldn't. Some people assumed he was pitiful because of the wheelchair, but they were wrong. Living in a wheelchair and managing to enjoy life, resisting the temptation to self-pity, requires character and grit.

After I'd finished sending, I poured myself a cup of tea, sank down onto the couch, and blurted out what was on my mind.

"Daddy, you have to talk to Mamma. You're the only one who can convince her." By that point I felt the two of us were like boxers who'd gone too many rounds, crouched in our corners, too bruised to get back in the ring.

"I have been talking to her," he said. "Most every night. The subject's not closed. Put your cup down for a minute and listen. There are things I should have told you a long time ago, reasons your mother is sometimes so intractable."

"Sometimes?"

We laughed.

"She rarely talks about her childhood. You know her parents died, one right after the other, of typhoid fever. She and Dora were just bitty kids, eleven and five. No relatives in Germany offered to take them in. That still feels heartless to me. They had to be fetching little things. Instead, they were sent to live with a cousin in America.

"When the boat docked in Boston Harbor, they were collected by the cousin, a blacksmith from Revere, north of the city. He had a bunch of kids, times were hard, and pretty quick he decided he didn't have room for two more. Once your Uncle Bernhard agreed to take them, that bastard from Revere shot them onto a steamer bound for California. When you visit Bern out at the ranch, I know he seems like a kindly old man, but back then he treated those little girls like servants, not children, especially your mother.

"When the boat docked in Panama, Mamma and Dora were loaded onto a donkey, part of a convoy traveling overland to take them to another steamer on the west coast. Yellow fever was the danger. Dora took sick, fever and chills, throwing up her insides, too dizzy to stand up.

"There was no doctor on board that tub. Your mother nursed Dora around the clock, wiping the sweat off her face with their mother's handkerchiefs, one of the few things they'd been able to bring with them. Mamma still keeps a couple of them, in the top drawer of her bureau. They were steerage of course. The passengers shunned them—can't say I blame them, must have been afeared the contagion would spread—except for one lady who had a good Christian heart. She spelled your mother now and then so she could catch a few hours' sleep.

"All your mother cared about was keeping Dora alive. Without her, she would have no one. On the third day, the crisis came. Dora was shaking fit to rattle her teeth out. Your mother had to hold her to keep her from falling off the cot. Suddenly, Dora took a huge breath. Mamma thought it was her last, but instead the child let out a lungful of air, and she quieted. In minutes, she was asleep. Hannah knelt by the cot and prayed to thank God for not taking her little sister.

"I've heard bits and pieces of this story from Dora, but a lot of it came from your mother. A couple of nights after you were born, she was still very weak, but she wanted to talk. The delivery was rough: I almost lost her. Would I have survived that? I wonder.

"She was joyful because you were a healthy little thing. Her heart opened when she held you in her arms. I sat with her, and she told me about her parents' dying and Dora's fever. I think she was trying to tell me why she has to keep so much inside. What I'm trying to tell you is: She has suffered more loss than she can bear. You are the most precious thing in the world to her. She lives to protect you, and for her, that means keeping you close. She never takes her eyes off you."

I knew how important Mamma's happiness was to my father. I thought he was telling me why I had to stay home. My efforts to hide my disappointment were a failure. He saw what was wrong and put it right. "Oh, sweetheart, I didn't explain that very well. It doesn't mean she has to have her way. I'm just trying to tell you why she is the way she is."

CHAPTER 7

That Sunday morning, getting ready for church, I decided it was time for a declaration of independence. After I put on my favorite dress, a slate-blue silk with sprigs of heather embroidered on the bodice, I made the mistake of looking at my face in the mirror. A smile softened the chiseled planes of my cheekbones and the long line of my jaw, but that was about it.

I counted up my good points: straight white teeth, well-defined eyebrows, and thick, wavy brown hair, darker than Billy's. My eyes were green like his, and I had long lashes. A small triangular mole marred my cheek. My nose was aquiline, but the bone had a little ripple right in the middle that made it look like it had been broken. My forehead was high, lips thin. Would anyone ever want to kiss such skinny lips?

Ugly or not, I was intent on proceeding with my plan. Deliberately, I unplaited my braids and twisted my hair into a soft knot at the base of my neck, pinning it carefully. In the privacy of my bedroom I'd tried a dozen different styles, and decided this knot was the most becoming. I put on my favorite hat, a navy-blue felt decorated with a black velvet ribbon and two dark pink roses. Tipping it this way and that until it was set at the most flattering angle, I anchored it with pearl-tipped hatpins. Looking in the mirror one last time, I stuck out my tongue and ran downstairs to join my parents for the short walk to church.

Daddy was wearing his suit and his favorite hat, a smart gray fedora. Mamma was waiting by his chair in her black bombazine cloak and kid boots, her habitual black straw planted squarely on top of her head. Her hatpins were adorned with jet beads, the only visible concession to femininity. But I knew underneath the high-necked collar of her dress she was wearing the gold necklace Daddy had given her on their wedding day. She never took it off.

I fully expected Mamma to tell me to march back upstairs and take my hair down. I was braced to resist. In fact, I was hoping she would insist because I was in the mood to refuse. Instead, after a tense moment, she said, "We need to get going or we'll be late."

Why had Mamma passed up the chance for a good fight? Enjoying my victory, I joined in the hymns, harmonizing my alto with Daddy's tenor.

The minister droned on—he deemed a half-hour of moral instruction the bare minimum—and my thoughts drifted until I heard his voice drop into a lower register, signaling the end was finally in sight. If I listened to the last few sentences, I'd be able to discuss the sermon at lunch and that would please Mamma, which seemed in my best interest since I'd provoked her that morning.

Usually his admonitions were toothless, but today they bit into me like the fangs of an adder: "What the Lord seeks to show us in today's lesson is the danger of setting our own desires above those of others. We are always in danger of taking the road to selfishness. Too often we justify that choice by calling it the path of righteousness. Poor fallen creatures that we are, blind to our vanities, we must learn to see the sacrifices that must be made if we want to call ourselves followers of Jesus Christ, the Son of God, who gave Himself for our salvation. We must embrace duties that are bitter and pledge ourselves, as He did, to drink from that bitter cup without complaint."

It felt as if he were speaking only to me because he knew how selfish and greedy I was. My mother was a follower of Christ, without question. No matter how hard she was on me she was at least as hard on herself. When I helped my father out of the pew, he put his hand on my arm and squeezed it quickly.

Later that night I overheard a conversation I was never meant to hear.

Every Sunday after dinner Mamma heated water on the stove for Daddy's bath. After she carried several gallons of hot water up the stairs to fill the tub, she helped him undress and climb in. When I was very small, I watched this ritual, which followed my own bath, because Mamma wanted to keep an eye on me so I didn't wander off and get into trouble.

Getting him in and out of the tub was hard. Lifting his body up and lowering it into the water put pressure on his spine. No matter how hard Mamma tried to support his back, sometimes he cried out. He'd look at me and say, "Don't worry, Peanut, I'm fine. You know me, always making a fuss."

On that Sunday, as I walked down the hall, I heard his voice. "Hannah, I've been thinking about what the Reverend said today. He was telling us we're being selfish."

"Selfish?" she said incredulously. "What are you talking about?"

"I think he meant we should let her go."

I couldn't resist the temptation to eavesdrop. Mamma said sharply, "Don't be a fool, William. He was telling her to put the needs of others above her own. She knew it. I read it in her face."

"Of course she took it to heart. She's a good girl. But her wish isn't about vanity or willfulness. The kinds of mathematics she'll be studying will be very difficult, and all she's asking for is the chance to do the work. Why can't you see she was born to do this?"

"Her place is here."

"I don't agree," he said. "Maybe I did, but I was wrong. I can't hide behind your skirts this time. Shouldn't she have the chance you never had? Aren't you stuck here, taking care of me and little else? Isn't that a shame? I won't ruin both your lives."

Mamma didn't deny what he'd said. Instead, she said, "What if I weren't here to care for you? Wouldn't you need her? That day may come, sooner than you think."

"What are you saying, Hannah? Are you ill?" I heard the fear in Daddy's voice.

"We never know when death will come knocking at our door," Mamma said. By this time, she sounded almost hysterical. "She was born into this life, and she will not escape it."

A few days later, Billy asked me to ride out to the orchards with him. We raced each other to the creek, where we threw ourselves on the ground and, using our hands as cups, drank from the swift-flowing creek and looked down into the cool water, searching for minnows. I offered him the cookies I'd saved in my lunch box, but he turned them down, a first. It turned out this little jaunt had an agenda.

"Told her yet, Ev?"

"You know I did, weeks ago."

"No, I don't mean did you tell her about Howard's offer. I mean have you told her you're going?"

"Told her? Nobody tells her anything. When did I ever bend her will to mine?"

"Rather recently, I'd say," he said, with a raised eyebrow. "The braids are gone."

"I mean about something serious. She's made it clear my leaving home would be the great betrayal."

"So, you're going to crump out," he said, "and let her ruin your life?"

"I've tried everything. Rationality, promises, tears—not that I meant to cry. I've lost my temper. I can just about match her there, but she's still the queen of fits. Miss Koenig tried to convince her. I heard Daddy arguing with her during his bath. They never argue. But he didn't back off. She told him he had it all wrong—my duty is to take care of him after she dies. I could have killed her, throwing it in his face like that. She literally said, 'Evelyn will never escape this life.' Think what that means. She believes a life consumed by caretaking is a punishment, and she means for me to be punished, just as she was."

"Mom tried to talk sense to her," Billy said. "They're barely speaking." He pressed me. "She can't stop you. She can't chain you to the bedpost."

"You don't get it. The chains that bind girls may be invisible, but they're forged of steel."

"Time to whip out your invisible hacksaw, Missy. Tell the old trout. Because I'm not going without you. I told my mother this morning . . . and I mean it, Squirt."

"You can't be serious? You'd stay home?"

"Absolutely. I won't let her keep you trapped here by yourself."

"But one of us has to go!" I said.

"Nope."

CHAPTER 8

The following Saturday morning, when we finished breakfast, Mamma said, matter-of-factly, as if she were telling me to pack up the winter woolens, "You're going to need two gowns for evening wear. I've got a piece of blue lace that should do for one."

I had no idea what she was talking about. I had no evening dress or any need for one, let alone two.

"Come up to my room," she said. "I brought it down from the attic to see if you like it."

Mystified, I watched her spread yards of periwinkle-blue lace across the coverlet on her bed.

"Dora gave it to me when I married," Mamma said. "I haven't lived the sort of life where there was much call for lace, but I take it out of the tissue every fall to make sure it's not fading. Now you need it."

"But why? In June I can wear the green silk for graduation, the one you made last summer."

"I expect there are a lot of evening parties at Stanford. You can't wear the same dress to every one."

Finally, it hit me. Not only had my mother imagined me going to Stanford she had imagined my going to parties there, too. I certainly hadn't.

I saw that she was waiting for a response. I was anxious that, if I didn't say the right thing, I might lose all I seemed to have gained. Eventually, I said meekly, "Thank you, Mamma, but I don't need another dress. They're so much work, and you're so busy."

"Nonsense. I love to sew. I have some ideas. Grab a paper and pencil. I want to show you a design I've been thinking about. Come sit on the bed."

I sat quietly, watching her sketch. She was speaking to me in the language of clothes, a kind of speech we both understood.

Winter 1913

I helped to make the blue lace dress, and that was just the beginning. While I'd never mastered knitting, my mother had taught me how to sew—back then there were so few ready-made clothes to buy that sewing was as essential a skill as cooking. The two of us spent hours together, stitching seams, facings, hems, buttons, and buttonholes. I learned to turn a sleeve properly, a skill that had always eluded me. We made new underclothing, and Mamma embroidered the white lawn chemises with lilies of the valley. She tailored a new traveling suit for me.

That year, because fashion dictated skirts should almost brush the floor, I insisted my hems clear the ground by just one inch. I seized the rare chance to abuse my power over my mother. I couldn't resist. The poor woman spent hours crawling around on the hardwood floor, holding a yardstick, straight pins in her mouth, reminding me to hold still. Then we shared the rest of this little purgatory, hemming my voluminous skirts with hundreds of small, neat stitches.

I wanted my mother to know I appreciated her seeming change of heart: Why would she have spent so many hours creating a beautiful new wardrobe for me if she wasn't pleased that I was going to have this chance to spread my wings? Her letting go of her ferocious objections was so out of character that I hoped her backing down might open a door long shut between us. If Mamma, Daddy, and I could believe in the adventure that lay ahead of me, perhaps we could find the closeness I longed for.

But my efforts to tell my mother I loved her for letting me go came to little. She cut me off.

"Your father insisted. He said it would be cruel to forbid you to go. I am not a cruel person. Nor could I go against his wishes. So I had no choice. It's settled. You may go."

The word "cruel" stunned me. I was amazed my father had gone so far. I was also hurt that, if he hadn't, apparently my mother would not have given in. Perhaps she'd been shamed by my father's judgment. But I've never been sure. Those lovely clothes told another story, wonderful but obscure. Who would embroider lilies of the valley out of a sense of duty? Perhaps she had heard Dora's message. Perhaps she knew Billy was stubborn enough to make good on his threat to stay home, and she couldn't hurt him or her sister that profoundly. I don't know. Maybe she didn't want to lose me—but she just couldn't admit it.

The summer slipped by, and I grew excited about all that lay ahead: teachers who would challenge me, students as smart as I was who might, with luck, become friends as well as sparring partners. I was eager to escape the pressure of being my mother's daughter. But I was painfully aware of Daddy's sadness. If I said anything, he made light of it, but he had no talent for hiding his feelings. Once I was gone, we wouldn't have tea together every afternoon, I wouldn't sit in his office while I did my homework, we wouldn't sit on the porch and gab on warm evenings. His love had been the salvation of my childhood. I had trouble finding the right words to tell him what I felt.

"Daddy, I'm going to miss you. I expect you'll miss me, too."

"Of course I will, darling, but I'm thrilled you're going. I want you to have this chance."

"I love you as much as I could ever love anyone, not least for standing by me when I needed you."

"I will always want the best for you, whatever that is. A parent should never cling to a child."

"That doesn't mean my going away won't be hard."

"A lot of important things are hard. But we still need to do them."

September 1913

As the day of my leaving drew near, my mother and I wrapped my clothes in tissue and laid them gently in an old steamer trunk. There was a sense of accomplishment in the air, but also of finality, and no little tension. We were both nervous. One harsh remark, one slip of the tongue, might rend the fragile veil of acceptance that had protected the two of us for the last few months.

The morning I left, Mamma said she didn't want to go to the station. On the porch, she wished me well while Daddy waited in the buggy. When he shook the reins to get the horse moving, I looked back and saw her wave, looking sadder than I'd ever seen her. That look was chastening. I'd had to fight so hard to leave I'd never considered she would miss me. If I hadn't looked back, I might never have known.

Will I ever understand why she went to such lengths to hide that she loved me? My father had explained the cost of showing affection was so high she could not risk it. But why? She succeeded in driving me away. Did she truly want that?

At the station, Dora and little Alice were already waiting on the platform. Because they were wearing matching navy overcoats Mamma had made for them last Christmas, Alice looked even more like a miniature of her mother than usual. Billy was stowing his luggage in the baggage car. Daddy busied himself, hailing a porter to carry my trunk, and then I gave him a quick hug.

I noticed Alice, standing on tippy toes, straining to see inside the train. I held her up high so she could get a good look at the interior of the car. As I was about to board, Dora slipped a little box in my pocket and whispered, "Don't worry, dear. I'll look after them. Go now, and live."

Offering me the seat next to the window, Billy said, "It's hard to leave. I don't like the idea of Mother and Alice alone in that house by themselves. But this is still a great day—we're getting out of this one-horse town."

Hell-bent on medical school, Billy knew exactly where he was headed. At that moment I wasn't so sure. Mathematics suddenly seemed an abstract love, home more precious. When I took Dora's box from my pocket and opened it, I found an old, delicate gold necklace hung with lilies of the valley, pearls folded into tiny gold leaves covered with green enamel. This necklace had to have a special meaning for Dora. She had taken very good care of it: Not a single leaf was chipped. It was jewelry better suited for a fairy princess than a hapless college student. I asked Billy if he recognized it, but he shook his head. After I returned it carefully to its box, I sat stroking the box's velvet surface, looking out the window and feeling forlorn.

"Think about it, Ev!" Billy said, intent on cheering me up. "We'll meet new people, kids from all over the state. No more teachers—we'll have professors. Ferocious old fossils, but you're going to knock 'em out."

No matter how hard he tried to jolly me into it, I couldn't share his enthusiasm. Until this morning I'd been so eager to leave. Now that I'd finally boarded the train, I felt bewildered and guilty. Billy opened his newspaper and settled in to wait for me to come back to him. I always did.

CHAPTER 9

On board the USS Huntington
April 1919

Throughout our tense and endless journey home from France, I rarely took my eyes off Billy. The contrast of the confident young man who'd calmly buried himself in his newspaper on that long-ago morning with the angry, moody man now pacing the deck hour after hour made me so sad. The ground of our lives was shifting under our feet. When I had agreed to marry Arthur, I had assumed I would be able to depend on Billy's strength, as I always had. But our roles were reversing: It looked as if I would be the one who had to provide the strength and faith we needed. If Billy was as broken as he seemed, how would I be able to go to Boston?

During the first semester of our freshman year at Stanford, I'd been the one who lacked confidence, not Billy. He studied hard but found plenty of time for the girls who flocked around him. Handsome, funny and kind, he could have had a date with a different girl every night if he'd wanted one.

I struggled in one class. Unfortunately, it was the only one I truly cared about, a course in number theory. Thanks to a perfect score on a placement test, I'd been invited to take a graduate seminar taught by Dr. David Page, an eccentric genius with no patience for fools, and little patience for anyone else. He'd walk into the classroom, turn to the blackboard and begin stabbing it with a stick of chalk, scribbling numbers and symbols, scarcely bothering to look at us. The chalk broke frequently. He kept extra sticks in the pockets of his trousers so he could grab a fresh one before he lost his train of thought. I often thought he was having a conversation with himself. At times his voice dropped so low it was hard to hear what he was saying. I'd rush to copy into my notebook everything he wrote on the blackboard, hoping I could make sense of it later.

He rarely said anything of a personal nature until the morning he mentioned he'd just received a letter from his friend Hardy at Cambridge. To get the class underway, he read us an extract from the letter. I knew G. H. Hardy was the most prominent number theorist in the world. It dawned on me: If Hardy wanted Page to know what he was thinking, Page wasn't just a giant at Stanford.

In the beginning I was confused by Page's style of teaching, or more precisely by his style of mind, which seemed chaotic. His words and the symbols he dashed on the board tended to diverge. His mind seemed to buzz around like a bumblebee. Eventually, I realized that he sometimes started talking about a second question, of greater interest to him, while he finished writing out the answer to the first question. Assuming his students could follow him wherever he went, he ignored evidence to the contrary. I sensed he was perfectly happy talking to himself.

In the first weeks of the term, his lectures scared me spitless—I didn't know if I would ever understand what he was trying to teach us. Before class, I skipped breakfast because I knew I might throw it up. I prayed he wouldn't call on me.

One day in November, Billy asked me to have lunch with him on the quad, where we joined the other students sitting on the lawn eating sandwiches. It was one of the last days of autumn, crisp with a clear blue sky, and we knew we'd be spending the rest of the afternoon cooped up inside, studying. Before we went inside, he suggested a walk down by the creek.

Once we were alone, he said, "Something's bothering you. If you don't want to talk about it, okay, but I wish you would."

"It's the same old thing. Page. I've never been afraid of anyone before, at least not anyone at school. My mind struggles to follow him. Sometimes I wobble and lose my way entirely."

Billy shook his head ruefully.

"Good Lord. The rest of us wobble all the time. You're used to everything coming easy—maybe that's not so great. You know how bored you get."

"Not in Page's class."

"Maybe that's a good thing."

"Hmm, boredom or terror. Great choices."

"Hang onto your shirt, Squirt." He made as if to pick me up by the collar of my blouse, but I saw the move coming and slipped out of his grasp. "I predict that, before it's over, Page will be afraid of you."

I was inspired to do something I hadn't done in years—tickle him until he rolled up into a ball and begged for mercy. For a couple of minutes we were eight again. Eventually, I quit and laid down on the grass next to him, the warmth of the sun filling me with contentment.

In time Billy was proved right. I saw that Page didn't always know what he'd be saying next—he was willing to take himself and his students on a journey without knowing for certain what he'd find at trail's end. If he could tolerate the possibility of a trip to nowhere, there was a lesson in that for me. At first I'd sat in the back of the lecture hall to avoid notice; by the end of the semester, I'd moved to the front row where it was easier to hear him. At the best moments, when I did comprehend what he meant, it felt as if I'd been right behind him, climbing a steep, rocky trail, and suddenly both of us could see the magnificence of the ocean stretching before us.

December 24, 1913

When exams were over, Billy and I were happy to head home.
On Christmas Eve, Billy, Alice, and Dora joined us for dinner as
they did every year. While our mothers worked in the kitchen,
the rest of us hung ornaments and put candles in the punched-tin
holders. We always lit the candles after dinner, when we sat
down in the parlor to open our gifts, because Mamma worried
a tree left untended might catch fire. The house filled with the
smell of roasting goose. Mashed potatoes and buttered lima beans
were kept warm on top of the stove until the bird was done.

When we gathered around the table, conversation was
general and easy until Daddy asked what we did for entertainment at college. Billy said I was a model of decorum, in the
library even on Saturday nights, which was a slight exagger-
ation. To make us laugh, he launched into the tale of a prank
he'd played on his roommates, rich boys from San Francisco.
A couple of pompous asses, they'd treated him like a hayseed.

One Saturday they had all been invited to a party at the
Sigma Nu house. Standing on the second-floor balcony, Billy
proposed a contest. He suggested the three of them drink as
much punch, a lethal mixture of gin and apricot brandy, as
they could. The first two who called it quits would have to pay
five dollars to the last man standing. He knew they wouldn't
be able to resist the dare since they prided themselves on how
well they handled their liquor. To set the pace, he drank two
cups at a fast clip. After that, while the others knocked back
cup after cup, he quietly poured the rest of his drinks over the
railing onto the rhododendrons below.

When they both passed out, Billy enlisted a friend to help
carry them back to the dorm. He left a note on their night
table: "I thoroughly enjoyed your company. No need to thank
me for the ride home, but it's going to cost you ten bucks."

Everybody at the table was laughing, except Mamma, whose
lips were set in a tight line. When the laughter died down, she
said, "I don't find that funny in the least."

"Oh, Mamma, Billy was tired of their childish antics. Those pipsqueaks deserved a comeuppance."

"Drunkenness is abominable," Mamma said. "Leading someone into drunkenness is worse. It's preying on weakness."

"Mamma, those idiots drink every chance they get. Billy didn't need to lead them anywhere."

Silence.

"Mamma, they treat Billy like he's a bumpkin. He just wanted a chance to even the playing field."

"I'm sure he did," Mamma said, "and, as I can see, you now know everything."

"That's outrageous."

"I don't see the outrage at all."

"You wouldn't," I spat out, stomping out of the room, leaving an overturned chair in my wake.

Later Dora came up to my room where I was lying on my bed rigid with anger. There was no fireplace in the room, so she shook out the quilt and tucked it in around me. Sitting on the edge of my bed, she stroked my back until I began to unwind a bit.

"You know she practiced on me first."

"Did you ever fight back?" I asked.

"Not really. That's why you confuse her. She expected her daughter to be as docile as I was."

"What was she like when you were young?"

"Not so different from the way she is now. Fierce, determined, certain about how to do everything, when to do it, and why. I needed the shelter of her certainty. Only later did I realize how much she needed it, as a fortress she built around us so we could be safe, inside the walls. Imagine what it was like for her when she realized we weren't wanted in Boston. She was my only protector. She must have been terrified, but she never let me see it. She's still scared. Her rage is a paper-thin cover for fear."

"But why? She has a home; she has Daddy and me, and you and Billy and Alice."

"Some wounds never heal, *Liebchen*. They're too deep. To convince herself she's invincible, she turns her fear outward and visits it as righteous anger on other people, especially you. It's not pretty. But I understand where it comes from."

"Why aren't you like her? You lost everything, the same as she did."

"No, I didn't. I had her."

"She had you."

"But who was the mother then?"

I had never thanked her for the necklace. Lifting the gold chain with one finger, I gently touched an enameled leaf. "It's so beautiful and so delicate I'm worried I'll break it. Where did it come from?"

"It belonged to our mother. I wore it in a little leather pouch around my neck on the trip from Germany. Now it's time for you to have it. I talked to Hannah before I gave it to you, and she agreed. Wear it. Don't lock it away in a jewelry box."

"But Billy's wife should have it someday."

"*Nein, Liebchen*. There will be plenty of lovely things for Billy's wife. My Mamma would have given it to you. She would have loved you so, and you're her blood. In the kitchen, while we were filling up the platters, did you feel your Mamma touching the clasp, on the back of your neck, ever so lightly, with her fingertips?"

I shook my head no.

"You look so much like our Mamma: the thick, curling, almost coppery hair, the ivory skin, the same quick, light movements. I can still see her sitting out on the porch, her feet tucked up underneath her, bent over her book, idly pushing back wisps of hair that had fallen out of their pins."

"I'm sorry I ruined dinner," I said, pushing myself up out of bed so we could go back downstairs. "I didn't mean to. I never mean to. I just couldn't bear her scolding Billy."

"Her anger rolls right off him like water off a duck's back. He swims away, preening his feathers, and it drives her wild." Dora giggled, and she reached for my hand.

"I wish I had a little of that," I said.

"You wouldn't be your mother's daughter if you did."

"No, I guess not. Daddy doesn't let her get to him either."

"You have many of your father's good qualities. But his gentleness is almost unearthly. If you didn't have that fieriness, you'd never have gotten out of here. A woman who's too soft will be crushed. Better off mad as hell."

CHAPTER 10

On board the USS Huntington
April 1919

The next morning the ship seemed to have outrun the storm front that had been pursuing her. I was grateful because I never had good sea legs—just being on board ship made me feel slightly nauseous. After a dreary breakfast in the mess of scrambled eggs, stale bread, and weak coffee, I went up on deck to get some air. As I gripped the railing, I watched the gulls circling our ship, wishing I was as free. Instead, I was enmeshed in a net woven by the war, by my love for Billy and by his love for me. I could see Arthur was trapped in this net, too, and unless I found a way to cut the ties that bound the three of us, I worried I might lose him, too.

The ease with which those birds were sailing through the air took me back to the day Billy made me feel like a bird, a perfect summer day in that last perfect summer of 1914, just weeks before the Germans swept through Belgium.

Billy was working at the cannery that year, and I was stationed behind the counter at the bakery, tying up boxes of cookies and cakes with red-and-white string. On his days off, Billy was nowhere to be found, and I missed his company. The previous summer he'd spent his spare time in the garage, lying underneath his dilapidated old jalopy, teaching himself by trial and error how the combustion engine worked. I had grown accustomed to his dropping by my house when he took a break from tinkering with his bucket of bolts.

On a hot afternoon in July, I was lazing on the wooden swing on our back porch, engrossed in the newspaper, when Billy landed next to me, pushing off hard with his foot, sending us flying.

"Always need to be airborne?" I said, a little exasperated.

Billy was uncharacteristically silent, not taking the bait I'd thrown him. "You might say that." He reached for my newspaper so he could read the headlines.

"There's more about the assassination in Sarajevo," I said. "When the Archduke and his wife were murdered, they were on their way to the hospital to visit the people hurt by the bomb that had missed their car earlier in the day. His wife was shot and killed trying to shield him from the gunman. Later, the assassin tried to shoot himself too, but the police stopped him. When he took cyanide, that didn't work either. Miserable little swine."

Billy grimaced as he studied the photograph of the assassin. "I have a bad feeling about this. A really bad feeling. But today I came to show you something that makes me very happy, and I will not be deterred. Can I tear you away from your seat on the porch?"

"Nope, sorry. I promised Mother I'd help her with a pile of mending. Most of the stockings in her basket are mine."

"Really? I can't tempt you?"

"Heaven knows I'd rather do anything fun, but if I don't do it, she'll blow her stack. I wouldn't even blame her. I've been stalling."

"Okay, Missy, I grant you a day's grace," he said. "But I will be here at six sharp tomorrow morning, when I won't take no for an answer."

"You're certainly mysterious. What are you up to?"

"Patience, poppet," he said, as he trotted down the steps of the porch. Turning to look back, he raised an eyebrow, grinned and said, "I have a little surprise in store. You must trust in William Greenfield, even when airborne."

True to his word, Billy knocked on our back door the next morning, so early I was hardly awake. I made him a cup of coffee, black, no sugar, and ran upstairs to dress. As soon as I reappeared, he whipped me into his car. He loved speed; I didn't. Fortunately, the streets were almost deserted.

Trying to keep my eyes off the road, I studied his profile. A perfectly proportioned brow led down to an aquiline nose, so like mine but minus the ripple; the rosy lips elegant and carefully cut, as if by an American Michelangelo carving his David, a boy from the West. The sun had turned his skin golden, his sandy hair blond, and his eyes more intensely green than they would seem next winter, after the tan faded. It had been so long since I had really looked at him—his face was so utterly familiar to me. He was part of the air I breathed. I'd forgotten how lovely he was.

We drove north, into the country, for the better part of an hour. I hadn't a clue where we were going, and when I asked, he just put a finger to his lips. Suddenly, he pulled over, turned off the engine and drew a scarf from his pocket, which he directed me to use as a blindfold.

"So what are we playing here, blind man's bluff?"

"Indulge me."

"Okay, but this better be good," I said, tying the scarf around my head.

Five minutes later, he stopped the car again, came around to open my door, and led me over the grass because the ground was uneven. He didn't want me to turn an ankle.

"So is this where I get sold into white slavery?"

"You wish."

"You're awful."

"But I am funny."

"That's true."

"Get those eyebrows out of your hairline. They increase the resemblance to your mother."

"Not fair!"

"But effective, my darling."

When he finally pulled off the scarf, I found myself so close to a small airplane I could almost touch it.

"I got my license yesterday!"

"Oh dear. Does this mean I'm your first passenger?"

"No need to worry. I guarantee you'll love it. It's the greatest feeling in the world."

"No need to worry? I haven't forgotten the day you convinced me to dive into the quarry pond, and I broke my arm."

"But I did jump in to save you, didn't I?"

"So you'll jump out of the plane if need be?"

"Of course."

"Good, now I'm completely calm."

He grabbed a helmet and goggles from the cockpit and helped me buckle them on, then pressed his hand into my back to help me scramble up into the passenger's seat. Jumping into the cockpit, he signaled, and a mechanic emerged from the hangar to pull the chocks out from under the wheels and wind the propeller.

The plane, built of wood, wire, and linen, so slight it looked like a huge cricket, taxied downfield. I was so nervous I stopped breathing. I was going to faint if I didn't force myself to breathe, so I made myself, but I also closed my eyes tightly. The plane rose slowly into the air. By the time I dared to open my eyes, Billy was banking gently in a long, smooth curve. We sailed above the orchards; then, as we reached the coastal range, we climbed steeply, up over the redwoods, until suddenly I saw the ocean, and the sun glinting off the water. I'd never felt so free. I wished my feet would never touch the ground again, that, instead, we could soar above the clouds forever, together.

When the plane began to run low on fuel, Billy had to head back. It seemed to me we were barely clearing the tops of the trees as we flew over the orchards. The field was so bumpy that, coming in to land, the plane bounced along the ground. Pilots today probably can't imagine landing on grass. Maybe bush pilots in Africa. California was pretty much bush then, a scrappy place trying to find its way.

Once we were back on the ground, he looked at me for approval. To hide my pleasure—I didn't want him to be too satisfied with himself—I teased him.

"Well, there are no broken bones. But I expect there are some gray hairs. Were you trying to make sure I'd never fly again?"

"No. I thought you would love it."

"I did. I was terrified, but I wouldn't have missed it for anything. It makes one jealous of birds, doesn't it?"

CHAPTER 11

Stanford University
1914

In August, when the Germans crossed the border into neutral Belgium, slaughtering her small army and shooting civilians who resisted, France and Britain had no choice but to declare war. That brazen, vicious attack was as riveting as it was horrifying, but in those early days we still had no idea how radically the war would change our lives—at least, I didn't.

One morning a couple of weeks before Thanksgiving, Billy stopped by the carrel in the library where I was studying and interrupted me, which I found aggravating because I needed to concentrate.

"Ev, can I talk to you?"

"We have a physics midterm tomorrow. Don't you need to study?"

"Maybe after dinner?"

"Are you in trouble?"

Heaven knows he had a genius for getting into trouble. Instead of answering my question, he just smiled and left me in peace. I didn't think much about it.

That night after dinner, we walked down into the woods behind the residence halls. The air was so clear the stars looked brighter than usual. The Milky Way in all its millions shone broadly across the sky. How vast is the universe and how little we understand it.

Without preamble, Billy said: "I'm not coming back to school after exams."

I couldn't believe my ears. "You what? You're quitting? What are you thinking? Forget that question. Clearly, you're not thinking."

"This war won't be fought by cavalry," he said. "Planes are going to win it. Pilots will be desperately needed. I need to be there, in the real fight. I can't play at being a schoolboy any longer."

"But America's not even in the war," I countered. "Wilson's dead set against it."

"It's only a matter of time. But even if America chickens out, I won't. My father came here from England. England's in, and so am I."

"What about your mother, who came here from Germany?" I asked, playing what I thought would be a strong card.

"A country that tossed her out like so much trash. I've been thinking about this since the ground war came to a halt, after the butchery at Ypres. The Brits who survived are trapped in the trenches. The only thing that's kept me here this long is worrying about my mother."

"You and Alice are her whole life," I said, slicing closer to the bone. Normally, I would never have used the happiness or welfare of his mother and sister to pressure him. But the danger to him felt so acute I was willing to use any weapon I could lay my hands on.

"That's the hell of it, but it's also why I have to go."

"I'm not sure I've ever heard anyone say anything so completely illogical."

"My mother raised me to be a certain kind of man, one who would not choose a life without honor."

I felt frantic. "What would her life be without you?" What I really meant was: What would *my* life be?

"Please, don't make me feel any more guilty than I already do," he said, his face pleading. "I need you to stand by me."

Grabbing his shoulders and pulling him close, I said furiously, "Not on your life." Afraid of what else I might say, I ran back toward the lights of the dormitory. Just before I opened the door, I turned and saw him sitting with his head in his hands.

The next afternoon we left the examination room together.

"You aren't going to change your mind, are you?" I asked.

He shook his head.

"Have you thought about how you're going to break this to your mother?"

"Haven't thought about much else," he said, "except for how mad you are." I thought, I'm only mad because you're making me so scared.

"So what are you going to do?"

"I was hoping you'd come home with me this weekend."

"All right," I said, "but I'm not going to be in the room when you tell her. You have to do that alone."

That Saturday afternoon I waited on our back porch while Billy talked to Dora. When he walked out the back door of his house, I could tell by the hunch of his shoulders how badly he felt about what he'd just done.

Sitting down beside me on the swing, he said, "I think she already knew I might do this."

"I guess she knows you better than I do."

"But I know I scared her. Would you go over and see her? She's upset, but she shut herself up tight, to hide it from me."

I squeezed his shoulder and set off across the garden. At the back door, I was on the point of calling out her name when I heard crying. Letting myself in, I set about making tea to give her time to collect herself. While I was buttering toast, she came in to help.

"There's nothing we can do to stop him, is there?" I asked.

"No, and I don't think we should."

"Really?"

"He has to live with himself. If he doesn't go, he'll spend the rest of his life regretting it. I can't do that to him, no matter how afraid I am. I am afraid. But I have to accept that he must do this."

I had to try to match her courage, but doubted I could.

CHAPTER 12

January 1915

Billy left for France on a cheerless winter morning. Dora, Alice, and I accompanied him to the train station to see him off. That night, instead of ordering me to help her make dinner, my mother asked if I would help her. While I scraped carrots, she came over and stood quietly beside me. When I turned to her, I could see that she, too, was close to tears.

"I made my life here in America. I am proud to be a citizen of the United States, but I never forget Germany is my homeland. Why Germany decides she has to fight again, I have no idea. My mother's brother was killed the last time they fought against the French, at the battle for Sedan. Run through by a saber. That was less than fifty years ago; apparently, they learned nothing. This will be just one more terrible waste of young lives. Billy, going to fight simply because his father was English. Think what it will mean to Dora if he's killed."

Our worries redoubled when, for weeks, we didn't know where Billy was. Back at school, I felt very much alone. Dora had promised she would get a message to me as soon as she heard from Billy.

France felt unimaginably far away. There were plenty of people in San Jose who had never visited San Francisco.

Eventually, we learned Billy had gone first to Toronto because he hoped to join the Royal Canadian Flying Corps. Letters and postcards trickled in, recounting his vain effort to sign up for the Corps. He wasn't Canadian, and there were already more young Canadians who wanted to fly than there were planes. Nonetheless, a sense of adventure and high purpose blazed through his letters as he searched for another way to serve.

We received a letter from him written the day before he boarded a steamer bound for Le Havre—which meant that by the time we read it he was already crossing the Atlantic. Anyone who read the newspapers knew the German kill rate for ships, naval and civilian, was high.

May 1915

Three months later, a letter from Billy arrived in my mailbox telling me he had reached Paris safely. As I read it, I thought about how we'd dreamed of visiting Paris one day. Now he was there alone, with little cause for gaiety because the Germans were almost at the gate.

When he arrived, he'd felt like a tramp. There'd been no showers on the boat and no way to wash clothes. But the city was filled with thousands of refugees as dusty and dirty as he was, who'd fled the countryside just ahead of the furious German advance. Looking at their exhausted, haunted faces, he saw how ridiculous he was to care how he looked.

Not sure where else to go, he'd made his way to the American Embassy in the Place du Trocadéro to ask if there was some way he could help. The following morning a young attaché introduced him to Beatrice Franklin, a wealthy American expatriate who'd lived in Paris for years, after leaving a disappointing husband behind in England. A formidable woman who could shame the most puffed-up bureaucrat into doing what she needed done, she was organizing relief for refugees, and she put Billy to work immediately, cooking and serving in the cafeteria she'd set up, staffed by people she paid out of her own pocket.

At first Billy felt chagrined to be doing "women's work." He illustrated his letters with comical sketches of himself wearing an apron, brandishing a skillet, burning his fingers. He tried to maintain the fiction he was the same devil-may-care Billy we'd always known, but I read between the lines. He was keenly alive to the desperation of those he was feeding, some of them widows already, others with husbands at the front, many with children. It broke his heart to see families reduced to living in dormitories, perched during the day on cots, with little but what they'd been able to carry in a suitcase shoved underneath their skimpy beds. Some proudly displayed an enameled clock or porcelain tureen, the only treasure they'd saved from homes left behind to an uncertain fate.

Few in the capital knew much about what was happening at the front. Rumors flew. As the Germans closed in on the city, many rich women who'd turned their homes into private hospitals shut down operations and fled to the south of France. Billy was proud of his Mrs. Franklin, who refused to budge from her townhouse in the Rue de Martignac, near the Invalides. She loved Paris and had no intention of deserting when the need was so great. I began to envy Billy and Mrs. Franklin for being where they were needed. When Billy wrote about Mrs. Franklin's courage and stamina, I felt jealous, stuck at home, still a schoolgirl.

As the rumor mill churned ever faster, she asked Billy if he'd drive with her toward the front to get an idea of what was going on. In a car loaded with food and gasoline, they headed east. They saw bodies—rotting, covered with flies—that had been moved to the side of the road to make way for troops and trucks.

Shelling had destroyed everything in its path. Trees had been leveled.

Only burnt stumps remained. Though the sight of ruined trees was upsetting, they felt these were the least of the losses in a countryside where homes, churches, and farms had been reduced to rubble, on a scale beyond anything they had imagined.

They found a village where the church had been hastily turned into a hospital, the nave strewn with straw to serve as a communal mattress for the wounded. While most patients were French, some were German. All of them were cared for not just by French but also by German doctors who could not bear to leave their countrymen behind.

Billy was touched to see these doctors, enemies in theory, operating side by side, as fast as they could, desperate to save anyone who could be saved, national differences forgotten. Billy and I lived with the difficult knowledge that our mothers were German. If their parents had not died when they were young, those little girls would have grown up in Germany and, no doubt, married there. If either had had a son, he might well have been lying here, on the floor of this church in a muddy, blood-soaked German uniform.

The hospital was short of everything: food, water, bandages, drugs, and blankets. Billy and Mrs. Franklin unloaded all they had brought in their car. They knelt on the floor and held glasses of water to the lips of thirsty men whose hands were bandaged or missing. At twilight, they headed back to Paris. They'd seen what they needed to see, and they were exhausted. Driving through the dark, they talked late into the night about what they could do to help.

The French had been entirely unprepared for Germany's attack. Every ambulance had been mobilized; then every automobile and truck had been commandeered to carry soldiers to the front and bring back the wounded. Neutrals were allowed to give humanitarian aid, so Billy and Mrs. Franklin planned a letter-writing campaign, asking everyone they knew to donate money to buy ambulances. By that summer of 1915, no one knew what the future held except more blood and pain.

While they were raising money, Billy trained in first aid, and he was assigned to meet the wounded at a suburban train station on the edge of Paris. The dozens of stretcher drills he'd done had not prepared him for the sight of men who'd spent weeks lying in the clothes in which they'd been wounded. Blood had glued the fabric to their skin, and that fabric had to be cut away at a dreadful cost in suffering as wounds were opened afresh and disinfected. In some cases, it was too late: Lockjaw had already set in—gangrene—which gave off a sickly sweet smell Billy never forgot.

His handwriting changed so much that reading his letters made me anxious. The old free, loping script became cramped hieroglyphics, which betrayed he was nowhere near as calm as he claimed to be.

We had read in the newspapers that, if the Germans came across a disabled ambulance, the wounded and drivers would be taken prisoner and the ambulance appropriated to carry injured Germans. Billy tried to reassure us; after all, he wrote, he was perfectly suited to drive an ambulance because, fixing his old car, he'd learned to take an engine apart and put it back together. Still, knowing Billy was no longer safe in Paris made my nights restless. Some nights I hardly slept at all.

Billy picked his way over roads torn up by heavy trucks and shelling, struggling to spare his passengers for whom every bump was agony.

One night he said yes to a request that altered his life forever. Pulling up at a field hospital, he jumped out to unload stretchers. Every nurse was busy. A surgeon in need of another pair of hands to close a gaping chest wound grabbed Billy and asked him to assist. Because of the many nights he'd spent helping his dad, he was able to leap right in.

When the surgeon saw how much Billy already knew, he asked if he would be willing to stay on. Billy didn't hesitate. From then on he was even busier than before, and the intervals between letters grew longer. He told us little of the gory realities of his life, but he did write that he was more certain than ever he wanted to be a doctor. The knowledge he could relieve suffering was his bulwark against horror. The one place he stopped worrying was the operating room where he had no time to think about anything but the work at hand.

I was relieved he was in a hospital; I thought this meant he would be safe because he was behind the front. I failed to understand how much of the damage inflicted by war is not physical.

CHAPTER 13

On board the USS Huntington
April 1919

I reminded myself that, even though Billy had lost his temper with me, before he'd gone below deck to sleep, he'd kissed me and called me Squirt. In the morning, we sat out in the sun and read; in the afternoon, we played a hard-fought game of gin, teasing and laughing, like old times. After dinner, feeling the barrier between us had come down, and we might be able to talk, I brought up the war again. Before long I saw how badly I had misread the situation.

Billy jumped out of his chair. Torment shot across his face like a jagged streak of lightning; I thought he might be having a seizure.

"Do you really want to know what happened? You're going to regret it." His voice broke on the word "regret." He hugged his chest with his arms; I could see he was trembling. "I want to protect you," he said, his face beseeching me to back down. "I need to protect you."

"That's not what I need," I said. "I need to know what happened. I can't help you if I have no idea what you are up against." Reaching out my hands to him, I tried to get him to sit down beside me. He refused, and my hands hung there in the air until finally I pulled them back and clasped them together in my lap.

"You have no idea what you're asking. But I know you so well I know you won't let this go. So I'll tell you why I don't sleep, but only just this once. When you want me to stop, say so. I wish you would."

I shook my head.

"I made a fatal mistake, last October, during the push through the Argonne Forest. Everybody was exhausted—it looked like we were losing, which meant the war would go into 1919, for a fifth year. Wounded were flooding in. We ran out of beds. We ran out of morphine. You could smell blood in the air. Men were screaming, crying, in pain. The quiet ones were quiet because they were in shock, which meant we would lose them if we didn't move fast. There weren't enough doctors, or nurses.

"I was on triage. They brought in a kid who'd caught a shell fragment in the gut. Blood was pouring out of him, but he was lucid. His platoon had been ordered to take out a machine gun hidden by a huge rock, at the top of a steep hill. A suicide mission, ordered by morons.

"I saw something in that kid. By that point I'd seen hundreds of wounds as bad as his. But, at that moment, he was the one I needed to save. He didn't look like me, but I thought, He could be my little brother. I poured reassurance into him, telling him to hang on, willing him to live.

"I was holding up the line, which was unfair to the men behind him, but I couldn't let go. I was convinced he had a chance if his bloody mess of intestines could be repaired. The doctor in charge disagreed. I ended up yelling at him, 'Everyone deserves a chance . . . You can't kill this kid.' I was scaring everyone in earshot. To shut me up, the doctor backed down. The boy survived the surgery, and I felt vindicated.

"I stopped by his bed every chance I got, checking his dressings and fluids, transfusing him, telling him he was going to make it. He died a slow, agonizing death, from peritonitis. That doctor knew what he was talking about. I should have listened. I caused that boy so much pain. My dad would never have made such a stupid mistake."

He had been right: I could hardly bear to listen to this story. But I had asked for it.

"After that, I tried to be careful, but I kept making mistakes because I was certain I'd make another disastrous error. I didn't want to be sent back. One slip and I could have killed someone else. I should've told the truth and asked to be relieved.

"Now I feel like there's acid running through my veins. I broke faith with my men. I was risking their lives because I was no longer trustworthy, and too much of a coward to admit it. They deserved better. Things were moving so fast nobody had time to notice what was going on with me, so I got away with it. Now, when I fall asleep, my patients visit me in dreams. I try not to sleep."

Before I had a chance to say anything, he hushed me, putting two fingers firmly against my lips. Then he turned and walked away. If I'd had the courage to talk to him right then, maybe his demons would have lost some of their power, but I didn't. Maybe no one could have helped him. My hand-wringing certainly never did him any good.

Over the next few days, he shut me out almost entirely. I was trapped in my own mind, with my own worries. I tried to write to Arthur, but night after night my waste-basket filled with crumpled sheets of stationery. The more I understood how hurt Billy was, the more I feared I would have to stay home to take care of him. I needed to write something of this to Arthur; otherwise, my silence might create distance between us. At the same time, I didn't want to betray Billy's confidence, so every letter I wrote felt wrong, unfair to someone, not even bearing witness to the truth—because I didn't know what the truth was. The whole time we were crossing the Atlantic, I never wrote a single satisfactory letter I could mail to Arthur, and that made me feel as if I had abandoned him. I certainly feared he would feel I had abandoned him.

But Billy was a greater concern for me then, for all I knew, a matter of life or death. He was fighting for his sanity each night. I worried I might wake up one morning to find he had slipped quietly over the side of the ship while I was sleeping.

CHAPTER 14

New York City
May 1919

When our ship docked, we headed straight to Penn Station and bought tickets for the next train west. The platform was packed with soldiers eager to get home, so we felt lucky when we wedged ourselves into a car, though we had to stand in the aisle. As the train pulled out of the station, we looked down on the faces of those left behind, some angry, some discouraged, others too tired to care.

Later that night Billy got hold of a seat, which he tried to give to me. Since he seemed to me far more exhausted than I was, I told him to keep it.

He lost patience. "Evelyn, that's ridiculous. I'm not going to let you stand while I sit." We'd come close to an explosion several times on this trip but usually pulled ourselves back from the edge. Now something as silly as a seat on a train set off the bomb.

"Stop treating me like a Dresden shepherdess," I hissed.

"I'll be damned if I'm going to sit here and watch you stand in the aisle," he said in a low voice. "Stop making a scene—be sensible and sit down right now."

"Be sensible" was the last straw. My mother had used those same two words to humiliate me too many times. Turning my back on him, I pushed through the crowd, elbowing people aside, ignoring wisecracks and curious looks. One pimply corporal called out, "Whatsamatter, sister? Lover boy treat you bad?"

I ran out of steam after a few cars. Tired and hurt, I found a spot on the floor. I thought about the pain waiting for Dora. I had considered writing from Paris to prepare her. Instead, I'd clung to the hope he would get better on the trip home.

Falling into a fitful sleep, I woke each time the train lurched and my head knocked against the side of the car. As sunlight finally crept in through the window, I saw stains on my skirt. During the night someone had kicked over a bottle of pop, and the sticky, sugary soda had run all over the floor. There was no way to wash it off. I wasn't even sure I could climb over enough people to get to the bathroom. Having had nothing to eat since we got on the train, I felt hollow.

Then Billy knelt down in front of me and lifted my chin with his fingertips. When he put his face close to mine, our noses touched.

I spread out my filthy, wet skirt for him to see. He sat down on the little square of floor next to me, snuggled up, and said, "Hungry?"

When I nodded, he produced a soggy ham sandwich from his pocket. "Cost me five cigarettes," he said, "but tough times require extreme measures!" Tearing it in two, he handed me the larger half. Last night we couldn't share a seat, but this morning we could share a sandwich. Maybe we would find our way back to each other.

As the train moved westward, there were fewer passengers, and more seats. Things seemed to ease between us. But I was still watching him constantly.

His fingernails were bitten down to the quick, something he'd never done in the old days. It made me feel helpless that I couldn't protect even his fingers. When our bodies pressed against each other, I felt waves of tension coursing through him, as he continually clenched the muscles in his arms and legs. When he tried to light a cigarette, his hand still trembled.

I hated how much he was smoking, and finally said so, which was stupid.

"I'm sorry, Evelyn, but I can't sit here watching you watch every move I make. *I can't take it anymore.*" With that, he got up and headed out of the car.

He'd made it plain I shouldn't go after him. I couldn't sit there by myself either, because I knew everyone around us was wondering what had caused his outburst. Did they think I was a shrew, hounding Billy and making his life miserable? It seemed absurd that I cared what anybody thought, but I could hear my mother's voice telling me I'd made a fool of myself in public.

Making my way to the front of the car, I opened the door, seeking the only privacy to be had on that train—between cars. Afraid I might fall, I gripped the railing tightly.

Ever since I could remember, Billy and I had done everything together. Then, without warning, the war had sent us hurtling to France, separately, stripped of all that was safe and familiar, into a world defined by death. We'd been among those lucky enough to make it through alive, and we should have been on our way home to live out our dreams. Instead, our dreams were moving out of reach, and each of us was grieving for all that had been lost.

From then on, we sat separately, often in different cars.

Two years ago, when I'd taken this same train, heading east to Washington instead of west toward home, I'd looked out on green shoots of new wheat just breaking through the ground. Now I sat alone and stared out the window, bored by the monotony of the plains, the wheat dry, bent stalks, just stubble. I tried to imagine how I would ever reveal the secret I was holding so closely—that I had fallen in love with Arthur and wanted to marry him. Would I ever again feel the pure happiness I'd known when I was with him?

I kept looking for a way forward, but all I could see ahead was loss, terrible loss, for me and for everyone I loved.

CHAPTER 15

Stanford University
1915-1917

After Billy left for France, I had studied harder than ever because that was the one time I could forget the dangers he faced. Unexpectedly, those years became golden ones for me. Professor Page invited me to drop by his office, and I was amazed to learn that, outside the classroom, he could be very good company. We shared a passion for mathematics, and he was eager to tell me about what he was working on. I felt lucky to be privy to his thought processes. He began loaning me journals so I could read about new developments in number theory.

Before long, I was spending most of my afternoons with him, after classes finished for the day. He charmed me by introducing me to the history of mathematics, a subject about which I knew precious little. Pythagoras had been a theorem to me; Euclid a dusty old Greek. I knew just as little about the mathematicians of the last two centuries. When Page told me their stories, they became real to me, people with worries, families, and quirks, not just geniuses.

Leonhard Euler was, he believed, the most important mathematician of modern times; he also told me Euler could hold a baby in his lap while he wrote equations and kept an eye on the older children who played on the floor of his study. If Euler could care for his kids and do his work at the same time,

I thought, then perhaps I, too, would find a way someday if I had a family of my own.

Carl Friedrich Gauss, on the other hand, ignored his family along with almost everyone else. Pursuing questions that interested him, he rarely published his conclusions. While he made significant discoveries in number theory, geometry, probability, astronomy, and theory of functions, many of them would have been lost if his son had not studied his papers and published them—after he died. Page and I, like many before us, found Gauss's behavior truly odd. We speculated about why he didn't share his work. Did he investigate only to amuse himself? Was he contemptuous of other men? Or did he want solitude in which to work? While he hadn't published his findings, neither had he burned them.

At the end of our conversations, Page often took me with him to the faculty club where he and his friends gathered for coffee at the end of the day. They always sat at the same table by a picture window that looked out on a stand of pine trees. A couple of the regulars, obsessed birdwatchers, introduced me to the pair of magnificent red-tailed hawks that nested nearby. At that hour, they would be hunting for dinner. I loved to see their swift, sharp descent as they dropped out of the sky to snatch their prey. But I couldn't bear to watch a hapless creature, usually a small rabbit or a mouse, wriggle desperately, as it tried, and failed, to escape their talons. I thought about how Billy would have wanted to save them, as he'd saved the mice he caught in his mother's kitchen.

When Page and his friends traded ideas, college became what I had wanted it to be—not just more school but a place where I could hear scholars explore their theories and test them out on each other.

The more time I spent in the company of these men—and they were all men—the more I came to see that, while most of them thought teaching important, what drove them was the need to break through the boundaries of knowledge.

I rarely volunteered anything, but I sometimes had to ask questions because I couldn't follow. I'd heard of Einstein and his special theory of relativity but knew little about it. When Dr. Page referred to it, I had to admit my ignorance. While explaining the theory, he mentioned he'd met Einstein when the great man had attended a guest lecture Page had been invited to deliver at the University of Berlin.

One afternoon while we were waiting for our coffee, he pulled a letter out of his pocket, written by a German friend, a mathematician, and read a detailed account of a lecture in which Einstein had made a spectacular and, to the letter writer, convincing argument that generalized his special theory of relativity to cover all cases. Special relativity had explained only the simplest case in which space and time affected each other—the case in which the velocity of an object remained constant. Now Einstein had found a way to extend his theory to cover accelerating velocities, decelerating velocities, and even variations in velocity.

This letter unleashed a fierce argument around the table. If the hypothesis was verified, classical physics would be turned on its head. One faction found the notion arrogant. How could a fellow toss aside three hundred years of work solidly grounded on Newton's laws? Page and his friend the brilliant chemist Max Weiler made the counterargument, defending Einstein's theory, arguing it was creative, possibly true, and, if so, the final, extraordinary step in the direction his work had been moving for more than a decade. At the very least, the theory was exciting and deserved a fair test. How could one just dismiss it?

If Page and Weiler were right, Einstein's insight marked a turning point in our understanding of the laws of nature. It was exhilarating to be in the company of people who debated such fundamental questions. I hoped to make startling discoveries of my own one day, but I kept the thought to myself.

One afternoon I asked Page when he'd started to do original work, hoping he wouldn't see the self-interest thinly veiled by my question. Of course, he saw right through me, but he didn't laugh; instead, he encouraged me, telling me it was never too early to try, and the sooner the better. Many great mathematicians had made their mark before they were thirty. Handing me a copy of his most recent paper, he mentioned he'd posed some questions at the end that still needed answers, and suggested I read the paper to see if I thought one of those questions might be worth my time. Worth my time?

Of course, I read the paper as soon as I left his office, skipping dinner. The questions he raised were worth pursuing, but, over the next several weeks, the more I thought about it, the more clearly I saw the danger of following obediently in Page's footsteps. I needed to strike out on my own, especially because I was a woman. If I didn't, I risked being seen as little more than his handmaiden.

When I was still in high school, Miss Koenig had made me read the famous lecture David Hilbert, the German mathematician, had delivered at a scholarly meeting in 1900. Hilbert had had the audacity to identify what he believed were the twenty-three most significant problems not yet solved by mathematicians. His lecture had not been translated into English, so Miss Koenig set me the task of reading the original German. Then she made me choose a question I thought might be within my grasp, and pushed me to think about how I might look for a solution. This work had been brutally hard— and it had proved beyond my range—but the effort had been invigorating. Miss Koenig tried to teach me the math I would need to attack the problem I chose. I see now what a brilliant stroke this was on her part: She allowed me to glimpse that I might one day be able to comprehend the challenges in my field, giving me confidence I could be in the thick of it all, striving to do work at the highest level. That had changed how I saw myself.

Page and I discussed Hilbert's conviction that Euclid's axioms were insufficiently fundamental. Hilbert believed it would be necessary to define a larger, deeper set of assumptions because mathematicians needed more powerful tools to solve problems. Page had come around to Hilbert's point of view. The idea that Euclid's axioms were not enough disturbed me. Until now I'd never found them wanting, and they underlay my sense of the order and perfection I craved in my work—and in my life.

I bristled at Hilbert's extravagant vision, convinced he had to be wrong, until it occurred to me that what he proposed was parallel to what Einstein had accomplished with the theory of relativity: a radical challenge that might well knock the slats out from under Newtonian physics. Hilbert's challenge to Euclid was just as fundamental, and deserved the same consideration and careful trials Einstein's theory did. My hours spent listening carefully in the faculty club had not been wasted—they had broadened my view of what was possible.

I proceeded to spend countless hours at my desk, trying to define one small trial, one effort to identify one principle that might lie beyond one axiom.

I armed myself by learning what was already known. I surveyed the literature. I talked to Page who had talked to Hilbert about where he saw weaknesses or insufficiencies in the axioms. But once I knew what Page had gleaned from Hilbert, I had to enter a solitary realm, within the confines of my own mind. Until now, there had always been someone to ask for help. But if this was going to be my own work, I had to do it by myself, which felt like being in a dark house, searching for a light switch. Not only was I unable to find a switch, I was not sure where the walls were or whether the floor was flat. I had to get down on my hands and knees and crawl, feeling the floor with my fingers, inching forward through the blackness.

I came to appreciate this awareness of my limitations. Many mathematicians believe the equations they write are the fruits of their own thinking. But I came to believe that we don't create equations. They exist, and it's our job to find and share them with others. I believe in the perfection of mathematics, a world that exists beyond and above the world of fallible humans.

I never despaired of seeing that perfection, though it involved mental labor so intense it bordered, at times, on the unbearable. Yet I craved it. I wanted to go to the heart of things.

I knew it might be years before I made progress, but, back then, that didn't daunt me. I thought I had a whole lifetime stretching out in front of me.

CHAPTER 16

April 12, 1917

F or more than two years the United States had refused to enter the war, even though the Allies begged for our help. We had supported them with war materiel but no troops. Unlike Billy, many Americans were eager to hide behind the protection of the Atlantic Ocean until the Germans finally forced our hand. I hated the war and just wanted it over soon enough for Billy to make it home alive.

Late in February 1917, two long years after Billy left for France, British intelligence agents arrived in Washington to show President Wilson a telegram they'd intercepted. The German ambassador had told the Mexican government that, if they allied themselves with Germany, after the war they would receive handsome prizes: Texas, New Mexico, and Arizona. Once that telegram was printed in American newspapers, the threat of invasion on our home shores became real, as even the staunchest isolationists had to concede. On April 2 Wilson asked Congress to declare war.

Ten days later, I found a handwritten note from Professor Page tacked to the door of my room, asking me to come to his office right away. I assumed Daddy had died or Billy had been killed.

I couldn't have been more wrong. Summoned to Washington to work in military intelligence, Page and Weiler wanted me to go with them—immediately. Page had arranged with the registrar for my withdrawal from the university and for my degree to be awarded in absentia.

Misinterpreting my silence as hesitation, Page said, "Excuse me, Miss Havilland, perhaps I've presumed. You certainly do not have to—"

"No, no, it was just . . . I mean, yes, of course I'll go. It would be . . . But are you sure I'll be up to the job?"

When Page laughed, I was thrown further off balance. Laughter sounded incongruous.

"Oh, my dear, to tell you the truth, there've been times I wished you were a little less acute—moments when it was difficult for me to keep up with you."

I listened with half an ear as he went over plans for departure, which station, which train, baggage restrictions. The idea I'd ever tested Page was distracting me. I was also wondering how to tell Mamma and Daddy where I was going. Trips cross country, especially for women, were almost unheard of—Billy's father, who'd gone to medical school at the University of Pennsylvania, was the only person in our family who had ever traveled back east.

Just when the conversation seemed to be winding down, Page's face reddened. "This is awkward. I hate to ask, but I must. Your mother was born in Germany. There are concerns about where her loyalties—and yours—may lie."

I was so angry I couldn't think straight until I realized this was not a question he was asking but a question someone else, a stranger, had forced him to ask. Swallowing my gorge, I said, "My mother loves the country where she was born. She also loves this country as much as you and I do."

"I don't doubt that. But I have to warn you. This issue may be raised again, in Washington. War whips up paranoia. Some folks will see a spy under every bed. But in the end, good sense should prevail. Please, forgive my bluntness. May I telephone your mother and father to assure them you will be under my protection?"

Rushing back to my room, I crammed as much as I could into a suitcase and ran for the train so I could say goodbye to my parents in person.

As I walked through the front door, I was apprehensive Mamma would balk because she'd had no part in my decision. Fortunately, Page had reached her, so she didn't feel excluded. "Of course, you must go," she said and turned her attention immediately to practical matters. She might not be able to voice her concern, but she could send a message through a gift of clothing. "You must take my wool coat. It's in the cedar closet. Winters back there are bitterly cold."

Once she left in search of the coat, I saw the stricken expression on Daddy's face.

"I should be happy you have this opportunity, darling," he said, patting my arm. "I am proud. It's just hard to see my little girl and . . . her country asking her to go so far away."

"Oh, Daddy, as soon as the war's over, I'll come straight home."

"You do that, Princess, and I'll be here waiting for you. Don't worry about that!" He tried to laugh, but the sound came out strangled because he was choking back tears.

Mamma bustled into the room, carrying her favorite coat, a perfectly tailored cream-and-brown tweed she'd made for herself. I finished cooking dinner while she sat at the kitchen table and lengthened the sleeves. "I'll ship you a trunk of clothes as fast as I can," she promised. "What you're bringing with you won't be nearly enough."

I left right after supper to cut short the pain of departure. We had no idea when we would see each other again or what the world would look like when we did. Dr. Page had said we were being rushed to Washington because the sand in the hourglass had almost run out—unless the United States could work a miracle the Germans were going to win the war. I wanted to throw myself into my father's arms. Until that night, I had imagined I could still be his little girl.

On board the Overland Limited

As our train to Washington climbed into the Sierras, I spent a long day looking out the window, imagining myself alone on the cliff face, at the mercy of nature. When we reached the top and the train began its descent, I had to close my eyes so I couldn't see the sheer drop down the side of the mountain. But when I closed them, images of Billy, somewhere in France, surrounded by the wounded and dying, appeared like a little horror movie projected on my lids.

Page and Weiler asked me to call them David and Max, as the rest of their colleagues did. I agreed, though "David" and "Max" never tripped easily off my tongue. In every respect they treated me as an equal—except for a certain solicitude they showed toward a young woman traveling on her own, a solicitude I appreciated because I did feel vulnerable.

One day when Page and I were alone, he brought up the conversation we'd had in his office about my mother and Germany.

"I owe you an apology."

"For what?"

"I insulted you. I insulted my own intelligence by bringing up any question of loyalty."

"I was upset," I said, "but then I realized somebody in Washington told you to do it."

"They did, but I should have said, 'If you can't trust my judgment of this young woman, you shouldn't be trusting me with military secrets.' After you left my office, I felt like a fool."

"Everything was happening too fast. You had no intention of hurting me."

"That's no excuse. When I was listening to that damned idiot on the telephone, I should have told him your fluency in German was exactly what we needed. But I was too cowed by his authority. You'll be the ideal interpreter to study enemy documents because you will understand the numbers *and* the words. If anybody bothers you about this again, come straight to me. I won't buckle under a second time."

In the evenings we ate together in the dining car and speculated about what we would be asked to do. Our work would no longer deal in abstractions. Our knowledge and analytic skills had to be harnessed to yield practical results.

The most horrifying prospect was poison gas research, almost inevitably the assignment for a chemist like Weiler. He'd known this day might come. Since the Germans had unleashed these vile new weapons early in the war, he'd learned all he could about them. When he described the suffering inflicted by these gases, I heard torment in his voice.

The Germans had tried chlorine, but then they'd switched to phosgene, more effective because it smelled benign, like dusty hay. At first, they'd had trouble with delivery systems. When the wind was blowing toward them, they gassed their own men. But all too quickly they figured out how to pack gas into artillery shells and drop them on the enemy with deadly accuracy. It could damage the lungs permanently; it could cause blindness. Diabolically, deploying it was more useful than killing a soldier outright with a bullet, because a gas victim took not just one soldier off the battlefield but also everyone who had to transport and care for him.

Chemical weapons had caught the Allies by surprise. The first primitive but effective gas masks weren't handed out to the troops until 1916, well into the war. Unfortunately, they were so cumbersome many men yanked them off in frustration and refused to wear them.

I couldn't help but picture Billy with scorched lungs, gasping for breath. Shoving this vision out of my mind, I prayed, instead, that the war would end soon. I don't think God was listening; I was just distracting myself in an attempt to ward off the reality: death, death, and more death.

When we reached Washington, the people plodding through Union Station looked somber, inward. Why I expected them to be cheerful I don't know. I began to see that the rest of the country was still living in a sentimental dream about the glorious quest ahead; here in the capital, dread hung in the air.

Porters carried our bags to taxis for the short trip to the Willard Hotel, where we would stay until we were assigned housing. The curtains in my room were blue-green satin, the walls covered with pickled green wainscoting. A fire roaring in the fireplace made the room toasty. As I sank into an armchair, the luxury was welcome; yet, it seemed inappropriate somehow. Everywhere else we were reminded to conserve every last scrap—every nail, every vegetable peeling—for the war effort.

I was surprised by a soft knock on my door—I wasn't expecting visitors. When I opened it, a waiter stood there, holding a silver tray of pastries and a steaming pot of jasmine tea, sent with the compliments of David Page. I would never have dared to order room service for myself; in fact, I'd never stayed in a hotel before. David was treating me like a princess. I was accustomed to my father giving me the royal treatment, but David was not my father, and he was, as I'd discovered on our journey, a most appealing man. I didn't know what to make of his generosity. I was so innocent in those days.

CHAPTER 17

When we tried to report for work, we encountered chaos. Thousands of people had been summoned urgently to Washington, but once they showed up, the person who'd asked them to come was often too busy to see them or saw them briefly, greeted them distractedly, and promised to get back to them sometime soon. The country had not only refused to enter the war until so late—we had also kept our heads in the sand, making no plans in case we ever did have to enter the war. The government and the military had closed their eyes to the fact that the weapons of warfare had changed profoundly. Many old soldiers, high up on the general staff, thought we would be sending regiments of cavalry across the ocean, men who would charge into battle holding the reins in one hand and flashing a saber in the other—one more charge up San Juan Hill. In fact, horses would be needed desperately—to drag machine guns we hadn't even manufactured yet up to the front. By this point in the war, the Allies and the Germans had hundreds of planes in the air. Their factories were cranking out machines as fast as they could to replace those shot down, while the United States military possessed fewer than a dozen planes.

After Page met with the new head of intelligence, he told me the two of us had been assigned to the department of cryptography. All we knew about Max was that he took the streetcar each day to a laboratory at American University. Exactly what he did we didn't know because he was forbidden to talk about his work, just as we would be.

In the weeks before Page and I started work, I walked all over the city. The formality of Washington was intimidating. Public buildings, gray stone monoliths that dwarfed pedestrians, suggested the work done inside them was more important than what ordinary humans did. Instead, I sought out neighborhoods where people lived. I fell in love with Georgetown, which looked a lot like home, on a grander scale. Some of the houses were built of soft red brick that had melted over the years, welcoming the eye, but many, like ours, were wood painted white with black shutters.

Searching the gardens for flowers my mother grew, I was startled by how pitifully small the roses were, but their scent still carried on the air, just like the roses in her garden. For a moment I could close my eyes, breathe in the scent, and imagine I was walking up our front path to the porch where Daddy would be waiting for me. One day my eyes lit on an astonishing rose, pearly white, with a faint blush of pink deep inside. Some roses are as gaudy and blowsy as a streetwalker advertising for customers; this one was the embodiment of virginal purity. I was taken aback because it had no scent. A man in a cream-colored linen suit popped up next to me. "No smell at all. Distressing, but still it gives great pleasure to the eye. Don't you agree?"

I was disconcerted by the forwardness of this stranger. His flowing gray hair and the violet scarf tied around his neck announced his eccentricity. But he was clearly a connoisseur of roses, and I wanted to identify this splendid specimen so I could tell Mamma about it. Also, I could see he planned to wait as long as necessary for an answer to his question.

"Yes, it is disappointing."

"Do you love roses so much?"

"I do, but I was thinking about my mother, who loves them a great deal more. I've never seen this one, and as far as I know, neither has she."

"Ah, then you must tell her about it. This is a new rose— Frau Karl Druschki—brought to market in 1901. I have one in my garden, up the street. Would you care to see my roses?"

I'd never entered the house of a man I didn't know by myself. He sensed my wariness.

"I could introduce you to my wife Elisabeth, who would give us tea. May I introduce myself? I am Karl Loewenstein, which makes my wife Frau Karl. I bought this rose for her birthday because I thought, if she were a rose, this is the one she would be."

Could he have been more courtly? I decided to trust there was a Frau Karl, but it was still a relief when, as soon as he unlocked the front door of a townhouse, I heard a woman's voice call, "Karl dear, is that you?"

A maid was instructed to bring tea to the garden, where we settled ourselves in chairs around a low wrought-iron table. It wasn't hard to see their roses were their children. They could have afforded a gardener, but they did all the work themselves, going out early every morning to deadhead and search for black spot, watering before the heat of the day, just as Mamma did.

In answer to a question from Mrs. Karl, I explained that I'd come to Washington to do some war work.

"Like you," Karl said, "I serve the government, but as a long-time civil servant. I'm a doddering old fixture at the State Department. I am also a connoisseur of hypocrisy. Usually, Elisabeth is the only one around to listen to my rants. Hypocrisy is a plant that grows so abundantly in this town you can't help but see it everywhere.

"Anyway, to get to my point. Since five minutes after Wilson declared war, the politicos have been running around, beating their chests and proclaiming that, for the duration, they are not party men but patriots, willing to make any sacrifice for our men in uniform. That, my dear young lady, is twaddle. Virtually every decision made by the Congress serves someone's political end and puts gold in various pockets. Anybody who tells you different is just a-whistlin' Dixie."

"He gets a little wound up on the subject," said Elisabeth, "but he's right. It's embarrassing to listen to them these days, talking through their hats." Then she thoughtfully turned the conversation back to me.

"Where are you from?"

"California."

"You must miss your family," she said, pouring me another cup of tea.

"More than I expected."

Seeing how lonely I was, she offered me a chance to talk about home. "Please tell me about your mother's roses."

"I hope you won't mind my saying this, but, if your roses are the size of saucers, hers are dinner plates. She attributes that to our perfect weather. 'They grow like weeds around here,' she says. 'Any fool with a trowel could do it.' Of course, that's not true."

As I walked back to the Willard, I thought about these two devoted gardeners, so obviously in love with each other and their roses. They often touched each other, to emphasize a point or to show affection, something I'd rarely seen at home. My mother's roses were one of few ways she let herself express her sensuous nature. She could sew me a beautiful blue lace dress, but, for herself, she chose black or brown serge. I thought, If only she'd been less remote, and more comfortable in her body, how happy our family might have been. I saw her bathe Daddy and dress him, but I never saw her hold his hand. I would have traded all the roses in the world for one memory of her cuddling me.

June 1917

Finally, we were summoned to a meeting by Herbert Yardley, chief of cryptography for the State Department. Yardley was an American original—one of those people who create themselves through sheer will and relentless determination. Born in Indiana, where his father worked, like my father, as a telegrapher for the railroad, he'd made it to the University of Chicago and then fled the Midwest, ending up in Washington. Humorous, with few pretensions, he never mentioned he was one of the best poker players in the country; someone else had to tell me. What a rare bird he was in the capital, a place filled with men who thought they bore the weight of the world on their shoulders and enjoyed nothing so much as reminding you of the fact.

He asked each of us to say a few words about the expertise we brought with us. The room was filled with scruffy academics, wearing cheap suits off the rack or ancient tweed jackets that should have been retired years ago. The exception was Dr. Arthur Bayard, whose suit had been hand-tailored by a master craftsman. As Hannah Havilland's daughter, I knew quality work when I saw it. I was interested in the suit, but more curious about the man wearing it.

On the fifth day of the war, Yardley said, the British Navy had severed all German transatlantic undersea cables, which meant the Germans had had to scramble for another way to communicate with their diplomats and allies. To solve the problem, they'd built a network of radio stations, including the largest transmitter in the world, at Nauen just outside Berlin, capable of broadcasting as far as Mexico. The French and the British had countered by building their own dense network of listening posts, where German radio signals were intercepted, transcribed, and passed along for decoding.

Yardley explained with chagrin that, until America's entrance into the war, the entire cryptography section of the State Department had consisted of himself and two clerks. There was a sense of bewilderment in the room. We'd assumed we were joining a department already in full swing. To remedy the situation, the Allies were sending experts to teach us about German codes and how to break them. They were en route but had not yet arrived. In the meantime, Yardley had pulled together a crash course for us with the help of Parker Hitt, the army's chief of cryptography, to teach fundamentals and familiarize us with the codes used by our military. Yardley would instruct us in his specialty, diplomatic codes, which were by far the most intricate. Military codes had to be simpler, because messages had to be encrypted and decrypted quickly, sometimes under fire.

He urged us to get to know one another. The better we knew how each other's minds worked, he said, the more fully we'd be able to draw on each other's strengths to compensate for our weaknesses. Needless to say, his directness was bracing to a roomful of academics more accustomed to hiding their vulnerabilities from each other.

As one of few women and the youngest person in the department, I needed to prove I could be an equal. In the office I kept my emotions under such tight control that, by the end of the day, my body ached. Even my skin hurt. I had no appetite. By late summer my clothes were hanging off me. In those days men liked women with generous curves. Now other women would begrudge me that boniness. The world I grew up in was healthier. Women were not meant to look like sticks.

In the evening I wrote long letters home. I didn't want them to know how lonely I was, so I recopied more than one page on which teardrops had blurred the ink. Goodness came out of that sadness: my discovery of the healing power of tears. I would think about Billy or miss my father, and tears would flow. For the first time I felt no shame: My mother wasn't lurking on the stairs ready to pounce and embarrass me if she heard me sob.

The collective brainpower in the room where we worked would have been the envy of any Ivy League school. Surrounded by men older, tougher, and, I suspected, smarter than I made me starkly aware my student days were over.

Until then I'd had few female friends, no doubt because my mother was so adversarial, which made it hard for me to see women as allies. That began to change one night when Nina Chapman, an older woman in the department, asked me to dinner.

That first evening was awkward, in part because Nina was excruciatingly shy. As we struggled to make conversation, I wondered why she was putting herself through this ordeal. We had little in common. She was a medieval scholar at the University of Chicago, while I'd barely heard of Chaucer.

Later, she explained she'd befriended me because she knew how difficult it was for a young woman, no matter how gifted, to make her way as a scholar. Well into her fifties when I met her, Nina had survived decades in the academic pond, where fractious male ducks preened at her expense, never missing a chance to tell her women didn't belong in the water at all. My professors had been unusually generous in this regard, but I didn't know that yet. The price she'd paid to become a tenured professor was evident. There wasn't an extra ounce of flesh on her. Her face was unnaturally pale, the high forehead etched with deep lines. She kept her short iron-gray hair tightly marcelled. The first time I saw her, two words flashed through my mind: death's head.

As I grew to know her better, I worried I might end up as damaged as she was. If I became one of the very few women in the world of mathematics, I might well live a life as isolated as hers had been. I'd enjoyed the encouragement of my professors, but I was no fool: I knew men treated older women differently. Girls were not yet threats.

CHAPTER 18

Once the cryptographers sent by the Allies arrived in Washington to instruct us, the tempo and difficulty of our work increased. Sorely needed back home, they raced through their lectures. As soon as they'd brought us up to speed on the latest developments in code breaking, they wished us Godspeed, turned on their heels and left.

I'd thought cryptography would be just one more branch of math I had to master. Until now, I'd always attacked a problem by searching for the logic that would lead to the solution. Instead, I found myself facing problems that defied logic. Encrypted messages were more like puzzles than problems, puzzles where the maker was intent on building in a random element that could not be identified. That element was called the key: It might be a word, a phrase or a string of numbers. By that point in the war the Germans were changing their keys at the front every few days. Diplomatic messages were harder to crack. Your mind had to stay open to the possibility that, if you found a key to one door, you might run smack into a second door secured by another key entirely.

I spent hours using frequency analysis, the blunt force instrument cryptographers relied upon back then, long before there were machines to do this dog work for you. Frequency analysis is exactly what it sounds like: You count how many times a letter or number is used in a message, and then, because an exhaustive study had been made of how often each letter is used in any given language, you make educated guesses about what actual letter an encoded letter or number represents. A code that used single letters would present only twenty-six possibilities for the identity of each letter. But by then code makers were using two or more symbols to represent a single letter, so there were thousands of possibilities, which meant the search was tedious in the extreme, and often led nowhere. I needed to move beyond frequency analysis, but couldn't see how.

In college I'd been able to feed off the enthusiasm and encouragement of others. Everyone had had great confidence in my abilities. There seemed to be limitless time stretching out in front of me, time for all sorts of adventures of the mind.

Now when I needed to think more clearly than I ever had in my life, my mind began to freeze, without warning. I'd sit at my desk, pencil in hand, and devise a plan of attack only to find that it led to a dead end. Looking for another approach, I'd hit a brick wall, then another, and another.

My failures embarrassed me acutely because everyone around me seemed imperturbable. I watched as they threw themselves at the same problem time and again, laughing at their failures, while I silently tore myself to pieces.

Later, I learned many of them had been relying on bravado, their joking just a screen to hide their anxieties. If I'd been more experienced, I would have figured that out a lot sooner. But that's not how it works, is it? You can't grow up until you grow up.

I began to worry that, once my supervisors realized how few successes I was having, I'd be sent home or, worse yet, relegated to clerical work, typing and filing while the rest of the team forged ahead without me.

I became obsessed with my shortcomings. Should I admit I wasn't cut out for the work? Finally, one awful night, I realized I'd turned failure into an absolute, which gave it great power over me. Before I finally fell asleep, I decided I was damned if I would give up. The stubbornness I'd inherited from my mother made quitting out of the question. I also saw that, unless I learned to tolerate failing, I would never be able to sustain the search for solutions.

It was also embarrassing to realize that I was being held back by intellectual pride, the sin my mother had so often accused me of. In this race, I was not the only thoroughbred, flying around the track, while the rest of the poor nags ate my dust. I had to accept there would be times when others streaked by me.

What's more, while I needed the drive of a thoroughbred, that, by itself, wouldn't be enough. Patience and aggression are not natural bedfellows, but I needed both to break code.

When I moved out of the Willard, I was lucky to get a room to myself. Thousands of people pouring into the city had to make do, sharing rooms, even beds, with strangers. The women got the worst of it: Men still thought of us as so many canaries, happy to twitter together in the same cage. Since most of the women flooding into Washington were being hired as secretaries, clerks, or telephone operators, it was easy for men to treat them as servants.

Page had used his clout to get me a front room on the second story of a boarding house in Georgetown, which had a bay window that looked out on a grand old maple tree. As autumn set in, I dragged my bed close to the window, where I could wake up to the sight of its leaves changing. For those few moments each morning, looking out on the golds and pinks and scarlets, I saw only beauty. No codes, no enemy, no war.

After weeks of making little headway, I swallowed my pride and asked Arthur Bayard for help. My failures to decode made me feel ordinary. But, as soon as I asked for help, he grinned and said yes, he'd be delighted to take me on. Besides, he added, I had all the earmarks of a promising pupil. Was he teasing me?

During lunch breaks he'd bring a pencil and notebook so he could write down his strategies as he explained how he used them to prise meaning out of the endless strings of apparently indiscriminate symbols.

One day when I had no idea what he was talking about, I blurted, "I'm just hopeless at this."

"Stop judging yourself so harshly," he said. "Those judgments are getting in your way. There are plenty of times when I have absolutely no idea what I'm doing. Surely you've seen me hunched over my desk tearing my hair out? I'm just showing you the part I do understand."

Arthur introduced me to his science, linguistics. He couldn't resist teasing me about how, as a mathematician, I thought numbers were the key to everything, and words just a poor second. He showed me how my knowledge of German could make cryptography easier for me, as David Page had predicted when he'd recruited me.

The highly routinized Teutonic mind was a gift: Placement of words proceeds in a strict, unvarying order. For instance, the last word in a sentence is always the verb. So the first thing one needed to do was to find the word STOP, the most frequently used word in almost every telegraphic transmission. At first the search party for STOP struck me as silly, but then I realized that, once I found it, I could locate the verbs, determine the length of sentences, and look for repeated verbs. I was on my way.

Arthur suggested I study French. If I understood a third language, he explained, it would be easier for him to teach me principles of syntax, so I could decrypt at a deeper level. He bought me a textbook, and I carried it everywhere. I fell in love with the language, no doubt because I had fallen in love with my instructor, and love is a very good teacher.

Mercifully, Arthur had oceans of patience. He not only showed me tricks of the trade, he took pains to make sure I mastered them. He showed me strategies for cracking the tough poly-alphabetic ciphers the Germans used, in which different alphabets are used in different places within a message as substitutions for the actual alphabet of that message, moving me well beyond frequency analysis.

But Arthur's strategies still required hours of concentration, and there were moments when I felt drained. Observing how he worked, I saw how essential the ability to withstand frustration was to the process. What one had to do wasn't exactly thinking, at least not any sort of thinking I was familiar with. I had to let my mind float until something that might be useful drifted to the surface, where I could grab it and create a new order, often an order entirely foreign to me. If none emerged, I had to start over, letting my brain drift again on the endless sea of symbols, waiting for a marlin—or a sand dab—to break the surface so I could hook it, in case it was what I needed. Eventually, I might find the right fish, or I might not.

Late one night, without Arthur's help, I broke a long message that demanded action, a cipher full of valuable, timely information. When I phoned the War Department, they sent a messenger immediately to collect my decrypt. From that night, I began to fly on my own, no longer needing Arthur by my side all the time.

Most often, for security reasons, we heard nothing about what was done with messages we decoded, but in that case an undersecretary at the War Department broke the rule and told Herbert Yardley he could congratulate me. Yardley invited me to take a walk with him in Lafayette Park. He could tell I thought this a little odd, so he explained that, in the open air, there was less danger of our being overheard. He gave me the undersecretary's congratulations and added he was proud to have me on his team. Because of the message I had decrypted, the police had rounded up a cadre of German spies and arrested them. The message had contained the location of an army warehouse, which was why I'd rung the alarm bell. The saboteurs had planned to steal dynamite from the warehouse to blow up department stores.

That night when Arthur and I walked home from work, I confided the fact of my breakthrough—though, respecting the need to maintain security, I gave him no details—and thanked him for all he had taught me. "Nonsense," he said. "You would have figured it out on your own. You're a lot smarter than you know."

CHAPTER 19

The two of us seemed to be getting closer, but Arthur still remained somewhat aloof. While he was keenly interested in everything about my life, when I asked him a question about himself, he'd usually put me off with a sentence or two. Once when he was explaining a subtlety of French pronunciation, I said, "You're almost as fluent in French as you are in English. Did you live in France?"

"No."

"How did you learn to speak like a native?"

"It was just summers."

"What does 'just summers' mean? Why are you being so cryptic?"

"I only meant my family spent a lot of summers there."

"You ask me dozens of questions about my family, and I answer every one. But you practically never talk about yourself."

"I guess I thought I was being polite. When you meet my mother, my silence will make more sense to you."

The news that Arthur expected to introduce me to his mother was surprising—and exhilarating.

"In her world, there's a proper way to do everything," he said. "Deviation brings criticism, even ostracism. To talk about oneself is pure selfishness and, even more humiliating, poor form. I've tried hard to break with that world because I hate the isolation it breeds. Even so, it's hard for me to get close to anyone. The one time I did, it ended badly. I want to trust you, but I'm scared. Please don't give up on me."

Patience I had, if that was all he needed. I tried to reassure him, but he stopped me.

"Good Lord, I've made this into just the sort of emotional chest-baring my mother would find appalling. The hardest part is I know there's a touch of vanity in my hesitation. If you'd grown up in Boston, you would know who the Bayards are. You'd know they were Brahmins of the deepest dye, and that would tell you a great deal." He laughed ruefully. "When I say Brahmin to you, I bet you think Hindu priest—or sacred cow."

I admitted he was right.

"We tend to live in our own little worlds and believe they're the whole world, don't we?" he said. "I expect a Hindu priest would be outraged to learn that the high-wallahs of Beantown appropriated the name of his caste to aggrandize themselves."

By now I was thoroughly confused and a bit embarrassed. All I knew for sure was that Beantown was Boston.

"I just keep making it worse, don't I?" he said. "If I lay this out baldly, it's going to sound absolutely dreadful, but God knows we deserve to be cut down to size. I don't mean you and me. I mean we, the Brahmins.

"The Brahmins of Boston are America's sacred cows, a select handful of families that came from England and managed to survive on the rocky shores of Massachusetts. They built a city and fortunes and a little college named after one of their own, the Reverend John Harvard. They're not all rich anymore, but remain great believers in their gentility. They believe their real fortune lies in the cultural and scholarly traditions they've built up over three centuries. They marry each other, which conserves the money, though they'd be outraged if you suggested that was their motive. Divorce is unthinkable; scandal is to be avoided at all costs. As you can imagine, this leads to a great deal of unhappiness and breeds more pomposity than children.

"Can you see why I shied away from displaying my family history to you? Your family possessed great daring. They made their own way to California—gritted their teeth, rolled up their sleeves, and worked hard. They would find my family insufferable. In most cases they would be right."

"But wouldn't I like your father?" I asked. "I'm sure he must be as kind as you are."

"You're right that my father was not impressed by himself. In fact, he found himself highly entertaining. You would have liked him tremendously, and he would have loved you. For however decent a fellow I am, he gets the credit. I miss him."

I hadn't known Arthur had lost his father, which underlined how little I knew about him. Why had he never told me? Was it a loss too painful to talk about? I couldn't imagine keeping anything of such magnitude secret from him. What else didn't I know?

One Sunday in Rock Creek Park, I said the word marriage. I don't remember what prompted me to say it, but I do remember seeing the muscles in Arthur's jaw clench. He turned away from me ever so slightly. Had I unwittingly crossed a boundary? Before I could apologize, he stopped me by putting up a hand.

"I've been lying to you."

I could no more imagine Arthur lying than I could imagine my father being dishonest, but it was plain he was serious. I crossed my arms over my chest, to protect myself. I sensed that what I was about to hear was going to cause me pain. I wanted him to touch me to reassure me we would get through this, but he didn't.

When he said, "I should have told you I was married," it felt like a knife slicing across my chest.

"How could you lie to me?" I spat out. "Or to her? I bet you haven't told her about me."

Arthur started to laugh, which seemed mean and made me more furious. When he tried to take my face in his hands, I slapped him. I didn't want him ever to touch me again.

He said quietly, "No, dear. I said, 'I was married.' I was married to Isabel, but she died. Seven years ago. I've thought so long and so hard about how to tell you, but I still managed to make a complete hash of it. I should have told you before this."

Relief surged through my body. My world had just been turned upside down, again and then again. Until Arthur said the word "wife," I'd been as happy as I'd ever been in my life. Then I was ambushed, and the arrows just kept on piercing me: Arthur was married; Arthur wasn't married; Arthur was laughing at me; Arthur was a widower. Had I been betrayed? I'd always trusted Arthur and needed to believe I still could. Taking me in his arms, he stroked my hair and comforted me as if I were an injured child, murmuring endearments: *my darling, my sweet girl, my little bunny.*

Once I calmed down, I realized I needed to hear more about Isabel. He said he was ready to tell me the whole story, if I thought I could bear it. In fact, it would be a relief to him. More silence on his part would only compound the lie.

"What lie are we talking about now?" I asked.

He was right to wonder whether I would be able to bear it. It was almost physically painful for me to watch him disappear into himself and return to his beloved past, a past that didn't include me.

"Isabel's family lived on Beacon Hill, a couple of blocks from us. The Bayards and the Paines had known each other for generations. I can't remember a time I didn't know Isabel. When we were children, we spent our afternoons playing in the square while our nursemaids gossiped on a bench and kept an eye on us."

He paused. "Are you sure you want to hear all this? You don't have to, you know." I nodded for him to go on.

"Everyone loved Isabel," he said. "It was impossible not to."

Everyone did not love me. Could he ever love someone as difficult as I was in the way he had loved her? It was hard to hear about his first love. Until then I'd naïvely assumed I was his only romance.

Isabel seemed to have no flaws. Gentle and thoughtful but always ready for fun, always the first to notice if someone felt left out. In my mind, I heard my mother pointing out how selfishness blinded me to everyone else's needs.

"As we got older, everyone took it for granted we would marry, as if it were part of the natural order of things. I never questioned it. I'd always loved her, and I knew I always would."

After he finished his bachelor's degree, they did marry, and spent a year traveling in Europe before settling down in Cambridge so he could start graduate school. They bought a house, an old three-decker, that became a gathering place for their friends.

"When Isabel shyly told me she was pregnant, I was thrilled. We wanted a houseful of children. The pregnancy was easy right up to the end. Isabel sensed the baby had stopped moving. I phoned the doctor, who came and assured her everything was fine. Babies often slept a lot in the last month, he said, because they're too big to move around very much.

"A couple of days later, the doctor stopped by to check on Isabel. When he came downstairs, he asked to speak to me alone in my study. Isabel's instinct had been right, he confessed. The baby was dead. I was horrified, and he read it on my face. 'No one did anything wrong,' he said. 'Sometimes these things just happen. Most likely, she'll have another healthy baby one day.'

"He warned me that getting this baby out would be difficult. Isabel would have to wait until her body was ready to give it up. The days we spent waiting will haunt me the rest of my life.

"When the contractions began, I phoned the doctor, but he was out on an emergency. I sat with her, dreading each pain, even while I prayed they would come closer together, to shorten her suffering. When the doctor arrived, he tried to send me out of the room, but I stayed. After a long night, the baby emerged, and Isabel began to bleed heavily. I watched the life drain out of her. In minutes, she was gone.

"Months earlier, when we had no idea what lay ahead, we had decided that, if the baby was a girl, we would call her Lily. She was as beautiful as her mother. I held her and whispered to her that her name was Lily, and I said goodbye."

He said nothing about how he had said goodbye to Isabel. He wasn't crying, but I was. I knew he was still in the room with the two of them, and I understood that that was where he should be. He had to say goodbye again.

After a few minutes, he came back to me. "I never expected to love anyone else, but then you came along and I was shocked by how easy it was to love you and . . . it was a happy shock."

I reached for his hand. With hesitation, I asked the question I had posed but he had failed to answer. "Where was the lie?"

"Part of me still loves her. I hid that from you."

Later that night, as I lay in bed going over this harrowing story, I realized Arthur wouldn't have been the person I loved if he'd ever stopped loving Isabel.

Knowing about Isabel made some things about Arthur easier to understand. Having heard about his difficult, exacting mother, I'd wondered how a man so reserved, so formal, could also be tender and affectionate. He was comfortable touching me. Physical intimacy was familiar to him; he'd journeyed in realms of which I knew nothing. I felt awkward around him until I realized his ease might be a blessing. He could lead me to places I wanted to go but was afraid of.

For this, I had Isabel to thank. I was grateful.

And jealous.

I kept on turning it all over in my head the next morning as I walked to work. There was no one I could talk to about this jealousy, not least because I was so ashamed of it. I tried to stamp it out, but it was fueled by too great an anger—that he'd waited so long to tell me, that he'd laughed when I misunderstood.

I found his description of Isabel hard to believe: She was too perfect to be human. Death often washes away the faults and failings of the beloved dead, and a death so terrible might well have cleansed his memories entirely. Wherever the truth lay, she would always be hovering over our heads, an angel holding a cherub.

Suddenly, I felt like banging my head against a wall. I said to myself, For God's sake, Evelyn, can you really resent a woman who died just as her life was beginning, in a way you can hardly bear to think about? Can you be so heartless? Apparently, the answer was yes.

I wanted Arthur for myself alone. Until that day of revelation in Rock Creek Park, I hadn't felt possessive of him. I hadn't needed to. Now I had to face how deeply I wanted him to belong to me. Fortunately, over time, I came to see I could never own Arthur. I accepted that Isabel and her baby were his most precious memories.

September 1917

One night as we were walking home from work, Arthur told me we'd been invited to dinner at his uncle's house in Georgetown. His willingness to introduce me to his family meant a great deal to me, not least because my feelings had been so bruised by finding out about Isabel.

Uncle Andrew, Arthur's father's brother, proved to be a diplomat who inhabited the upper regions of the State Department. Along with his wife Helena, he lived on N Street, in a very beautiful, very old row house filled with English antiques and American furniture, Hepplewhite and Duncan Phyfe, things I'd hitherto seen only as drawings in books. These pieces, handed down and cherished, were a far cry from the scratchy horsehair couches and well-scrubbed pine tables that filled our house in California.

The couple welcomed me and introduced me to the other guests: a senator and his wife, some people who worked with Andrew, and a historian from the Smithsonian, an expert in early American lusterware. Since the historian was enamored of his subject, it was easy to strike up a conversation with him, which gave me a little breathing room. I was trying to act like I went to elegant dinner parties all the time, but I was sure everybody else in the room could see how green I was.

When dinner was finished, the ladies retired to the living room so the gentlemen could drink brandy and smoke cigars around the table, which made me feel like a character in a Jane Austen novel.

We went to the house on N Street for other parties and to dine alone with Andrew and Helena. I can still picture those evenings: the green velvet curtains, the furniture upholstered in blue and ivory damask, the faint smell of lavender polish, the portraits of formidable forebears, the evening gowns, and jewels—not just garnets and jet but emeralds, diamonds, and rubies. An Aladdin's palace for the girl who had tied up boxes of cookies with red-and-white string to earn her pocket money.

CHAPTER 20

December 1917

A s Christmas approached, Yardley knew we were all worn out, so he gave us a few days' leave.

Arthur asked if I would be willing to come to Boston, giving me fair warning his mother, Rose, would be relentless in her effort to detect my flaws. The smile on his face when I said yes was worth any amount of maternal grilling. Besides, could Rose be any harder to handle than my mother? He arranged for me to stay in Cambridge at the home of his Aunt Lily, instead of at his mother's house, so I could have a respite from Rose's scrutiny.

As we waited for the train at Union Station, Arthur described the house in Louisburg Square where he'd grown up. When I heard him mention the drawing room, which we called the parlor, I began to realize how deep was the sea into which I was about to plunge.

The train stopped and started while other trains, carrying troops, took precedence. I didn't mind. Each delay put off the meeting with Mrs. Bayard, which was fine by me. Being alone in a train compartment was a luxury—we had absolutely nothing to do but enjoy our time together. I had leisure to study Arthur's hands, each finger long and beautifully tapered, each nail with its perfect half-moon. As the train flew past snow-covered marshes and naked trees—forlorn on any other day—Arthur took my face in his hands and kissed me gently.

When he said he thought meeting his mother might put me right off him, I told him he was being ridiculous.

Shaking his head, Arthur said, "Reserve judgment. There's a lot of evidence to the contrary. When a friend of mine didn't come up to scratch, Mother always found a way to get rid of him.

"When I was a child, I tried so hard to please her but rarely succeeded. I never stopped trying; she never missed a chance to let me know how badly I'd failed. That sense she had a third eye, trained on me at all times, made it impossible for me to be the self-possessed little man she wanted.

"The strange thing was she never seemed to bother Nathaniel. I envied him more than a little. I tried to copy him, but never quite got the hang of it."

Nathaniel, the brother who knew how to let his mother's slings and arrows fly by, sounded a lot like Billy. Both were confident in a way Arthur and I were not. Perhaps Arthur's insecurity helped him to understand me in a way most people wouldn't have. Maybe that was part of his attraction for me.

"After my father died," Arthur said, "Mother held herself together, but I couldn't hide my grief. It sounds absurd now, but at the time my sense of letting her down was unbearable." I was appalled. My own mother, as hard as she could be, would not have behaved so heartlessly, especially to a child. Underneath Arthur's appearance of calm self-possession, there had to be rivers of hurt I had not yet seen, and I knew I had to keep this in mind. The pressure to be a perfect child and perfect son can inflict damage that never heals.

I asked him to tell me about his father's death. Taking one of my hands in his and feeling how icy cold it was, he took my other hand, too, and rubbed them gently to warm them up.

"It was the day after my fifteenth birthday. To celebrate, my father had taken me to his tailor to be measured for a suit, a rite of passage that we had both thoroughly enjoyed. Until then, my mother had chosen all my clothes, which made me feel like a child. I was desperate to leave childhood behind, and gain a measure of control over my life.

"The next morning, on my way down to breakfast, I passed by the library where I saw Father sitting in his favorite armchair. That was odd. He should have been in the dining room, drinking coffee and reading his newspaper. Usually, when I sat down at the table, he'd put down the paper and tell me the news of the day so we could discuss it. Nathaniel was away at boarding school, and Mother started her day with a tray in her room, where she read her mail before getting up to dress. The hour my father and I spent together at the breakfast table was my favorite time of the day. I had his complete attention and no threat of reproach from my mother. He treated me like a good friend rather than a child, and I loved that. It helped to balance my mother's frequent disapproval.

"He looked so peaceful there, in his chair, that at first I thought he was asleep. But when I teased him about being late to breakfast, there was no response. When I shook his shoulder and he didn't wake up, I shouted for help. Mrs. Turner, the cook, took one look at Father and yelled for Mother. I'd never lost anyone before, not even a pet. I didn't know someone you loved could disappear without warning. The suddenness of his death left a deep scar: It's hard for me to say goodbye to anyone I care for.

"The rest of the family was nowhere near as shaken as I was. They'd colluded in hiding from me the fact Father had a weak heart—at his insistence. He wanted me to have a carefree childhood. Nathaniel explained this later, when I asked why they'd kept me in the dark. I still have mixed feelings about their keeping that secret. Sometimes I wish they'd been more honest—I would have treasured more moments with him. But their collusion was probably a blessing. If I'd known, my childhood might have been blighted by my fear of losing him.

"When Mother came into the room, she saw at once what had happened and took charge, telling Mrs. Turner to see to my breakfast while she made some calls. I couldn't eat but sat obediently at the table. I couldn't help myself. I began to cry.

"As soon as Mother came into the dining room, she said, 'Stop that right now. Your father would be ashamed. Do not carry on like a baby!' I quickly dried my face with my napkin and picked up my fork, though I knew I would gag on the scrambled eggs if I had to take a mouthful. My mother glared at me, but then, fortunately, she swept out of the room before the eggs had to cross my lips. Years later I realized her stoniness had gotten her through. Behind the cold mask she put on, she had loved my father. Her loss was as grievous as mine."

I found myself distracted, imagining my mother and me left alone together someday if Daddy died, a grim prospect indeed. "What was it like, later, for the two of you?" I asked.

"She withdrew into herself for months. With Nathaniel away, it was just the two of us in that big old house. We hardly spoke. Outwardly, I remained the dutiful son who did whatever she asked.

"As time passed, little signs crept in that she needed me. Not that she would ever have acknowledged it. When the two of us were invited to a dinner party, once we rang the doorbell, she'd grab my arm and hold it very tight.

"When I had to decide whether to go to Harvard or Yale, she insisted on the superiority of Harvard and belittled Yale. This was a perfectly defensible prejudice, held by almost everyone we knew, but her intensity seemed peculiar. Maybe she didn't want me to go as far away as New Haven. I figured I was kidding myself, so I put the question to Nathaniel. He laughed: 'Listen, old buddy, this is not the first time you've had trouble seeing the nose on your face. She'd move to Cambridge if you said the word—or New Haven.' I asked if he was serious, and he cuffed me on the side of the head.

"When I offered to live at home, she dismissed the idea as so much nonsense. But I felt compelled to stick close to home, so I went to Harvard. I had dinner in Louisburg Square on Sundays, and Mother came to my room for tea every Wednesday. The notion she needed me began to change the equation between us. I began to feel I wasn't altogether hopeless and that, in time, I might become my own man."

The mention of tea made me think of Daddy and our afternoons together, and I found myself missing him, especially because it was Christmas. Arthur saw that tide of feeling pass over my face and asked if I was all right. I brushed aside his concern. After all, I still had a father.

When I asked him to tell me about Aunt Lily, the very mention of her name made him smile. "Lily's house was my refuge, the one place no one ever punished or criticized me. Lily never married. She had no husband or children to distract her from lavishing attention on Nat and me.

"What was really spectacular about her was that she enjoyed mischief as much as little boys did. She encouraged me to step out, try things, cross lines. Nothing dangerous. She just encouraged me to untie the straitjacket my mother had strapped so tightly across my chest. I was allowed to pitch a tent in her backyard and sleep there, even when there was snow on the ground, something my mother wouldn't have allowed in a million years. She showed me how to build a fire and roast marshmallows. When my mother forbade me to have a dog, Lily bought a spaniel puppy. I named her Penny because she had white fur with brown spots, and we agreed that Penny was mine—she just happened to live at Lily's house, so Lily had to take care of her when I wasn't there. We had a clear understanding about this."

At Back Bay Station, Arthur asked a porter to collect our bags. His mother had sent a splendid carriage to pick us up—black walnut with seats covered in glove leather. The coachman welcomed Mr. Arthur home and wished us both a happy Christmas. Next to the windows in the back of the carriage, little silver vases held white violets. Arthur asked the coachman to drive us around so I could see the Common and the State House. I was enchanted.

This little detour delayed our arrival. Rose Bayard maintained civility until the maid left the room and closed the door, at which point she stared at Arthur and said coldly, "Was your train late?" The frost in the air was thick. Arthur refused to take the bait. He crossed the room, put his hands on her shoulders and gave her a kiss on the cheek, which she did not return.

Even as Arthur introduced me, I could feel her taking my measure. She made no effort whatsoever to be friendly.

A handsome, imposing woman, she was tall, but shorter than I was, which I expect didn't sit well with her. She seemed accustomed to dominating women by looming imperiously over them. The seat of her chair was a few inches higher than the other seats in the room, which gave her an advantage. She looked like a queen on her throne, a queen who wouldn't hesitate to throw a miscreant into the dungeon and forget all about her.

Like Arthur, she had rich, thick black hair but, unlike his, it was threaded with gray, and she wore it in a neatly arranged chignon, pinned high on the back of her head. She and Arthur had the same dark blue eyes. Her face was the same shape as his, her cheekbones poised at the same angle. One knew instantly they were mother and son.

Her drawing room was intimidating. By contrast, our parlor at home was simple and straightforward, its rough walls covered with whitewash, windows hung with curtains of beige linen, sewn by my mother. Rose's walls were sheathed in pale green damask, her windows covered by deep-red jacquard silk curtains tied back with silk ropes. On the walls hung two paintings and several carefully chosen drawings. On close questioning later that night, Arthur identified the paintings as a Constable and a Sargent, the red-chalk drawings as "school of Rembrandt." The same trace of lavender polish that hung in the air at Aunt Helena's house in Georgetown was strong here too. One thing felt off to me: There wasn't a single personal item on view, no family portraits, no mementos of their travels, not even a photograph of her sons.

I knew what happened this afternoon might well determine her opinion of me and the odds were stacked against me. My one advantage was she'd probably never met anyone remotely like me, so it might take her a while to figure out what I was made of.

Despite the need to concentrate, I found myself distracted. What, I wondered, must it have been like for Arthur to spend his childhood in this room? He and Nathaniel would have listened politely to the conversation of his mother's callers, though I was sure they would rather have been running around outside. What games had they played? It was hard to imagine them spending their afternoons playing cowboys and Indians as Billy and I and our friends had done. In a place as formal as Louisburg Square, they would never have been allowed to build anything as ramshackle as our fort.

While Rose poured out tea and offered petit fours iced with a B, we felt our way awkwardly, trying to find common ground for conversation. The war kept us going for a while. We discussed whether the United States could get enough troops to France before the Germans crushed the Allies. She'd gotten a letter that morning from Nathaniel, which she read to us, the only time that afternoon she let her guard down. I remember noticing Nathaniel was funnier than Arthur. The letter was full of wry observations, which gave the three of us a much needed chance for laughter.

Rose began poking around, asking me what it was like to live in Washington and what I thought of the East Coast, which, she said, had to be so terribly different from California.

"It must be so hard for your parents that you're so far away. Are you sure they did the right thing, letting you travel so far from home? Alone?"

"I traveled quite safely, under the watchful eyes of my professors."

"All men, I suppose?"

"Yes," I said, struggling to remain polite. "Most mathematicians are men. In fact, most scientists are men." I wanted to poke back a good deal harder by pointing out that I had to be rather intelligent or I would never have been accepted into that august male fraternity. But I refrained.

Then she zeroed in on what she was really curious about.

"What does your father do?"

That did it. I wasn't about to apologize for my family, so I said coolly, "He's a dispatcher for the Southern Pacific Railroad."

A look of triumph flickered across her face, and I knew the game was on.

She was not planning to let Arthur marry a girl so infinitely far beneath him in class. Although I was confident Arthur loved me, there was no question in my mind that Rose would be a formidable foe, accustomed as she was to bending Arthur to her will. As far as I knew, he had never defied her in any significant way. While I'd had plenty of practice defying my mother, I had the brains to see that, for me, locking horns with Rose would be stupid in the extreme because it would only give her fresh cause for attacking Arthur.

Common sense told me my best hope was to bite my tongue, no matter what she did to provoke me. Mamma and Rose were different sorts of adversaries. When Mamma was angry, she didn't hold back. If you wanted something, you had to fight it out with her in the open. In the end, you might still lose the battle. But if you didn't engage, you had no chance. I doubted Rose would ever take me on so directly. She'd bide her time. Then one day I'd look down and see blood on the floor, my throat cut so deftly I hadn't seen her do it.

Thankfully, we did not have to spend the evening with Rose. Just as I felt the strain becoming intolerable, Arthur told his mother we had to leave or we'd be late for dinner at Lily's. No doubt Rose was as relieved to see us go as I was to hear the front door shut behind us.

As soon as the carriage rounded the corner, Arthur said, "I am so sorry. I thought she'd let us have at least one civilized afternoon before she started checking the pedigree. I purposely arranged for us to dine with Lily tonight because I was afraid an entire evening with my mother as soon as we arrived might be more than you could take. My choice backfired. She was insulted we weren't dining with her. I didn't mean to hurt her feelings."

I was furious at her, but I didn't want to take it out on Arthur. I wished he had defended me; it worried me he hadn't. On the other hand, I could see his mother's home wasn't the sort of place where one could rip the social fabric by saying, "Mother, stop it, you're being rude." That conversation was going to happen in private, if it ever did, and I knew, at least for now, I had to leave it to Arthur.

The carriage pulled up in front of a small Federal-style house, angular, with columns on either side of the front door, white with shutters painted a green so dark they looked black in the twilight. The white picket fence along the sidewalk was heavy with Christmas roses, a phenomenon I'd heard about but never seen. Set against the whiteness of the snow, their blooms were the velvety dark red of fresh blood.

Before we had time to climb down the steps of the carriage, a small figure rushed out to meet us. One could almost see the excitement radiating off her—it was a frosty winter evening and she hadn't even bothered with a coat. She threw herself into Arthur's arms and turned happily to me.

"Oh, my dear, I have to get you inside, out of this miserable cold. I'm so thrilled to meet you. This is such a great day." It was hard to believe she was Rose's sister.

While Lily hung up our coats, we settled into cozy armchairs in the sitting room, decorated with watercolors painted by Arthur, and a wealth of small treasures, chosen because they reminded Lily of people she loved. On the mantel she had arranged a cluster of brightly colored clay animals Arthur and Nathaniel had modeled at her kitchen table when they were little.

"I know you had plenty of tea at Rose's, so I'm offering sherry—or something a little stronger. I bet you could use a bracer after that encounter!" I started to say something polite about Mrs. Bayard, but Arthur cut me off.

"Whisky, please—straight, no ice. And, oh, Lily, she was dreadful. Even at my advanced age, I still can't handle her when she goes on a tear. She jumped to 'And what does your daddy do?' before we'd been sitting long enough to warm the cushions on the sofa."

"Outdid herself, did she?" Lily said, raising an eyebrow. "What you need to remember, Evelyn dear, is that the nastier my sister is, the more threatened she must be. I'll have a few words with her."

I asked her not to, because, I said, I wanted to make friends with Rose if I could. Arthur and Lily looked at each other and said in unison, "Good luck!" Over dinner Lily asked about my parents, but her interest was to know what they were like as people, not their social standing. It was abundantly clear she planned to be my friend.

She told me about Arthur when he was a boy and how much she had looked forward to his visits. He talked about the sweaters she'd knitted for him. He laughed, telling me about the drawer in her kitchen stocked with candy and how no one ever mentioned anything about candy disappearing from that drawer. During summer visits to Maine she had spent hours with him and Nat examining tidal pools along the shore. The rest of the adults loathed the freezing water and refused even to dip their toes in it, so Lily taught both brothers and all their cousins how to swim.

By the time we finished dinner, I felt at home, and Rose's remarks had lost a good deal of their sting. Lily excused herself from the table, under the pretext that she had letters to write before turning in, but really so Arthur and I could be alone. We went through to the sitting room and sat together on the squashy old sofa, where Arthur apologized again for his mother. I told him to forget it, that I couldn't control my mother any more than he could control Rose.

After that, little more was said until it grew late and Arthur bade me goodnight so I could go upstairs to my room and get some badly needed sleep. I'd been stifling my yawns so he wouldn't leave.

Just as I reached to switch off my reading light, Lily came in and sat down on the edge of the bed.

"You must be worn out. I know you've been worked to death down there in Washington. Then the train journey, then Rose. Oh dear. I assume Arthur warned you, but the actual meeting had to be worse than what you imagined. Well, you're a strong person. I can see that, and he adores you. That's obvious from the way he looks at you when you aren't looking at him."

CHAPTER 21

I was embarrassed the next morning when I woke up after ten. When I apologized, Lily laughed and said hers was a house with no fixed schedule. Guests were free to come and go as they pleased. While she whipped up eggs scrambled with cream, I phoned Arthur, and it was wonderful to hear his voice. Then Lily poured each of us a cup of coffee and sat down to keep me company while I ate, buttering my toast for me and asking whether I'd prefer blueberry jam or marmalade.

"If it doesn't seem too nosy," she said, "I'd love to know how you met Arthur." I knew that what she was really curious about was how we fell in love. For me it was a rare opportunity to talk about Arthur to someone who loved him dearly.

I told her about running into him outside the P Street laundry and that if I hadn't been stubbornly insistent that I was safe walking at night by myself, and he hadn't been even more stubbornly insistent that I wasn't, we'd probably still be strangers.

"So you can be stubborn—that's good," she said. "Arthur is so polite and so off in his own world that people sometimes think they can run right over him. But stubborn can be his middle name, at times. I don't think nature intended him to be that way—it was something he learned at great cost when he was growing up. From his father he learned kindness—Philip was a sweet-natured soul. Now there was a man who was run over. Philip decided early in the marriage that life would not be worth living if he tried to go up against Rose.

"Nathaniel was the one she could never bring to heel. It never bothered him when she went on the warpath. She'd be having a fit about something he'd done, and, when her head was turned, he'd give me a droll little smile that said, 'Yes, we both know she's impossible, but don't worry, I'm fine.'

"Arthur paid the price. Somehow he couldn't follow Nathaniel's lead, though it wasn't from lack of trying. Their temperaments were too different. Arthur did his damnedest to please his mother, but it was never enough. When I tried to speak to her about it, she threw it back in my face, saying I spoiled him rotten, I had no children of my own, and I knew nothing about raising a child properly. She thought that would shut me up, but, at first, it didn't. I kept on trying to get through to her until I saw that, whenever I said something, she just brought the lash down harder on the child, because she knew nothing would hurt me more."

"That sounds so sad."

"It was. But then along came Isabel. She loved him without reservation. I hate to think of what might have become of him without her. Once he had Izzie, he had to learn to stand up to Rose in order to protect his young wife. The year after she died, he hardly spoke at all. When I'd try to talk to him, he'd say, 'Please, Lily, I just *cannot*.' Every morning he walked to his office in Harvard Yard, and he taught his classes, but when you were with him, you knew he was somewhere else."

The doorbell rang. Signing to me that we would talk more later, she answered the door. Arthur rushed in, cheeks bright red from the cold, and told me to bundle up because there was an icy wind coming off the river. Once I was swaddled to his satisfaction, Lily having wrapped shawls and scarves over Mamma's winter coat, we set out so he could show me Cambridge and the college.

It was well below freezing. The snow was deep, but the sun was shining and the sky blue and cloudless. Arthur led me to an austere brick building in Harvard Yard where we visited his office. Silvery light shone into the room. He asked if I could picture myself working here, after the war, at a desk of my own. I said I didn't think so—I felt too much like an outsider. He looked upset, but didn't say anything. I had no idea he was picturing me as an instructor at Radcliffe, down the street.

"What are you thinking about right now?" he asked me. "I feel like you're far away, and I don't know why."

"I'm just thinking about home. That is far away."

"When you close your eyes, what do you see?"

"The mountains on the east side of our valley. This time of year they're golden brown, dotted by single oak trees, beautiful, like Japanese paintings. They have dusty, dark green leaves, gnarled in a way that creates extremely complex shapes. I've tried to work out a mathematical formula to describe those shapes, but I haven't made much headway. Maybe someday."

"Are you sure you need to?" Arthur said. "Not everything needs to be reduced to a formula. Sometimes it's enough just to see something. To touch it."

"I guess it's not always so easy for me to live in the present," I said. "I like the idea of representing everything in a way that is permanent, even eternal."

"It all slips away, you know," he said.

Of course he was right, but I didn't like hearing it. I couldn't bear the thought of loss, especially at this moment when I felt that happiness might be within my grasp.

"Tell me about your favorite place," he said, in an attempt to distract me from my unease.

"Our private swimming hole, the one place Billy and I never shared with our friends. After school we'd ride our bikes through the orchards down to the creek, to a place where it got wider and deeper, deep enough for swimming. Floating under branches bowed down by peach blossom, I used to think this must be what heaven is like."

"A city kid like me can't imagine that kind of pleasure, or freedom."

"Our life wasn't all play," I said. "As soon as my cousin and I were old enough, we had to work in the summer. At the cannery Billy unloaded railcars stacked with crates of fruit, and I worked behind the counter at a bakery. The summer I was sixteen, I begged to work at the cannery, too, because it paid better, but my mother forbade it. According to her, such nasty, menial work was simply too far beneath 'our class.' "

Laughing, Arthur said, "Your mother and my mother would have a lot to talk about."

For the rest of the afternoon, we wandered around Cambridge, and Arthur showed me his favorite spots along the river, the boathouses and the bridges. When the sun began to sink lower in the sky, Arthur said we had to walk back quickly to pick up Lily if we were going to make it to Louisburg Square in time for dinner. Every Christmas Eve the Bayards gathered around Rose's hearth, if the grand carved marble monument that was Rose's fireplace could be called a hearth. As much as I hated to end our lovely afternoon, I knew showing up late two days in a row would be a bad idea. At Lily's I rushed to change into my gown so I wouldn't be the one who held us up. Catching a glimpse of myself in the mirror as I left the room, I was surprised by what I saw: a radiant young woman, obviously in love, running toward life.

The drawing room in Louisburg Square was filled with relatives sipping sherry from small cut-crystal glasses. As I crossed the room on Arthur's arm, one head after another turned to give me a brief, cool glance until I felt the chill creep right through me. Turning to Arthur, Lily said, "Let me handle this. We start with Jedidiah, before the harpies have a chance to swoop in." In the carriage Arthur had advised me to follow Lily's lead. "She'll know exactly what to say. She's much better at this sort of thing than I am."

Sotto voce, Lily did her best to damp the flames of my anxiety as she led me through the roomful of Bayards. "Some of them are actually quite nice, if a bit dim, and a few are excellent people. You'll figure out who's who in no time. As for Jedidiah, he loves playing the old curmudgeon. If you were one of the tribe and he didn't approve, he'd happily make your life a merry hell. But you're not. He'll be curious. If he blusters, that's just Jed. Ignore it. Remember, everyone feels awkward much of the time. And I do mean everyone. Including my sister."

Jedidiah was the patriarch of the Bayard clan, and he looked the part—towering over everyone in the room, stick-thin, with high cheekbones and a pointed chin to match his pointed skull, edged by wisps of white hair. His suit, so ancient it looked rusty, hung on him as if he were a hanger. Standing by the fireplace, he surveyed the room with a raised eyebrow, almost a permanent feature, it turned out, because he spent so much time looking at the world askance.

After pecking her cousin on the cheek, Lily said, "Jedidiah, this is Evelyn Havilland, Arthur's friend. They met in Washington."

"No need for explanations, Lily. I've already had an earful on the subject from Rose, and I can't say I envy the girl. Take a look around the room, Miss Havilland. They seem normal enough, for Boston, but I promise half of 'em are mad as hatters. I'd steer clear myself. Centuries of inbreeding."

What could I say to that? Fortunately, Arthur walked up behind me and said, "Evening, Jedidiah, good to see you. From what I just heard, you've decided to give Evelyn the straight dope."

"Ought to know what she's getting into."

Now I had even less idea what to say. Was everyone assuming that Arthur and I were already engaged? Was I the only one who knew Arthur hadn't asked me to marry him yet? Whatever was happening, it didn't seem like a good idea to agree that the family was mostly mad before I'd even met them. On the other hand, if I didn't agree with Jedidiah, I might seem like a complete ass.

Feeling a need to show I was not bereft of the power of speech, I said, "I am curious. Though that might not be the politic thing to say."

"Politic? Hardly my strong suit. Don't expect it's yours either. You're from the West. People there put a high value on frankness. Shoot first and ask questions later."

"I do, indeed. But tonight I thought it best to leave my shotgun at home. Maybe you'd like to identify some of those who are carrying at this party, so I can steer clear." I wanted to give him rein to vent his spleen and myself time to get my bearings. I also wanted to make him laugh. Most of all, I knew I wanted him to like me.

"Over there, talking to Rose, that's Louisa, married into the family. An Adams, never lets you forget. 'Bayards didn't sign the Declaration. Hence, they're nobodies.' Tongue like a razor. Nod and smile, that's my advice, since you're obviously not an Adams either."

Lily sighed.

"Spade's a spade, Lily. You know it, I know it, and this very intelligent young lady knows it. What's the point of pretending?

"Drives Rose crazy Bayards didn't sign the Declaration. Even worse, Rose was born Rose Hart, Rose Elizabeth Hart— lovely name but no relation whatsoever to John, the Hart who did sign the Declaration. Humph," he said, his face positively gleeful, but the look Lily shot him caused him to curb his tongue. "All right, Lily. I'll change tack. Ready about, 'ar-to-lee. Hmm, a safer subject . . . Well, it's not England, so we can't talk about the weather. You're from California, Miss Havilland, if I'm not mistaken?"

I said yes, but before I could get another word in, he said, "My point exactly. Anyone who made it to California, like your family, has more gumption than this whole crowd put together, present company excepted, of course, Lily, Arthur. Besides, to point out the obvious, any woman called to Washington to do the kind of work Arthur is doing, well, she'd have to be blazin' smart. Bayards're desperately in need of fresh blood. In any case," he said, looking at me with mischief in his eye, "if Rose doesn't like you, that's good enough for me."

Thoroughly pleased with himself, Jedidiah was feeling expansive, and followed up on his triumph with an invitation. "Arthur, bring young Miss Havilland out to Concord after Christmas. It's a bit of a trip—stay over if you like. There's not a lot to do, young lady, but you can ride. I have a spirited new bay in my stable that I believe Arthur will approve of."

I was enjoying this lively old man and his take-no-prisoners style, so I winked at him.

"You'll spare this poor woman the torment of making a round of calls with Rose," he added to Arthur, casting a glance in my direction and winking back. "My personal idea of a morning in hell." Then he paused for a moment, and I could feel the atmosphere changing. "Since my wife died, I rattle around in my old barn of a place. You'd be doing me a kindness." With that admission, Jedidiah revealed the sensitivity that lay beneath his sardonic manner, and I began to like him even more. It was quickly agreed we'd visit, and I felt as if I'd been spared. I hadn't heard about the round of calls, and the very thought froze my blood.

Lily whisked me around the room, introducing me deftly to just about everyone before we went in to dinner. Seated between male cousins about whom I knew absolutely nothing, I found the conversation a tough go. I knew, and I'm sure Rose knew that I knew, she had intentionally set me between two nonentities at the bottom of the table.

At the other end of the table, Arthur was seated between his mother and a subtly stunning young woman I hadn't been introduced to. Her dove-gray satin gown, discreet in the extreme, was nonetheless draped so artfully that one couldn't help noticing the lovely body inside the dress. A demure string of pearls drew attention to her soft, creamy bosom.

Arthur was addressing a good many remarks to her. "Thick as thieves" was the phrase that kept running through my head. I tried not to spy on them, which would have seemed childish, searching instead for any topic that might elicit a sentence or two from one of my dinner partners. We'd exhausted the war—they weren't in favor of it—California—they didn't think much of it, had never been there, had no interest in going—my work—I couldn't talk about it—their work—they didn't work. I was running out of ideas, but then I thought to ask when the Bayards came to America. Family history proved to be of apparently infinite interest to them, and it floated us along until Rose stood up and announced it was time for the ladies to leave the men.

Oh my God, I thought, this evening is like an endless steeple-chase, and now there's another hurdle to clear, with no doubt a stream on the other side where the nag I'm riding might well break a leg. But I was wrong: Every woman in the party spoke to me, civilly, including the woman in the exquisite gray dress. I didn't pose a threat to her.

Finally, Lily said, "Rose, dear, thank you for a lovely evening. I'll be taking Evelyn home now. It's been a long day, and she needs rest before she has to go back to Washington." When Rose said I should come to stay with her after Christmas, Lily trumped her ace. "I'm so sorry, that won't be possible. Jedidiah has insisted Arthur and Evelyn come to visit him for a couple of days."

I could see steam coming out of Rose's ears. She'd been thwarted of a chance to warn me off Arthur.

Back at Lily's, I asked her the question that had been on my mind all evening: Who was the gorgeous creature seated at the table on Arthur's left? Her name, Lily said, was Abigail

Cranford, and she was indeed Rose's choice for the second Mrs. Arthur Bayard. She'd also been Isabel's close friend.

My confidence that Arthur loved me began to crumble. Was Abigail the reason Arthur hadn't proposed to me? I hoped I was being ridiculous. He had brought me home for Christmas. He had spent the day showing his world to me, not to Abigail. But, of course, she wouldn't have needed to see his world. She was part of it. I remembered how jealous I'd been when I heard about Isabel. Why was jealousy so quick to poison my love? Was this weekend a competition in which I was being judged against Abigail, who had the inside track?

Abigail, Lily said, had not yet married. After graduating from Mount Holyoke some years ago, she'd moved home, to live with her parents. Appalled at the prospect of a life of paying calls, good works, and embroidery, she'd found a job as an instructor of French language and history at a private school for girls. It was evident Lily liked and respected Abigail. She sounded perfect for Arthur, a woman who understood his world and already had a natural place there. Lily didn't come in to say goodnight. The sudden absence of her reassurances, on which I'd been leaning so heavily, made me feel even more vulnerable, and I went to bed sick at heart.

The next morning Lily and I set out for Christmas lunch at Rose's house. The first person I saw when I walked into the drawing room was Abigail, chatting merrily with Rose.

Even the food in this house was intimidating. In the center of the table rested a dessert I'd never seen: bûche de Noël, a chocolate roll frosted to look like a Yule log, decorated with marzipan squirrels and flowers—a far cry from what my mother would be serving that night, mince pie with a crust she'd rolled out herself. The meal started with vichyssoise, followed by partridges accompanied by white wine, puffed pastry filled with duck and a red wine, followed by a salad and an orange soufflé with champagne. This was the most sumptuous meal

I'd ever eaten, but I could see that for everyone else in the room except the serving girls it was common fare. By the time we finished, I felt like a stuffed pig.

Afterward, we gathered in the drawing room to exchange gifts. I'd put a lot deal of thought into choosing mine because I was eager to make a good impression, and feared appearing gauche. For Rose, a new book by H. G. Wells, *Mr. Britling Sees It Through*. For Lily, a small porcelain box painted with forget-me-nots. Because I'd wanted to give Arthur a present that wouldn't be awkward to open in front of his mother but would make it apparent how precious he was to me, I'd chosen a pair of small gold cuff links, set with lapis lazuli. When he opened them, he immediately took off the cuff links he was wearing and changed them for the ones I'd given him.

Then I opened Arthur's gift to me, a paisley shawl, red, green, and gold on a cream-colored ground, woven in Kashmir, that said to me: I will array you in beautiful garments—here is the first of many. Lily explained that when the memsahibs returned to England from India, they loved to flaunt their genuine Kashmiri shawls, knowing that the women at home had to make do with poor imitations loomed in Scotland. Having wrapped myself in the shawl, I felt lovely until I saw Abigail unwrap the box containing the gift Arthur had chosen for her: a long silk scarf, diaphanous and feminine, painted with lilacs in tender blues and violets. Suddenly, I felt like a middle-aged matron, just back from India, clutching her expensive wool shawl while watching a young girl tie a filmy, feather-light bit of silk around her swanlike neck. At that moment I could happily have used the scarf as a rope, though I'm not sure whether I would have hung Abigail or myself. Or maybe Arthur.

I succeeded in hiding my misery—Arthur gave no sign he knew anything was wrong. I would have felt better if he had noticed I was upset, but I wasn't going to tell him. My pride was too wounded. But I also had to ask myself if I was too ready to jump to conclusions. Despite all the proofs of Arthur's love for me over the last months, I had already decided, in just two days, Abigail was his first choice.

This wasn't the first time I'd assumed Arthur didn't love me enough. Was I hurting myself? Was I going to ruin our romance because I couldn't believe he truly cared for me? I doubted my mother loved me, but I was absolutely certain my father did. Had this welter of conflicting messages made it impossible for me to trust?

That night my sleep was ragged. When the sun finally rose, I gave up the pretense of sleep and dressed quickly, creeping downstairs and slipping out the back door. I needed time by myself, to consider my situation. I was upset with Arthur for bringing me here on such uncertain terms. I felt on trial, and resented it. But observing Abigail's easy self-assurance forced me to wonder why Arthur would have any interest in an artless, uncultured girl like me. As far as I knew he didn't have an unkind bone in his body. It seemed unlikely he'd brought me here to make a fool of me, and yet I felt like a fool. To ask Arthur whether he had feelings for Abigail meant risking an unbearable exposure. I couldn't make myself that vulnerable, and yet waiting to find out whether he did was equally unbearable.

Suddenly, I wished I'd been home yesterday, with Mamma and Daddy, in our house where each place at the table was set with one knife, one fork and one spoon, eating the simple meal we had every Christmas: roast goose or turkey, stuffing, and buttered beans. I would have washed the dishes while Billy dried. But Billy was in France, and I was here, among strangers.

Wherever the truth lay, there was no stuffing the genie back in the bottle. I started to make my way back to Lily's house. Turning off Appian Way onto Brattle Street, I was startled to see Arthur rushing toward me. Lily had phoned him because I'd gone out without telling her I was leaving, and she was worried. I pretended I was pleased to see him. How quickly I was learning to dissemble.

CHAPTER 22

What Jedidiah had dismissed as his "barn" turned out to be a delightfully mysterious old house that looked like something out of a Norse fairy tale. It was half-timbered; the first floor, painted olive green, was decorated with a pattern of diamond-shaped terra-cotta tiles sculpted with faces, some of which had melted away over the years. The stucco on the timbered upper half, once painted cream, had weathered to a mossy greenish-gray that made one feel the house had grown up right out of the ground.

The interior of the house made me think of a monastery. The beams were painted the same dark brown as the timbers of the façade, and the ceiling was high, the walls hung with tapestries Jedidiah and his wife had bought on their honeymoon in France. He took me into the library to show me his greatest treasure, a portrait of a stout old man painted, he told me proudly, by the great Flemish artist Hans Memling. The sun poured in through mullioned windows. The austere beauty of this house suggested Jedidiah was more a romantic than the no-nonsense New Englander he pretended to be.

We sat down to lunch at a long table in a dining room so vast I felt like one of three small children huddled at the end of an otherwise empty Viking ship.

Jedidiah tried to engage me in conversation, but his efforts to draw me out fell flat. I was too tense to banter. The meal grew ever more awkward, and I'm sure our host began to regret the invitation he'd issued so enthusiastically two days earlier. When we finished drinking our coffee, he announced he had some business to attend to that afternoon. We were free to amuse ourselves until dinner. If we wished, we were welcome to borrow horses from the stable.

Even though it was a glorious day, I didn't have the heart for riding. I told Arthur I would rather walk in the woods, despite the deep snow on the ground. Finally, Arthur asked, "What's wrong, dear?"

I hesitated to give voice to the questions tormenting me: Was I kidding myself to think you loved me? Are you in love with Abigail? I was angry. Yet I felt stupid being angry at Arthur who had told me he loved me and shown me he loved me. I dreaded that I might have misjudged his intentions and was afraid to hear what he would say if I asked whether I had.

He tried again. "Evelyn, something is wrong. I don't know what it is, and I can't fix it unless I know what's broken."

"I don't know how to talk about this."

"Just tell me." The look on his face was so sad.

"I think you're planning to marry Abigail."

"Marry Abigail? What on earth gave you that idea?"

"A lot of things. At dinner you were sitting next to her, and I saw how comfortable she was with you and your mother. I thought the three of you must have an understanding."

"Oh my God," he said. "I am sorry. You're right that I am comfortable with Abby. Her family lives on the square, too. Our nannies were friends, and we played together, often with Isabel. As we grew older, Abby became one of my closest friends, the kind of friend you rely on and confide in. But the notion of marrying her never entered my mind."

"Really?" I had to ask. "I think your mother wants you to marry her. She put her right next to you at the dinner table, and the three of you were all laughing and chatting away."

"I'm not an idiot—I see my mother doing her best to engineer a marriage. She knows it annoys me, but that doesn't stop her. That doesn't mean I don't care about Abigail—which is what you saw last night at the table. But how did such a wild thought enter your head? Don't you trust me at all?"

"To start with, I don't fit in here. You need a wife who can navigate the Bayard family as easily as Abigail does."

"I can see I've thoroughly bollixed this up. I thought it wouldn't be fair to ask you to marry me before you'd seen how treacherous the family waters are. Our boat is loaded with a great deal of baggage."

"Isn't everyone's?"

"But your world is different from mine—straighter, more earnest. Oh my darling, can you forgive me? Am I too late? Could you live this life and be happy? I care about your happiness, apparently more than you know."

"If you made any mistake," I said, "it was thinking too much."

"My darling, will you marry me and be my wife?"

I burst into tears, more from relief than from joy.

"Yes. Of course I will marry you."

I finally saw that possession is not love. My mother's insistence that it was had blinded me far too long.

CHAPTER 23

I spent the following day with Lily while Arthur told his mother he and I were going to be married. The plan was that I would join them in Louisburg Square for dinner. I told Lily I despaired of the evening to come, and she counseled forbearance. "I won't kid you. Rose isn't going to take this well. But keep in mind this is her problem. It becomes your problem only if you let her bait you. When she tells you how to live your life, you're going to have to do just what I do. Smile and nod and do exactly what you want to do."

I pointed out it might be easier for a sister to ignore Rose's admonitions than it would be for a new and unwanted daughter-in-law, but Lily dismissed the notion. "You are more than a match for Rose. She doesn't know it yet, but I do."

I wasn't sure she was right. Given my stupidity about Abigail, I wondered how long it would take me to learn to read the signs, let alone to post my own signboard with letters large enough for Rose to read.

Dinner was a disaster. As soon as the maid had finished setting bowls of turtle soup in front of us and the butler had filled our glasses with claret, they withdrew. Affecting an air of concern so phony it would not have deceived a child, Rose said, "Evelyn, I am worried about you. I feel your mother would not think well of me if she knew I was allowing you to travel without a chaperone."

Arthur counter-punched. "Mother, really, I'm hardly a threat. And if Evelyn and I are to be married, surely some latitude can be allowed, even on Beacon Hill."

Dropping all pretense, Rose countered: "Whether you are going to be married has yet to be decided."

Arthur didn't disabuse her of that notion, which alarmed me, but I had vowed to stay calm. "Mrs. Bayard, I've already made plenty of train trips by myself," I said in an even tone, but I couldn't resist the impulse to needle her. "I'd be well able to defend myself from anyone's advances on a train should the need arise."

Rose picked up the gauntlet. "Wouldn't your mother would be shocked to learn you were traveling with a man who was not a close relative?"

"Mrs. Bayard, when my mother's parents died, she and her sister were eleven and five. They sailed, without a chaperone, on a tramp steamer from Germany to America. They were the only children on board the ship. I wasn't raised to be a scaredy-cat."

Rose was speechless. I'd upped the ante. She couldn't see how tightly I was twisting the napkin in my lap. Trying another tack, she said: "I can't imagine you would want to live in a place like Boston where you have no family."

Finally, Arthur returned to the fray. "Mother, we would be Evelyn's family.

Rose cut him dead. "Choose for yourself, Arthur. Be careful. Choose wisely."

"I think both of us had better be careful about our choices, Mother. Right now, in this conversation."

I began to feel like a birdie in a furious game of badminton. For my own comfort, I wanted to defuse this confrontation, but I knew burying our differences would not lay them to rest. Despite Arthur's warnings that his mother would be difficult, I had naïvely hoped she and I might find common ground because we both loved her son. Instead, I found myself detesting this woman who was so ready to humiliate him in front of a woman he loved enough to marry.

Rose and Mamma would have been outraged if I'd dared to point it out, but they had a good deal in common—headstrong, harsh, and willing to say just about anything to win an argument. With my mother, I'd learned to stick up for myself, but it had taken me years. I'd had Daddy to explain the vulnerability that lay beneath her anger, and I saw how much he loved her. I thought Arthur loved Rose, and, if you had asked her, I'm sure she would have insisted she loved him, too. Whether she did was a question it might take me years to answer. Rose saw this situation as a competition, and she believed declaring herself the winner straight out of the gate would suffice. It seemed not to have occurred to her that this tactic might alienate Arthur and strengthen his alliance with me. Perhaps she wasn't as deft an opponent as I'd thought.

We made it through dinner somehow. After the maid had cleared away the bowls in which trifle had been served, Arthur told his mother he wanted to spend some time alone with me before he took me back to Lily's. I was mightily relieved to hear him say this because I had dreaded what might happen if I had to sit alone with Rose after dinner, sparring like a couple of characters in some nerve-tearing scene from a Galsworthy novel. Though he asked her to leave us in a courteous way, the touch of iron in his voice delivered his message. She left the room with a modicum of grace.

After she'd gone, he suggested we move to the sitting room that looked out on the back garden. We settled ourselves on the sofa, and he turned the lamps low so it would be easy to see the snow weighing down a wall of rhododendrons. Putting his arm around me, he described the day they'd been planted. The gardener had done the work while Arthur and his father watched.

"There, in a nutshell, lies the difference between my mother and my father. He thoroughly enjoyed joking around with the gardener who was digging holes for those spindly twigs. My mother would have given the man sharp, clear directions and left him to himself. I'm not sure she believes servants are quite human."

I sighed, and Arthur asked what was wrong.

"Nothing really," I said.

Ignoring an obvious lie, he asked: "Tired of walking the tightrope with my mother?"

"It's more than that. It's all the ghosts crowding this room."

"Ghosts? I'd say the one making you miserable is very much alive. Besides, this is my problem, not yours."

"Don't you see that, if we marry, your problems will become my problems?" I said. "You must think about whether this marriage could succeed. I'm not sure someone as much an outsider as I am would ever be accepted, or even tolerated, by the insiders. One day you might regret marrying me. Even if the Bayards failed to sign the Declaration, they knew plenty who did. All those ancestors watching over you. To make them happy, you should marry one of their own. Like your mother, they aren't going to rest easy if you marry a harum-scarum girl from a place they think of as too primitive to visit."

Now at full flood, I was sharing with Arthur the truth of my experience over the last few days, but I wondered if I should shut up. I pressed on, although I was scaring myself. Was I trying to convince him marrying me was a bad idea?

"I'm not imagining all this. At the table on Christmas Eve, cousin Everett, could hardly keep his mind on my chatter, especially after I suggested he consider a trip west to what he then referred to as 'that crude state' of California. To him, California is a place that those who had no social position in Boston fled to, in hopes of grubbing money."

"Good God, who are you marrying? Me, who loves you to distraction, or some tedious old toad who hasn't had an original thought since the day he was born? Everett is a witless snob. You should hear Jedidiah on the subject.

"I was horrified by my mother's behavior this evening, though hardly surprised. I will have to have it out with her again. I won't lie—when I told her I was going to marry you, she had a fit. But I thought I'd made it crystal clear that I had made my decision and that it was mine to make. I insisted she treat you with respect, but apparently she wasn't listening too closely. She never treated Isabel like this. And as lovely as Isabel was, she was no saint."

I should have held my tongue, but I couldn't stop myself. "Until she died. Death turned Isabel into a saint. Forgive me, that sounds awful. I don't mean to disparage her. But Lily told me how gently she took your mother's advice about everything from what kind of gloves to buy to what she should read to who she should invite—or not invite—when she entertained."

I expected Arthur to explode because I'd been so rude. Instead, he took my hands in his and put the blame squarely on himself. "Isabel did let Mother run over her. I was so young sometimes I didn't even notice there was a problem until I found Izzie sobbing quietly in her sitting room. You will—and I want you to be—the beneficiary of what I learned at great cost to her."

"I don't want to be a constant source of friction between you and your mother," I said. "You would be caught between the two of us, forced to choose sides or to mediate. It could become intolerable."

"Romance has certainly taken a back seat tonight, hasn't it?" Arthur observed, which made me smile.

"Come here, sweetheart," he said, drawing me toward him. "I knew this visit would be hard for you because my mother—"

I cut in. "It's been hard for both of us because I didn't trust you. I don't know what it says about me—you've never shown yourself to be an inch short of entirely honorable."

Arthur said, "Shhh." He drew a small green leather box from the pocket of his waistcoat and opened it. "I hope you'll think it's pretty."

I looked at the exquisitely cut oval sapphire set in a tiny wreath of gold leaves and held my breath. Until now, even though he had asked me to marry him the day before, I'd felt I might still be skating over a pond plagued with spots of soft ice. But when he took the ring and slipped it on my finger, I started to believe I was going to have my chance to be happy.

We passed the rest of the evening in each other's arms until it grew so late Arthur said he had to take me back to Lily's. There would be little sleep for either of us that night since our train to Washington was scheduled to leave at the crack of dawn. I would have been happy to stay up all night and nap on the train the next day. But Arthur was still too much the gentleman to tear the last frail edges of propriety.

In the months ahead those edges would be torn to shreds, as the war pushed us to grab what pleasure we could while we had the chance. That night we were still, in some sense, innocent. Neither of us had any idea we'd soon be on our way to France, nor could we have conceived the annihilation we were about to witness.

I'm glad we had those few months of happiness all to ourselves. We were in love, and I felt safe because we were still protected from the war by an ocean. That was the happiest time of my life, a time when Rose was the biggest problem we faced, and we still had our Sundays to wander in Rock Creek Park, arm in arm.

CHAPTER 24

When Arthur and I returned from Boston after Christmas, a bitter wind was blowing off the Potomac. In the District the sidewalks were slick as glass: Globally, the winter of 1918 was the coldest in the history of recorded weather. I thought about Billy stuck in France in a field hospital built of canvas tents. He hated the cold and could barely handle California winters.

The tweed coat my mother loaned me would have served as a fine spring jacket in Washington. Trudging to the office in the mornings, the cold air whistling up my sleeves, I wrapped my arms around my ribs and told myself to quit whining. Were men freezing in the trenches whining? Swearing more likely.

One morning I arrived at the office in time to hold the door open for Nina Chapman. In the months since our first tentative dinner, she'd become my good friend. The sight of her cheered me up. She took one look at me and said: "Good heavens, child, how red your cheeks are. Those look like chilblains! Let me see those gloves. Why, they're not even lined! You'll get sick running around like that. We're going shopping at lunchtime to get you some real winter clothing. I know where to go and what to buy. Arthur will survive one lunch without you."

I was shocked to learn she knew about Arthur. I thought we'd been so discreet, but clearly I'd been kidding myself.

She was as good as her word: At noon she marched me to Garfinckel's department store. This kind of shopping was new to me: I'd never owned a ready-made coat. She made me try on coat after coat until we found one I loved, a navy chesterfield that reached mid-calf. I couldn't actually afford the coat, nor could I find a way to stem her enthusiasm. She helped me pick out sturdy boots with deep treads, black leather gloves lined with rabbit fur, a red felt cloche that covered my ears, and a cream-colored cashmere scarf. When we'd made our choices, Nina said, "I want to ask you a favor. Let me buy these for you."

I felt I had to say no. "You can't possibly do that. Your gift was bringing me here and showing me what to buy."

She looked hurt. "I don't have a daughter, or any children. I never will. Please let me do this."

I nodded because I couldn't find words sufficient to thank her. She gave a little nod in return. She knew I couldn't afford these clothes, and she could, but what she gave me was more valuable than money. Her gift was given in the spirit that a mother gives love to a daughter, and I hungered for that generosity. I've never forgotten the smile on her face or how I felt when we exchanged those nods. That coat still hangs in my closet. The hat is carefully wrapped in tissue, and both are protected from moths. Sometimes I take them out and put them on to help me remember Nina.

CHAPTER 25

A t the start of that year, 1918, the rate at which the enemy's
radio signals were being intercepted went through the
roof. New stacks of flimsy yellow sheets printed with endless
columns of symbols appeared on our desks every morning. We
knew not a minute could be wasted: Every one of those sheets
might contain information that portended death and defeat.

One night in the depths of winter, as we walked home
picking our way over the ice, Arthur hemmed and hawed until
I finally said, "What is on your mind?"

He took a deep breath and told me he'd been assigned to
the American Expeditionary Force in France as a linguist and
cryptographer. His commission, secured with help from Uncle
Andrew, had been approved. When he saw how upset I was, he
assured me he would be absurdly safe, stationed at Pershing's
headquarters in Chaumont, far from the action. Then he made
the mistake of adding he wasn't entirely happy with this
assignment because he still wouldn't be in the real fighting.

"Why do all you men want to go and get killed?" I said, a
question I often asked myself. "Why do you love war so much?
You don't seem to care about wasting your life. Did it ever
occur to you that you would destroy my life, too?"

I felt abandoned, excluded from what might well have
been the most important decision of his life. Once I saw the
guilt-stricken look on his face, though, I calmed down. I'd
learned that melodrama only made things worse. The night
Billy told me he was going to France, I'd run off, to punish

him for frightening me. I didn't want to repeat that mistake. But I was mad at Arthur for asking his uncle to pull strings and wondered how he had convinced him to do it. I doubted Andrew wanted Arthur to go to France any more than I did.

By now I knew most men believed that, because there was a war on, they had to kill or be killed as a matter of self-respect. In my heart, I understood nothing of this sick logic. Women see the sheer wrongness, the stupidity of war; it is our tragedy we are expected to stay home and wait for bad news. Unlike many mothers and daughters—perhaps because I was my mother's daughter—I didn't feel the need to remain silent, validating men's heroism by condoning their foolhardy choices.

On the other hand, I had hurt and alienated Billy when I criticized his decision. Arthur would go to France no matter what I said, and I didn't want us to part in anger. I tried to control my voice when I asked when he would be leaving, though we both heard it tremble. Any day, he said. If his orders were already in the pipeline, his plans were more advanced than he'd been letting on, and it upset me even more to know how long he'd been keeping this awful secret from me.

We walked the rest of the way home, the sides of our arms discreetly touching as we moved slightly apart and then back together, the signal lovers use to remind each other of their desire. At my door, I reached for his hand, the hand still within my reach, even if only for a short while.

"Good night, my darling," he said with such tenderness that all I could say was "I love you." He put his arms around me right there on the steps of my boarding house and held me. When he pulled back a few inches, he looked at me with great sweetness and whispered, "I know."

As he disappeared up the street, I thought ahead to the day he'd walk up the gangplank of some desolate gray troopship, on his way to a fate neither of us could foresee.

That night I lay in bed, staring out the window, studying the intricate patterns of leafless branches, looking for stars, thinking about the people I loved. I worried if Billy was safe and whether my parents were all right. I thought about poor Dora and little Alice, at home, alone, far from Billy. Mostly I thought about the fact that Arthur and I would soon be separated, which meant I'd be worrying about him as well as Billy.

Knowing Arthur was leaving soon heightened the intensity of everything that passed between us. Our hunger for each other grew so keen we began to take chances we would never have considered before. After Arthur walked me home in the evening, instead of just kissing him and saying goodnight, I made him come upstairs with me. He followed me quietly to my room where we touched each other in the ways I craved. He hesitated at first, not wanting to put me at risk, but I wanted him, and, as the day of his leaving approached, I cared less and less about the consequences of our lovemaking. My virginity had become a burden to me. The only time I could blot out my fears was when our bodies were on fire. That heat wiped out my consciousness of everything but the need to quench it.

Arthur argued we should wait. If I found out after he left that I was pregnant, I would be in an impossible position. I insisted I didn't care, I could cope with whatever happened, but he countered I was being heedless. My child and I would be shunned. I argued that, to allay his concern, we could marry quickly, before he left. He hated the idea I might end up a widow. I said I'd far rather be a grieving widow than an almost bride.

The first time we made love I was nervous. I was afraid of the pain, but it lasted only a moment, and I felt silly to have worried about such a small thing. Over the next few days we each learned what the other wanted, and my pleasure grew and grew.

At the office I did my best to maintain the intense level of concentration required for the work, but my mind would stray to thoughts of our lovemaking. Someone else might have thought me irresponsible, but I didn't care. I was trying to store up this fullness to carry me through the long emptiness ahead. Touch is fleeting, but memories of touch are longer-lived, and sometimes they are all one has.

At the end of March, Arthur received his orders. I couldn't get leave, so he had to take the train to New York by himself. He said perhaps that was just as well since he hated goodbyes. I made a great effort to be cheerful when I gave him a last kiss at Union Station. But as the train disappeared into the distance, I cursed the war. That night, alone in bed, missing him bitterly, I also felt guilty when I thought about the mothers and fathers whose sons had already been killed. I was just a young woman, with her whole life ahead of her, worrying about a cousin and a lover, not a parent gutted by the loss of a child.

Yet why shouldn't I grieve for what I might lose? I was furious at a God who allowed so much tragedy to blanket the earth. Arthur had never done anything to hurt anyone. Nor had Billy. They were good men who wanted only to lead good lives.

CHAPTER 26

By the time the sun rose, I had decided I would figure out how to get to France. The army was extremely unlikely to give a female cryptographer a commission overseas. In Washington, most of the cryptographers, male or female, were civilians. But there might be other ways.

There were American women, referred to as Hello Girls, supporting the army in France. They'd been recruited as telephone operators when the army realized how few French women spoke English and what an urgent need there was going to be for quick, reliable communication. I was a little embarrassed by the idea of being a Hello Girl. But I'd be in France, where I might see Arthur and Billy. Rose would be thrilled to have one more proof of how unsuitable a choice I was for her Arthur. My mother would be horrified at my taking such a menial job, but she couldn't stop me.

I might also be able to find work in France as a nurse or an ambulance driver. American women had been doing these jobs since the beginning of the war. Billy's friend Mrs. Franklin, the expatriate American who'd given him work in Paris, had organized an entire ambulance corps.

I decided to ask Uncle Andrew for help. He had enormous influence; without him, Arthur would still be in Washington. He and Helena were so close they disliked being separated for a single night. I was sure they would understand why I had to be near Arthur.

That morning, I called Helena from the office and asked her to meet me for lunch. After soup and sandwiches at a coffee shop, I asked her to walk with me in Lafayette Park. I didn't want anyone to overhear my request.

I'd blithely assumed she'd offer to help, but instead she turned pale and sank her teeth into her lower lip. "You know I can't do that. Andrew and Arthur would be furious with me."

Seeing my distress, she softened, promising to think about it. Almost immediately she reversed herself. "I understand why you want to go, dear, but I believe women should not get in the way."

In the way! For a woman of her generation, knowing one's place was part of the training, absorbed through the skin in childhood, before a girl even knew she was taking it in. Since my mother had often used the very same words to criticize me, the phrase "in the way" grated. But Helena didn't know that. I thanked her for listening, and we parted as friends.

Not knowing what was happening to Arthur became a new kind of purgatory. Without him, I would have no lover and no future. He might be injured. He might be a prisoner. He might be killed. And my worries about Billy never lessened.

Though Arthur had made me promise to take the streetcar home at night, I usually walked—walking was one of few ways I could relieve my restlessness. Night after night, as I made my way home from work, I looked up at the stars and begged them for a letter, only to be greeted when I reached my door by an empty mailbox. Finally, on a night when I was close to the end of my tether, I found a letter from Arthur, written weeks earlier in his bold, even hand, telling me he'd reached France and was living in the barracks at Pershing's headquarters in Chaumont. For reasons of security, he could tell me little about what he was doing, which did not surprise me. Seeing his handwriting told me all I really needed to know—at the moment he took up pen and paper he was safe and he was thinking about me.

All that I couldn't know redoubled my intensity about getting to France. I arranged to spend an evening with Andrew and Helena. Over dinner I tried to persuade them to help, but their patience was wearing thin. They found it hard to understand why I refused to see they could not put me in danger.

I'm not sure I ate anything. Heedless, I carried on about how I had to go to France. I must have seemed like a thing possessed, but they indulged me because they knew how much I cared for Arthur. Later, I was mortified when I realized how unreasonable I'd been.

April 1918

Growing up, I'd striven to be a "good girl," doing chores, respecting parents' wishes, following teachers' directions, but I certainly wasn't a good girl anymore, and I wasn't going to back down. I decided to seek help at work. Yardley wouldn't help me leave—he needed every cryptographer he had—but I thought I might try Major Barkley, one of the officers who supervised the work in our department and had a reputation for getting things done without ruffling feathers.

The major was interested in me; I'd turned down more than one invitation to dine with him. I decided that, in the interest of my project, I would take him up on his offer. I was exploiting him, and I didn't feel good about it. But I couldn't see any other route to try. Of course he said yes, and we fixed an evening, the following Sunday.

Rather late in the day, I'd begun to realize the power I had over men. To keep up with Billy, I'd been a thoroughgoing tomboy. Growing up with plain-Jane braids, dressed by my mother in starched shirtwaists, I'd thought of myself as homely. Besides, my mind had been on math, not on boys. At Stanford I'd spent my time with Page and his friends, men who treated me with decorum and respect. But after I met

Arthur, his delight led me to see myself differently. He loved the little ripple in my nose. To him, the mole on my cheek was a beauty mark. He couldn't get enough of my soft, silky hair. Before we made love, he'd pull out the hairpins so it would fall on my shoulders and he could run his hands through it. When I mentioned I was thinking of bobbing it to make life simpler, he was appalled.

Now I was on my own again, I noticed other men were drawn to me. This could easily have gone to my head, but Arthur was the star toward which I had charted my course, and I had no intention of straying. Major Barkley was a casualty of my desire.

I dressed myself in the elegant blue-lace gown my mother and I had made before I went away to college. It was out of fashion, but men rarely have any idea what is in fashion. What mattered was that it was the most appealing dress I owned and, therefore, most likely to dazzle the major. I brushed my hair until it shone and slipped on my silver kid dancing shoes.

Major Barkley had booked a table for us at the restaurant in the Willard, a place to see and be seen in Washington. As I walked into the lobby on his arm, I thought about how much my life had changed since those first nervous weeks I'd stayed at this hotel. Nice Lutheran girls like me were supposed to marry their childhood sweethearts, but I was no longer slated for a sober, virginal promenade down the aisle. I would never be a high school teacher like my beloved Miss Koenig.

At the end of the meal, it was time to be more honest with the major. As gracefully as I could, I told him I needed a favor, and once I'd put the question to him, he saw how completely he'd misinterpreted my intentions. He was a gentleman—his face betrayed only flickers of disappointment. He said he might be able to help but would need time to consult with a friend or two.

I knew that, even though the major had promised to do his best, it wouldn't be easy to convince anyone to send me to France just because I wanted to go. I settled in to wait, but with each day that passed my hopes dwindled.

One afternoon, at the end of June, I saw the major standing in the doorway of the office, motioning for me to step out into the hall. To my surprise, he handed over an envelope and explained that it contained orders sending me overseas on the next available ship.

"Yardley is fit to be tied that he's losing you. But it was made clear to him how badly cryptographers are needed in France. So he had no choice but to let you go."

Somehow the major had gotten me appointed as an instructor of cryptography at the Army Staff College at Langres, not far from Pershing's headquarters in Chaumont where Arthur was stationed. Patting my arm in a fatherly way, he said, "Be careful, Miss Havilland, and good luck. I have to say I envy you, going over there. By the way, he's a lucky guy."

CHAPTER 27

My luck was born of tragedy, and, looking back, that is not lost on me. If it hadn't been for the battle of Belleau Wood, I probably would never have reached France. Now labeled a triumphant turning point in the war, the Marines who fought there knew it was a profligate waste of American lives.

Belleau Wood, one of the first battles fought by American troops in France, was not engaged until June 6, 1918, thirteen months after Congress declared war on Germany. The decision to fight there had been made under extreme pressure: The Allies were infuriated by what they saw as endless American pussyfooting. In fact, we'd been so ill-prepared that there were few officers who had any combat experience, and almost all our troops, newly drafted, were so green Pershing had delayed putting them into the line until they received a modicum of training.

At long last, an assault was planned that was expected to yield an easy victory, a matter of a day or two. Instead of a quick win, the fight turned into a deadly siege that lasted more than three weeks because of the American failure to gather vital information beforehand.

If one of our intelligence officers had talked to a single farmer who lived in the area, he would have found out how foolhardy our plan was. Deep in the forest, atop a hill, two hundred German machine guns, hidden by massive rock formations, were embedded in ancient briars. From these protected positions, the gunners mowed down wave after wave of American soldiers as they marched in formation across a wide, open field of golden wheat, dotted with red poppies, that surrounded the hill.

By the time the Marines took the hill, ten thousand men had been wounded and twelve hundred were dead. In the wake of that unforgivable error, there had been a call to train more intelligence officers immediately, which led to my appointment at Langres where I could teach the rudiments of cryptography.

July 1918

The morning I left on a troopship out of Hoboken, I wired my parents to let them know where I was going, promising a letter of explanation would follow. I'd considered telephoning, but didn't want to end up arguing with my mother about whether I was going to France so that the last sound she'd hear before I left would be the click of my hanging up.

Because my train was held up near Philadelphia, I didn't catch the ferry from Manhattan to the dock in Hoboken until six that evening. I was frantic because my ship was scheduled to cast off at six. It turned out I need not have hurried: U-boats had been sighted lurking near the entrance to New York harbor. To take advantage of the cover of darkness, we didn't weigh anchor until midnight. Though I was apprehensive about the crossing, I would have died rather than admit it. I wasn't going to give anyone a reason to put me off that ship.

A storm blew up as soon as we were at sea, and the boat was tossed around like a rubber duck in an angry child's bathtub. Because we had to maintain a blackout on the ship, we flailed around in utter darkness. The only illumination was provided by violent cracks of lightning that lit up the sky. When the lightning stopped, I dragged myself up on deck in a benighted attempt to calm my churning stomach. The stars and the moon were hidden behind storm clouds.

When I saw sheets of water pouring across the deck, I went right back down to my cabin. As soon as I crossed the threshold, I threw up everything in my stomach, while looking fruitlessly for a pail or a wastebasket. Finally, I reached the bathroom. Afterward, I made a feeble attempt to clear up the mess, but the French dictionary I'd brought with me ended up under the bed, where I found it days later, flecked with vomit.

Once I'd tried to wash myself, I tossed my clothes and the towels I'd used to mop up the revolting floor into a corner of the cabin. Taking a clean chemise out of my suitcase, I pulled it over my head and fell into bed. For the rest of the night the boat rose and fell over massive waves, and I clung to the rails of my bunk. Disoriented by the darkness, I was grateful when a glimmer of sunrise appeared through my porthole. The next day was a good deal calmer, and, exhausted, I spent most of it asleep.

That night the storm blew up again. I lay half in a trance, hallucinating sea creatures climbing from the depths up the sides of the ship, over the rails onto the deck, and down the stairs into my room where they could feast on me. That sounds absurd, like a scary story made up by a child, but I assure you it was quite real to me at the time.

Finally, a steward came to check on me, took one look and said he would be right back with the ship's doctor. By then I was too miserable to pretend I was all right. After the doctor examined me, he told the steward to sponge my sweaty forehead and handed him a powder to be mixed with water, to settle my stomach and calm my nerves. Even though I gulped it down and the storm subsided, my seasickness never stopped.

On the eighth day our ship rendezvoused with a convoy of destroyers. I hadn't realized we'd had no escort crossing the Atlantic, which was just as well because, had I known, I would have been even more frightened. On the afternoon of the tenth day we made it safely into the harbor at Brest, near the westernmost tip of France. Climbing down the gangplank, everyone, including me, affected to look casual, but I bet I wasn't the only one pleased to put a foot on solid ground. While we waited for a troop train to Paris, I found a rickety wooden bench where I tried to work on my French vocabulary, hopeful that anybody who looked over my shoulder would think the pages of my dictionary were stained with coffee.

Worried I'd miss the train if I fell asleep, I kept returning to the station café, drinking cup after cup of bitter ersatz coffee, so hot that the first sip burned the roof of my mouth. Waiting is never easy; in war, it is a series of endless little hells—countless delays, waiting for trains, for trucks, food, tea, letters, blankets, socks, every little thing.

These annoyances were of course trivial. When I arrived in France, no one knew how much more true hell lay ahead, battles that would claim thousands more lives, killing, wounding, and maiming: Château-Thierry, Soissons, the Second Somme, Amiens, Second Arras, the list goes on and on, ending only with the last desperate fight to take back the Argonne Forest and cross the River Meuse. Better, perhaps, not to have known.

Once we finally boarded the train, it proceeded by fits and starts across Brittany and Normandy. I was too distracted to pay much attention to the beautifully kept fields of western France, still untouched by the German guns that had decimated the east. All I wanted was to get to Langres so I could get to work—and search for Arthur and Billy.

Finally, we reached our destination, Blois, an Army camp a hundred miles southwest of Paris, the first stop for American military in France. Here I had to wait—yet again—until I was dispatched to the Staff College. Blois was a beehive filled with eager young Americans, newly commissioned officers buzzing with energy and determination. By contrast, the French officers were grayer, older, and had little patience for this stream of callow youth pouring in from the States. The war had reached a desperate point: For the second time, the German Army was pushing hard toward the river Marne. At the start of the war, the Germans had crossed the river and only narrowly missed seizing Paris. If they succeeded this time, it would be all over for France.

At Blois, one could hear the German guns, though the front was more than two hundred miles to the east. Later, I learned the barrage could sometimes be heard across the Channel, even in London. Both sides used shelling before every major offensive to kill—or at least terrify—their enemies before they attacked. This barrage meant hours, even days, of continuous, deafening explosions. I couldn't comprehend how men waiting to go over the top bore this assault on their nerves.

I had long been troubled by the fact that, because I was female, I would never be tested in battle. Why should an accident of birth, of gender, protect me from this ultimate trial? Now that even the sound of guns scared me, I was grateful no one would ever ask me to pick up a rifle and shoot another human being.

My halting train ride to Langres was another lesson in patience. The need to share the few rail lines that had to carry hundreds of tons of supplies and thousands of soldiers to the front created continual chaos. Our train spent hours on a siding, to allow another train carrying more urgently needed goods to go through ahead of us. A connection was missed; then, without explanation, we were told to get off the train and wait for another one. Nobody had any idea when the next train would be coming through. How badly the army needed people like my father, I thought, who could have helped to sort out the confusion and would have been thrilled to be here, helpful, in the middle of the action.

When the other train finally passed by, I peered into its windows. It felt ghostly; there were no passengers, just hundreds of boxes and crates of God knows what unholy things: guns? ammunition? barbed wire? poison gas?

CHAPTER 28

I'd barely settled into my new job when I was ordered to attend a series of briefings and dinner at Pershing's headquarters, exactly where Arthur had been posted. I had been asked to report about the progress made by our teaching staff. As I awaited my turn to speak, the prospect of addressing a roomful of high-ranking officers was nerve-wracking. There was so much I didn't understand about military culture I often felt like a deaf person in a room full of hearing people. Nonetheless, my eyes darted around the room, hoping to light on Arthur, but no such luck.

When the meeting finished, there was an hour left before we had to re-assemble for dinner. An orderly showed me to a room and offered to bring me hot water so I could wash up. Instead, I said coolly, hiding my excitement as best I could, that I needed to speak first with Captain Arthur Bayard on urgent business. The young man led me down two flights of stairs to a frosted glass door. My nerves were so keyed up I opened the door without even thinking to knock. Fortunately, Arthur was alone, bent over his work. Without raising his head, he said sharply, "Yes, what is it you want?"

When he lifted his head and saw that it was me, he was astounded, just as I had hoped. Jumping up from his chair, he rushed over and held me tightly in his embrace.

"*Where* did you come from?"

"Follow me," I said and led him upstairs. We said nothing in the hallways, maintaining the pretense we were colleagues.

But when we reached my room, he picked me up and carried me to the bed, no small feat, while covering my face with kisses.

I could scarcely believe he was actually there, with me, where I could touch him. I'd schemed relentlessly for this reunion. But now I was keenly aware I was in a bedroom with a man not my husband, which had to violate a slew of military regulations. I was worried I'd get Arthur into trouble. I also smelled awful because I'd nervously sweated through my clothes during my presentation. His hands were everywhere, exploring my body with the intensity a blind man might bring to the task, touching me as if to make sure I was the real thing, not an impostor.

When I barely responded, he stopped, perplexed. "I've been imagining this moment for months, longing to touch you, sure you felt the same, but suddenly you're an ice goddess." There was an edge of anger to his voice.

"Oh no, no, when you hear the unladylike plots I hatched to get here, you'll know how badly I wanted to see you. But I'm grubby and I stink!"

"Oh for God's sake, who cares?" he said, rushing to pull the pins out of my hair. I was eagerly returning his affection when, too soon, the inevitable, embarrassing knock on my door interrupted us at the worst possible moment. I threw on some clothes and opened the door a few inches, hoping the orderly who'd finally arrived with the pitcher of hot water wouldn't catch a glimpse of Arthur—or my bare feet.

Soon we had to go downstairs for cocktails. When Pershing appeared, a hush fell over the room. After he'd surveyed the crowd, he asked to be introduced to me, which made me feel uncomfortably conspicuous. I'd heard women found him irresistible, and I could see he was handsome and very tall, with a chiseled face and the erect, graceful posture that comes from endless marching and drilling. But it was not just his good looks or his power: commander of the American Expeditionary Forces, that drew both men and women to him—he had true charm, not the phony article so often mistaken for it.

He knew how to listen. He asked about my family, my education, the discipline of cryptography, and how I managed to end up in France. His attention had its intended effect—I was no more immune than any other woman. At the end of the evening, he sought me out and said that, if I needed anything, I should let his aide de camp know and it would be seen to immediately. His driver took me back to Langres in a sleek, fast car. This didn't go down well with my colleagues who made the same trip crammed into a supply truck.

Two days later, I was called back to Chaumont and shown into an office where I recognized the man behind the desk as the major who'd sat next to me at dinner. We exchanged a few pleasantries. The general wanted to make sure I had a comfortable billet at Langres and everything I needed. I insisted I had no need for special treatment; in fact, it would be a sign of respect if I weren't accorded any. Getting down to the real business of the morning, the major explained that, while we ate our steaks, he'd been sizing me up, and he felt certain the army could make better use of my skills.

Nervous but excited, I wondered where this was leading. Our conversation became a complicated dance because I realized he was trying to ascertain whether he could trust me. Since my mother had been born near Hamburg, I had to endure one more inquiry about her allegiance to Germany—and mine.

Though I'd been down this path more than once, these assaultive questions could still rile me. The room was so icy and damp the walls were sweating. I blew on my hands to warm them up and took a deep breath to force myself to stop shaking. I had to show self-possession.

Once I passed his loyalty test, he asked if I would be willing to work near the front—interviewing German soldiers. In the field, intelligence officers talked to prisoners as soon as they were captured to see if they could convince or coerce the captives into revealing useful information, anything from battle plans to the condition of war materiel. Even a simple fact, say, that a patrol was going out that night, might give us an advantage.

Of course I said yes.

I would remain a civilian, he said, but I would act in the role of an intelligence officer, attached to whatever unit needed me. He believed prisoners would open up to a sympathetic woman who spoke their language as fluently as if she'd been born in their homeland. Most officers who conducted these interviews had to rely on translators, which created a barrier. "Miss Havilland," he concluded, "you're a rare bird, a woman with great intelligence, language skills, and psychological acumen."

At first I was flattered, but then I saw that his comments might well be condescending. Was he saying that I, Evelyn, had an unusual confluence of knowledge and skills? Or was he saying that few, if any, women had this kind of intelligence? My aggravation got buried under my anxiety. Did I have psychological insight? That certainly wasn't how I thought of myself. The way I saw it was I'd always had trouble understanding what makes other people tick.

CHAPTER 29

O nce I got a chance to move up to the front, I knew I would face a great test, one I might fail: Did I have courage under fire?

Within days I'd been assigned to a sector where a big push was underway. Everything was moving so fast I'd had no chance to tell Arthur where I was going and why. But he'd gotten wind of my new assignment at headquarters before I had time even to write to him, and he showed up, in a rage, at my office in the staff college at Langres.

"Evelyn, you cannot do this—it's too dangerous. They should not be sending a woman to the front. I bet you've never even shot a gun."

I didn't take this well. "Actually, Billy and I had learned to shoot coyotes out at the ranch by the time we were twelve. Anyway, I'm not going to be part of the shooting war. I'll be interviewing prisoners. Why would a man be any better at that than a woman? I thought you wanted me to have every chance, the same chances you've had."

"Of course, you're right, in principle."

"In principle?!"

"I should be going, not you," Arthur said.

"But Major Nolan asked me, and I said I would."

I crossed over from behind my desk and reached out to take him in my arms.

"I won't be able to write and tell you where I am, but I promise whenever I know someone is returning to Chaumont, I'll send news."

"Are you going to tell Billy what you're doing?"

"I'm not sure. I am sure I'm not going to tell my parents. Even if the letter got past the censors, which it shouldn't, it would do no good to add to their worries."

We spent a quiet evening together while I packed my few belongings. The next morning I climbed aboard a truck headed north and waved goodbye to Arthur as it pulled out of the courtyard. I watched his figure grow smaller and smaller until I could not see him at all.

After that, I moved frequently, from one hot spot to another, billeted just behind the lines, usually in a farmhouse that had to one degree or another survived the shelling.

I didn't turn out to be a coward, which was almost my greatest fear. I learned to hit the ground as soon as I heard incoming fire, just like everyone else. A sergeant told me that when they were being shelled, he tried to picture himself in a place where he felt safe. I tried his strategy, and it did help, sometimes. I'd imagine myself sitting on the couch in Daddy's office or swimming in the creek with Billy. But when it seemed like the barrage was never going to end, nothing helped. I'd shut my eyes so tight that all I could see was white—like a whiteout in a snow storm.

When we gained ground, our troops brought back the prisoners they'd rounded up. Many of those I talked to were so old or so young they should never have been drafted. By that stage in the war, every male in the Fatherland who could walk and carry a rifle was being sent to the front. Some of the boys I talked to were no more than thirteen or fourteen, and most were terrified. Their officers had forced them to fight on by saying that, if the Americans captured them, they would torture them before they shot them. Once these boys reached me, I tried to assure them that no one was going to hurt them, that they were prisoners of war, entitled to food, shelter, and packages from home, but they remained wary. To build a little trust, I tried telling them I was scared, too, but I rarely succeeded in reaching them.

The first soldier I questioned was just a boy, a towhead with piercing gray-green eyes, who reminded me of Billy when he was young, which made it hard for me to see him as an enemy. A corporal dragged him through the door of the farmhouse where I was waiting. He refused to sit down in the sad little chair he was offered. I found myself imagining how cheerful that chair must have looked once upon a time. Long ago someone had plaited its rush seat, most likely the woman who had lived in that house—a woman probably as hardworking as this boy's mother—who had loved her family every bit as much as his mother had. Flakes of blue and red still clung to the wood, but one day long ago, before the war had blighted all our lives, she'd painted it bright, gay colors. Finally, the corporal grabbed the boy's shoulders and shoved him down onto the chair.

The boy sat, sullen, not saying a word. If he'd been home, and happy, as he should have been, he would be playing sports after school and studying hard in the evenings. He'd have had an impish grin, like Billy. But that day he didn't have a single smile left in him. I could feel his anger, like a huge wave, crashing over me.

I tried to talk to him as if he were Billy, but I couldn't pierce his fury. Fighting his contempt, I felt I had no choice but to goad him into speech. "I think you're afraid of talking to me."

He exploded. Being taken prisoner, he said, was shameful. Death or victory were the only honorable outcomes for a soldier in the Kaiser's army. I told him everyone in his unit had been rounded up and many had surrendered. I told him I would have surrendered.

"'Of course you would—you're a woman!' he hissed.

I argued that we all had to do our part. His part was to be a good prisoner. I could see him consider spitting at me, then think better of it. He hated me, but he still had an instinct for survival. He stonewalled until I gave up. My failure to draw anything from him shook my confidence. If I couldn't even pry secrets from a child, would I ever uncover any useful information?

The intelligence team to which I'd been assigned moved as the battlefront moved, not far behind the lines. Even when we were lucky enough to find quarters in a chateau, the Germans who had occupied them before us had often wrecked them before retreating. Rooms might be perfectly proportioned and stone walls beautifully hewn, but the furniture would be broken, the sheets disgusting, the china smashed. They took the silver with them.

The pressure was unrelenting, and I was bone-tired. My hair was filthy, my fingernails cracked, my clothes stained and sometimes torn. At night, if I wasn't too tired, I'd turn my garments inside out and run my thumb along seams where the lice liked to hide so I could crush them between thumb and forefinger.

One rare morning, just after sunrise, I grabbed a chance to wash my hair in a stream near where we were billeted. The water was ice cold, but so swift and clear I didn't mind. After I rinsed the soap out of my hair, I stripped down to my underclothes and lay in the stream, letting the water run over me. It felt glorious to be clean, even though my teeth were chattering. My luck held: Once I got back inside, breakfast was waiting and a fire had been lit.

Fortunately, there was almost always enough food. The army worked hard to make sure everyone had decent rations, at least behind the lines. Men in the trenches were served hot meals whenever possible, but when supply lines broke down they ate cold, greasy muck out of tins and drank lukewarm brown water passed off as coffee. Next to them, I was living the good life.

Some of the prisoners I talked to had been so dehumanized by their years in the trenches they seemed more like wolves than men. They'd survived by doing whatever they were told to do, no matter how brutal.

I learned to assess, with a fair degree of accuracy, who would talk to me, although sometimes they surprised me. One angry, hard-bitten man with a bad hip hauled himself into the tent where I was waiting. Watching him limp made me think of my father. "How painful it must have been for you when your platoon was on the march," I said. This elicited no response. Sympathy was not going to get me anywhere.

After we sat for some minutes in stony silence, he whispered, "*Haare, sehr schön*" and touched my hair. To my relief, he pulled back his hand, and amazed me by whispering in German, "Your shining hair is the same color as my wife's and just as beautiful. I try never to think about her. But, looking at you, I can't stop myself. I haven't seen her for three years, when I had leave, the only time."

I listened as he poured out a story about his beautiful young *fräulein*. She'd been a schoolteacher, he said, who'd been fool enough to fall in love with him, an ignorant, middle-aged mechanic. Her family had not approved, but she'd married him all the same, and he still couldn't believe his luck. He figured when he died in the war, she'd be able to marry some fellow younger, more her class, more cultured and able to give her the life she deserved. "I doubt that's what she would want," I said. "Besides you're not going to die. You're safe now. You'll be a prisoner until the war is over. No matter who wins, you'll be repatriated to Germany."

His disbelief was palpable. I kept pressing him, asking about plans for patrols or troop movements.

"I can't tell you. I can't put my friends in danger."

I respected his desire to protect them, although I wasn't supposed to. I didn't wring every last scrap of information out of him. He wasn't the only one I let slip through. By then

I pitied them all, Germans as well as Americans. I should have been tougher. I live with that on my conscience. But even those pangs have been a luxury. I have been alive to feel them.

One evening after dinner, I was writing up reports of the interviews I'd conducted that day when I heard a rustling outside my door and the sound of the knob turning softly. Despite the rugged conditions in which we lived, people generally respected my closed door—they were careful not to intrude on a lady's privacy. I wished I had turned the key in the lock.

When I turned to see who was there, Billy was peeking around the door, none too clean and badly in need of a haircut, but grinning ear to ear, unmistakably my Billy. I leaped out of my chair, and he gathered me into his arms.

It's been years since I've cried, but back then I was so young and emotions were heightened by the war. I let happy tears flow that night. He was here, we were together, and that was all that mattered.

I asked him how he'd found me, and he smiled. "I have my ways, little lady! . . . Actually, the grapevine is quite effective. What I don't know is how you landed yourself right behind the line. I'm not happy about how close you are to the shelling."

"Who dared me to swim out beyond the end of the wharf the same week a shark was sighted in the bay?"

"Ev, this is serious."

"Yes, I know it is, and you, my friend, are too thin. You look exhausted."

"Actually, I've never felt better in my life. For three years I've been longing for a sight of you, and I'm pleased to see what a strapping girl you've become. Apparently, you've been gorging on *le bifteck et les truffes* since you've arrived in France." I had to laugh.

The evening flew by. We found an *estaminet* where we could get a late dinner—an omelet, a salad, a bottle of rough red wine—and Billy declared it the best meal he'd had since leaving Paris. A small band of musicians were playing an old spinet, a trumpet, and a clarinet. When we finished eating, Billy rose from his chair and asked, "Mam'selle, may I have this dance?"

Before I knew it, I was being whirled around in his arms. He sang the words of the tune, so softly only I could hear: "If I were the only boy in the world, and you were the only girl/ Nothing else would matter in the world today/We could go on loving in the same sweet way . . . " Resting my head on his shoulder, I wished the song would never end and we'd never have to stop dancing.

Billy didn't want to talk about the hospital, but he was happy to catch me up on other news. Mrs. Franklin, friend and mentor from his earliest days in France, was still living in Paris, in her house on the Rue de Martignac, and she visited the hospital to check on him when she could. My ancient jealousy vanished like mist—I realized she was just a kindly, older American woman who'd befriended a young man far from home. I asked if I could meet her.

"*Mais bien entendu!*" he said, promising to get in touch with her right away. "*J'enverrai une carte postale à l'instant!*" I was startled to hear Billy speaking French; of course, he would have had to learn it to find his way here. It dawned on me how little I knew about his life in France.

He wasn't a boy anymore. Who was he now? How had he been changed by what he'd seen? He seemed like the old Billy. He might have fallen in love with a nurse. He might marry her when the war was over. He wouldn't always belong just to me. I started to tell him about Arthur, but something stopped me. I wanted this night to belong just to us.

We drank the wine slowly, to draw out our time together. He was convivial, but when I asked again about his work at the hospital, he said, "Tonight, we're not talking about what I do. It would only make you sad, and I refuse to do that." He made one slip, referring to his hospital as a field hospital. I'd learned enough to know that a field hospital was the first stop after the casualty clearing station, so it had to be set up right behind the front lines, which meant Billy had long been in greater danger than I had realized.

Before we knew it, it was time for him to catch his ride back to the hospital. After he left, I sat by myself at our table thinking about how precarious life is.

CHAPTER 30

September 1918

I wanted to see Billy's hospital, and I finally had the chance on a crisp, blue-skied autumn day, a day still burned into my memory.

I'd imagined another cheerful reunion, but I couldn't have picked a worse time to turn up. New patients were streaming in as fast as stretcher-bearers could carry them. The wounded and dying were lined up in rows on the ground, some quiet, others moaning and begging for help. It was a chilly day, but few had blankets. Their clothes were crusted with blood and dirt. In some cases, the blood had turned dark brown; in others, it was bright red, leaking through hastily applied bandages.

I found Billy, on his knees, bent over a boy missing a hand who also had blood leaking from his thigh. Billy was applying a tourniquet to the leg, but I could also see blood flowing from the hand.

When Billy saw me, all he said was, "Put pressure on the leg." The boy looked up at the sky, trying not to see what was happening to his body. He must have known he'd lost the hand. Once the bleeding was more or less controlled, Billy summoned orderlies to carry him to the head of the line so a doctor could decide whether to send him directly to the operating room. Then he dragged me off to some ragged shrubbery where no one could hear us. "What in the name of God are you doing here where you might get killed?"

I had no good answer.

"Okay, I'm damned glad to see you, despite everything," he said. "But I'm also worrying about how I'll explain to your mother if you get killed while visiting me."

"Just don't tell her!" For a moment we laughed at the sheer absurdity of what I had said.

"Since I am here, can I make myself useful?"

"Sit with the soldiers who are waiting to be taken farther behind the lines to the convalescent hospital. Write letters to their families. Even the ones who aren't badly wounded are often so shaky they can't write."

What struck me about the soldiers waiting for the transport train was how calm, even peaceful, most of them were, despite their wounds. It occurred to me that, for now, they wouldn't have to wake up each morning wondering if today would be their last. A young man from Oklahoma said as much. "Call me a coward if you want to, but I'm damn happy I caught one. Docs think they might be able to patch up my leg. Even if they cain't, I'll still see my Ma and my girl, and my dog. Blue coonhound. Trained him myself. We hunt rabbits and squirrels. Ever tasted squirrel?"

I allowed as how I hadn't had the pleasure. Then I wrote a letter to his girl. Even had his hands been steady, I'm not sure he'd have been able to turn out much of a letter. He probably hadn't made it beyond grade school. But I could tell he loved that girl. He blushed right to the roots of his hair when he asked me to sign the letter "with a kiss from Jimmy."

There was another boy I don't like to think about but can never forget. He'd seen his sergeant's head torn off when he took a direct hit from a German shell. The boy kept returning to the moment when he saw a fountain of blood gush up out of the sergeant's neck. When he first described it, I almost threw up. When he brought it up again, I realized he desperately needed to talk about what he'd seen. Maybe, I thought, talking would help him let go of some of the horror he felt, but I had completely misread the situation. Repetitions of this memory made the horror balloon in his mind.

When a nurse came by, I whispered to her that some sort of sedative might be a mercy for this boy, and she agreed to give him one right away. I'm sure of one thing—it was a mercy for me.

Needing a break, I wandered off to a clearing nearby. It comforted me that tiny blue cornflowers bloomed there amid the destruction. Eventually, I walked back to the hospital and made my way into a different tent, careful not to go back into the same one where my horror-stricken soldier might be awake, despite the sedative. I didn't think my seeing him again would do either of us any good. Probably I was just afraid to talk to him anymore.

The first bed in this tent was occupied by a man in his thirties, older than most of the wounded. A lieutenant from Montana, he'd led his men out of the trench and over the top before dawn and had no idea if any of them had survived—but he felt sure that few had. His platoon had been shelled heavily as they made their way across No Man's Land without cover. He was furious because he'd been ordered to lead them "like a pack of lambs to slaughter." Perhaps, he said, he should have risked court-martial to save them. It was plain he felt guilty for surviving.

He asked me to write to his parents, telling them he had only a minor wound—a lie—that his war was over and he looked forward to seeing them soon. That was another lie: Given how badly he'd been wounded, there was little chance he would recover. But he wasn't ready to give up yet. If he could will himself to live, he would. When I finished the letter, we sat together quietly for a while until stretcher-bearers arrived to load him onto the train. I can still see the look on his face, curious and distant, as they carried him off. I never knew if he beat the odds. Our lives in France were littered with such mysteries.

By late afternoon I was desperately tired. How did Billy do this day after day? I stopped talking to the men waiting for the train, and hung back in the shadows where I could watch Billy. This was my chance to see him at work, a chance that might not come again.

As he moved from one patient to the next, I saw a Billy I'd never seen before, deft and calm, cleaning a deep gash and sewing it up with quick, neat stitches, dressing wounds, changing bandages, one hand gently lifting the hair out of a patient's eyes while the other casually checked a blackened hole in the chest. He could coax a smile out of a patient at his wits' end. At the next bed, if the situation was beyond humor, he adjusted instantly. When everyone had been tended to, he returned to the beds where death was hovering. He sat with those men, held their hands, listened, and sometimes said a few words. I was not close enough to hear, but watching their faces I sensed he was helping them to let go of this world.

In that hour I saw Billy fully alive, in a way few of us ever are. In the years he'd been nursing, he had learned to do exactly what was needed. He'd been right to risk everything and go to France, not just for the sake of those he could help but for himself. Left at home, he would have felt like a eunuch. He'd have stewed and fretted and made himself miserable. One day he would be a great doctor. What he'd learned in war would be valuable in time of peace. There were going to be so many wounded in body and spirit: men without limbs, without sight, without mouths or ears or noses, who would need doctors to repair the damage as best they could, doctors who understood how hard it would be for their souls to heal.

Once he had a moment to breathe, Billy came looking for me. I hadn't had any food since breakfast, and I doubt he had either, but he said he couldn't take time to eat nor could he help me get back to my billet. I would have to figure out how to make my way alone.

At that moment I glimpsed that Billy wouldn't always be there to protect me, something I'd counted on as long as I could remember. If some boy hurt my feelings, Billy beat him up. When my mother tore into me, Billy coached me to hold my ground. Once he dared me, I could never back down. But the days of dares and hugs were over.

I wanted to be worthy of his trust, though I was still smarting from the angry sparks that had shot out of his eyes earlier in the day. Not wanting to add to the strain he was under, I said, "Sure, I'll be fine." He made me promise to send word if I got back safely.

After a good deal of asking around, I found a soldier who knew an ambulance driver who could take me as far as the casualty clearing station. It was almost midnight, and they hadn't finished picking up the wounded. Luckily, I found a second ride to take me the rest of the way.

Progress was slow because the road was pitted with shell holes, and ours was one of dozens of trucks inching forward in a convoy. Most trucks and soldiers traveled at night to hide their movements from German reconnaissance planes. No headlights were allowed, which occasionally meant drifting off the road into a ditch. Despite every precaution, the Germans often found out where troops and supplies were moving— effective espionage, I guess. At about three in the morning, the truck in front of us took a direct hit from a mortar. I watched, in horror, as everyone else jumped off our truck to move the bodies and the wrecked truck to the side of the road so we could continue on our way.

Just after dawn I reached the farmhouse where I'd been staying and fell into bed, exhausted. An hour later I was roused by a young lieutenant knocking on my door. When I answered, sodden with sleep, he told me to pack my bags immediately, because I was being transferred to Pershing's new headquarters in the town of Souilly. I didn't know it, but half a million American soldiers were already marching, double-time, toward the Argonne Forest where the last great battle of the war was under way. Later, I realized this mighty push explained why patients had been pouring into Billy's hospital.

For reasons I never understood, American soldiers fighting at Saint-Mihiel had been pulled out of the line before that battle was finished and rushed to the Argonne Forest where Pershing had committed them to a far greater fight, for which they were ill-prepared.

The steep ridges of the forest, pocked with rocks and deep ravines, were devilishly hard to climb and impossible terrain on which to fight. Nonetheless, Pershing had decreed his men would break through the German lines in thirty-six hours and begin the march to Berlin. Briefly, American troops made that rapid kind of progress, but when their advance ground to a halt the initial euphoria vanished.

Before long, it became clear that Pershing had been whistling in the dark. The casualties were astronomical. German guns were not the only killers. Men drowned in mud. Sometimes the rain and fog were so thick a soldier couldn't see his comrade marching two yards in front of him. Shell holes were everywhere, and if a soldier fell into one, he might never make it out. Those who survived were sopping wet for weeks on end, crawling every night into sleeping bags that never dried. Dysentery was rampant, and mold grew on their feet.

Early in the war the Germans had fortified the forest, which had long been regarded as impenetrable, by digging four rows of trenches that were miles long and, in places, forty feet deep. They'd embedded machine guns everywhere. As the Americans struggled to crawl up the ridges, German gunners hid behind boulders and sprayed bullets, mowing them down relentlessly.

Tension grew at headquarters in Souilly as weeks went by with little progress. Though we tried not to talk about it, we secretly wondered if this battle would prove as hopeless and ill-conceived as so many others.

No one knew if the Americans could hold out—even though more than a million soldiers had been committed to the fight— but, in the end, they gained ground, slowly and at great cost. Over forty-seven ghastly days and nights, twenty-six thousand Americans died and four times that many were wounded. But their sacrifices secured the last, essential victory. Against all odds, U.S. troops reached the top of the last ridge and made their way down the other side, crossing the River Meuse and cutting off the enemy's supply lines so fully that the Germans had to admit their war was over.

CHAPTER 31

Many nights when I have trouble falling asleep, I still torment myself by reliving my last evenings in France with Arthur. He, too, had been stationed at Souilly for that final, murderous battle, reassigned as a liaison officer, which meant he traveled constantly, dispatched to the front where he would gather intelligence to bring back to headquarters, then returning to the front with new orders for the troops.

One night, he turned up at my office to say he had the evening free. His commanding officer had told him to get lost, grab a good meal, and get a real night's sleep for a change.

After eating dinner in the mess, we retreated to my room. Arthur wanted to go to bed, but I insisted on talking. I'd never seen him so edgy, and I wanted to know why. Avoiding what was troubling him by making love, which was what he wanted to do, made me tense, too.

He evaded my questions. I didn't know how long it would be before I saw him again. Until now we'd shared so much, with fewer and fewer barriers between us, but that night he held himself aloof. I kept pushing. When he refused outright to tell me what he was upset about—insisting he wouldn't distress me because that would do neither of us any good—I lost my temper.

"What do you think I hear all day long? The prisoners don't want to talk to me about anything military. They're scared, and most of them haven't talked to a woman since they left home. Some are so young I'm sure the last woman they confided in was their mother. I am nothing if not a confessional for men riddled with fear. I expect I've heard more gory details than you think.

"There are only a few hard cases left, men who started out as sadists or have been driven mad by all the killing they've done. Once I see a certain creepy look in their eyes, I send them straight back to detention. I don't want to hear their fantasies about the monstrous things they want to do to French women—or have done. They're beyond redemption, enraged not because they've been captured but because they've lost the opportunity to indulge their bloodlust. What could you tell me that would frighten me more than that?"

"Oh my darling, you should never have heard such things. I hate the war; I hate that you should be so degraded."

"Degraded? What are you talking about? Maybe you're the one who's been degraded, because you no longer see me as I truly am. You think I've been dirtied because I heard these revolting stories? I'm just one more person who's been forced to witness the consequences of endless butchery. If I'm degraded, we all are."

Seeing him shrink from me, I wondered: Had I gone too far? The Arthur who'd taught me to love Beethoven, who'd introduced me to Eakins and Sargent, who'd taken me home to meet his mother and asked me to marry him, was the same man sitting beside me on a worn chintz-covered settee, tired, filthy, and near collapse. I'd forgotten that, at the best of times, love is a fragile plant.

When I put an arm around him, he rested his head on my shoulder. Feeling his bony ribs through the fabric of his shirt, I realized he was dangerously thin. Flu was sweeping through the ranks, killing more efficiently than guns.

What if he died while we were at odds? I apologized. "Shhh," he whispered, "stop now. I know you didn't mean it. The strain has to come out somewhere. Who can you yell at but me? I don't mind, at least nowhere near as much as you think. Maybe your yelling is a good thing. If you can let yourself get this angry, maybe you've begun to trust me."

Did he still think I didn't trust him? His empathy was humbling. "You're the person I should treat best in the world," I said.

"Stop being so harsh to yourself. Only people in novels behave as nobly as you think you should. Anybody can lose their temper when they're hurt or scared. Even the sainted Isabel yelled now and then." I recalled the first time he'd told me Isabel was not a saint—at Rose's house only last Christmas. I could picture us looking out on the rhododendrons weighed down by the snow falling in the garden. That memory reminded me how happy we could be, and I smiled. Once Arthur saw me smile, his face relaxed, no doubt relieved this painful moment was passing.

He unbuttoned my blouse, and for a while we forgot the war. Afterward, we fell into a deep sleep, and didn't wake till the first light was creeping in around the edges of the blackout curtains. I watched him dress, wishing he could stay. Sitting on the edge of the bed, he stroked my hair, kissed me on the forehead, and slipped out the door.

His words stayed with me, tipping a delicate balance in my mind. He wasn't all wrong. There was a degree to which I had been degraded—and blinded—by the work I was doing. I'd kept going by convincing myself the work I did was valuable, and, if it saved anyone's life, which it may have sometimes, then it was. But there was another more gruesome way to look at what I did. I was just one of thousands of cogs in a giant machine that ground forward, destroying everything in its path, fueled at moments by bits of information I fed it. My idealism about the war had withered away. It had started to die when I'd seen the agonies Billy's patients endured. After that, I'd read the casualty reports every morning. How much difference was there between my work and that of a sniper who waited for a head to show above the parapet? Not as much as I'd thought. But there was no turning back.

I saw Arthur only once more before the armistice, on another night when he came back from the front to report to his commanding officer. I was brushing my hair, getting ready for bed, when the landlady knocked on my door to tell me "a friend" had come to visit. She did not approve, but I was past caring. Throwing on a dressing gown, I ran downstairs to greet Arthur.

Up in my room we made love with a fierceness new to us. Our need was so great there were few endearments, just a wild grappling, an attempt to obliterate consciousness. This time, when we talked, Arthur held nothing back.

That morning a German soldier had surrendered and come forward to beg for water. Instead of handing him a canteen, the lieutenant had blown the prisoner's brains out, while the lieutenant's platoon watched him. Arthur had gone into the woods and thrown up.

"That man was terrified. He'd done nothing to threaten the lieutenant. He'd climbed out of the trench with his hands up—it was abundantly clear he was giving himself up. We haven't had enough water for weeks. That bastard couldn't see he could just as easily have been the one begging for water. Our men drink rainwater. They check shell holes for frogs. If they don't see any, they figure the water isn't pond scum yet, so it's safe enough to drink. That sounds crazy, but it makes more sense than a lot of things happening out there.

"We're fighting over ground where thousands of Frenchmen have already died. There are broken weapons, unexploded shells, and decayed bodies among the rotting leaves, stinking carcasses of horses, the poor dumb beasts. It's all one vile stew. It gets into your clothes and your hair. Even after I waded across a clear-running stream, water as high as my chest, I still stank. When there's a barrage, shells send body parts flying into the air. I've seen men scrape gobs of human flesh off their clothes and hands and faces.

"I wish I thought there was any point to what we're doing. If it all comes down to shooting a thirsty stranger in the head to amuse yourself, it's evil. We've taught young men to enjoy killing. Not all of them, but enough that it scares me. I don't want to go home to a world where there are men who think shooting another man is entertainment.

"Pershing and his callous underlings are responsible," he said, shivering uncontrollably. "The orders come down the line: 'Attack! Attack! Attack! Damn the losses!' Anything but relentless aggression is branded failure—and cowardice. They ought to get off their asses and go up to the front. They should have to watch men get torn to pieces while they try to take back a village that doesn't even exist because it was already bombed into rubble." The ardent patriot who had envied his brother Nathaniel for fighting in France had died in the Argonne Forest. As I sat there with him in his wretchedness, I hated to think what the death of our idealism meant.

Wrung out, he fell asleep in my arms. Gently, I lowered him onto the bed and slipped a pillow under his head. I laid his greatcoat over him—the fire had gone out, and there was no more coal. I sat on the floor next to him and studied his face, seeing how it had been changed by the strain of the war: the plum-colored shadows under the eyes, the drawn, yellow cast of his skin, gray hairs among the brown. Arthur was too young to go gray. But in comparison to what many had suffered, it was a small price.

After six weeks of carnage, the Allies captured Sedan and Mézières. Controlling the critical railway junctions in these cities deprived the Germans of troops, food, and ammunition. On November 7, Marshal Foch, commander in chief of the Allied Armies, received a telegram from Hindenburg, the German chief of staff, asking for a secret meeting to arrange terms for an armistice, news that traveled through headquarters like lightning.

On the 11th of November, at eleven in the morning, the armistice was signed in Foch's railroad car in the forest of Compiègne, and the war was officially at an end. Germany and Austria had gained nothing but the enmity of the rest of the world. Millions had died, their families left brokenhearted in every country that had taken part in the fight. But on that day, we were happy, raucously, riotously happy. It was over, and we were going home. Nothing else mattered.

Arthur was somewhere up near the front, but I knew I would see him soon.

I wanted to see Billy, but I knew his hospital was overflowing with patients, so I held off. The wounded kept arriving at the casualty clearing stations well after eleven o'clock and the victorious ringing of thousands of church bells. Think of parents who heard that their son had died that day, after eleven. What a bitter card to be dealt by fate.

The next few days were filled with relief but also with strain as we began to understand how exhausted we were. I wrote to my parents to tell them I was no longer in danger. I didn't know how I was going to tell them about Arthur and Boston, but I believed it would all work out somehow. In comparison to the toll taken by the war, a skirmish with Mamma seemed like a flea bite. In those first days after the Germans gave up, I still imagined that love could conquer all.

CHAPTER 32

December 1918

Not long after the armistice, when I got that scribbled postcard from Billy, its handwriting almost illegible, I decided I had to pay him a visit. The absence of his usually free, loping script shouted there was trouble.

I needed to tell him I was going to marry Arthur. I'd been lying, by omission. When I'd seen him at the hospital months before, there'd been so much death in the air that talk of marriage had felt frivolous. I hadn't wanted to tell him in a letter: This news should be delivered face-to-face. It would be best to tell him before we left France. If I waited until we got back to the States, he'd be hurt I'd waited so long.

I put in for a few days' leave. The roads were still clogged with army vehicles, but nobody minded anymore because they were not headed back to the front. Last time I'd made this trip, the men in the truck had been jumpy and irritable, but now the swearing about flat tires and traffic jams was good-natured. As the only woman on board, I endured a good deal of ribbing, but I didn't mind. Once, that kind of banter would have gotten my back up, but no longer. I'd lived through the shelling, just as they had. I felt like one of them, and I had learned the value of the dumbest joke as a means of distraction.

When I reached the hospital, I was struck by how quiet it was: no thundering barrage, no ambulances pulling in, packed with wounded. Nurses and doctors spoke almost in whispers, as if they were so tired they'd lost their full voices. Some looked stooped, as if bowed down by the effort of bending over too many beds. If a few faces looked cheerful, many appeared grim. I knew every one of them had been scarred by what they'd seen, whether it was apparent or not.

Someone directed me to Billy's ward, where I found him chatting with a patient who'd lost an arm. Billy was lighting a cigarette for the man and passed it to his remaining good hand.

When I touched Billy's arm to get his attention, he turned and saw me. I'd anticipated a smile, so I was horrified when I saw only a deadness in his eyes, a look that suggested something inside him had burnt out and little but ashes remained.

He asked me to wait while he checked on one more patient. I followed him down the aisle between the cots but stayed back a little when he stopped at the bed of a pale, thin young man who seemed to be resting quietly. No bandages or plaster cast were visible, so I wondered what had happened to him. Using hand signals, Billy asked the boy a series of questions. He held up a tin cup and tipped it to his mouth as if he were taking a sip—to find out whether the boy wanted water. He nodded. When the boy was through drinking, Billy put his hands together, as if in prayer, laid them on his cheek and tipped his head and hands—to ask if the boy was ready to sleep. After he nodded again, Billy turned him on his side, took the twisted sheet and blanket off the bed, smoothed them out and remade the bed properly.

Billy guided me out of the tent into the sunshine where a few chairs waited for those who had time to sit.

"Did that boy lose his hearing?" I asked.

"Not as far as the doctors can determine: His ear drums are fine, and the auditory nerve isn't damaged. But I've seen this before. I'd testify in court he can't hear anything. I believe he couldn't bear to—not another barrage, not one more incoming shell, one more machine gun. His best friend got caught on the wire trying to get back to the line. He had to listen to him scream, in agony, from where he was hung up on the barbed wire, begging for help, until he died. The lieutenant refused him permission to crawl out and bring his friend back. A sniper was waiting to pick off anyone who attempted a rescue. The lieutenant said he wouldn't let him commit suicide. I think those were the last words he heard."

After he finished his cigarette, Billy said he was so busy he had to get back to work. I sensed he wanted to get away before I could ask any questions. When I asked if he would have dinner with me, he started to say no, but thought better of it. Maybe he knew he couldn't avoid me forever. I wonder.

My afternoon was spent walking in the fields around the hospital, trying to figure out what to do. I'd been counting on Billy to stand by me when I told my mother I had married Arthur. I'd sketched out a future for all of us that worked to my advantage. I would settle in Boston, and Billy would look out for my parents. He'd go to medical school at Stanford and become a doctor, like his dad. He'd marry, have children, and buy a house in San Jose big enough that Dora could move in with his family when she needed to.

With little warning, the ground was shifting beneath me. To an extent, I was prepared for such shifts: The war had taught us to be quick because there was never time to grieve. Should you fail to see the danger that lay right in front of you, it was at your peril. But this turn of events, in my small world, was far greater than any I had anticipated. I felt tremendous pressure to figure out what I could do to save Billy, but I had no idea what to do. For the first time in my life, he seemed a thousand miles away from me. I thought of the long-ago day when he'd taken me up in his plane and flown over the mountains so I could see the ocean. Would we ever know that kind of pure joy again?

At sunset I walked back to meet him for dinner. We chatted about this and that, not much of anything really. It felt as if he had put on a mask to hide the dreadful conflict inside him, a mask that scared me because I didn't know why he needed to hide from me of all people. I didn't say anything about Arthur. How could I talk about happiness that lay ahead for me when Billy appeared to be falling into a hole so deep I knew not where the bottom lay? I tried to tell myself I was jumping too quickly to conclusions. But then I would look at him and be frightened all over again by the same deadness that had greeted me when I arrived. When I ventured to ask if he was all right, the kind of question he hated, he dismissed my concern with a wave of his hand.

I slept in the hospital that night. Because there were no empty beds, I had to make do with blankets stretched out on the dirt floor of the tent. The pain of my hipbones sticking into the hard dirt kept me awake for a long time. When I finally did slip into a light sleep, I had the worst dream. I was walking by myself on a sidewalk, in a city where there were no buildings, just a wrought-iron fence that separated me from a vast expanse of supernaturally green grass. The moonlight shone, too brightly. I felt endangered, so I walked faster and faster, but no matter how far I walked there were no houses, no cars, no people. I was horribly alone until a wolf with gleaming white fur and ice-blue eyes ran down the hill, howling, and jumped the fence with ease, landing in front of me. As it sank its teeth into my neck, I jerked myself awake and lay there panting, my heart racing.

I'd planned to stay a couple of days, but the next morning I told Billy I was leaving, using as my excuse that he had no time for visitors. He was visibly relieved to see me go. In the old days, we'd never wanted to be separated. But something had changed, something dangerous had come between us, and we both knew it.

CHAPTER 33

When I got back to Souilly, Arthur was pleased I'd returned early. At first, in a teasing voice, he said I must have missed him too much to stay away—but when he noticed I was unusually quiet he asked if something was wrong. I said only that the visit had been difficult. I needed to think. Considerate to a fault, Arthur respected my wishes and gave me time to work out what was troubling me. I wish he hadn't. If only he'd insisted, if only we'd talked right then and made plans together.

For the next few days I kept not telling Arthur what I had realized on the way back from the hospital: Instead of traveling with him to Boston so we could be married right away, I was going to have to go back to California. I feared letting Billy travel on his own. He seemed too damaged. I wrote to ask Billy what was wrong but received no reply. His silence was foreboding. Eventually, I realized my delays were going to feel cruel to Arthur. I was doing something much like what he'd done in the early days of our courtship, holding myself aloof, but this time the stakes were far higher.

With the benefit of hindsight, I ask myself: What in the name of heaven did I think I was doing by keeping my worry from Arthur? Protecting him? I think I thought so, but, if I did, it's another proof of how little I understood the nature of intimacy. I was too proud to ask Arthur for his help, to come with me to California if he could. I needed him to offer that help without my asking. Of course, I wasn't conscious of how this pride got in my way until years later. No doubt at the time I was protecting myself, but even in that I failed. Arthur would have helped me. All I had to do was ask.

Finally, when I faced that I had to tell him, I passed a hard night. Wrapped in my dressing gown to ward off the biting cold, I sat in an armchair and looked out my bedroom window onto the small apple orchard I'd come to know so well over the course of many sleepless nights. The trees were bereft of leaves. There were no clouds and no moon. Somewhere nearby a barn owl hooted mournfully.

If I did not go home with Billy, I would not be the person Arthur believed me to be. I tried to convince myself Billy would come through this crisis, but my instincts told me I was wrong. I had always been able to feel his feelings, and inside me there was a great darkness. Yet I wanted nothing so much as my beloved Arthur, marriage, and the life of intellectual companionship and physical happiness we would have.

I knew I would never marry anyone but Arthur. But what if I couldn't? What would it be not to hear his voice, not to see his face or feel his touch? Never to share a house with him, a bed? Never have his children? I loved Billy and our fates were linked, but this was a fate I had never imagined, just as none of us could ever have imagined the tragedy of the war.

When the sun rose, I saw a pair of wood-pigeons on the lawn below. As I stood up, they took flight.

When I asked Arthur if he would be free in the evening, I was stricken by his cheery "Of course."

While we ate dinner, he threw a new wrinkle into our plans. His Uncle Andrew had cabled to ask if he would be able to assist him at the peace conference that would start in France as soon as President Wilson arrived from America. Andrew needed him because his linguistic skills would be valuable: There would be several languages at the table and, no doubt, complex disagreements that had to be resolved. What's more, Arthur had been on the ground in France for almost a year, much of it spent at Pershing's headquarters, so he could advise Andrew about rivalries and factions that had grown up between countries, even within countries.

Of course, Arthur had said yes—he was buoyed by the idea of helping to build a good peace to end this disastrous war. But, unfortunately, helping Andrew meant Arthur would have to join him at headquarters in Chaumont almost immediately while I remained behind in Souilly to finish up my work. No one knew how long the conference would last, but it was likely the negotiations would take at least half a year, and he hated the idea of anything that would delay our marriage. When he mentioned how much he was looking forward to the honeymoon he envisioned for us, a trip to California so he could meet my family, I wanted to cry.

As I sat there listening to his concerns, pretending I would be able to share everything with him felt deceitful.

After we finished eating, we went for a walk into the woods west of town. The bleakness of winter was bearing down on us. I didn't know where to start. Finally, I plunged into a description of the miserable time I'd had with Billy, avoiding what I needed to say, until Arthur broke in. "So what are you trying to tell me?"

"He seemed so frail, so beaten. Maybe he will come back to himself, but I can't let him travel home alone. The worst thing, for us, is I don't know when I'll be able to come to Boston."

At first, Arthur was speechless. Then he said, "You were only there for a day. I believe Billy needs rest, and deserves it, but he's a strong man. He made it through four years, most of them near the front; he's still at the hospital nursing the wounded who can't be sent home yet. That hardly sounds like someone who's falling apart. If he heard what you are saying, I think he would feel humiliated—and probably angry. I know I would."

"If you saw him, I don't think you'd say that."

"I accept that's what you saw. I accept that you believe you must travel home with him. I'll be at the peace conference in Versailles, but that can't go on forever. You promised to marry me. Didn't you?"

If he'd told me I couldn't come to Boston, I would have been devastated. I struggled to explain.

"Of course, I did. But will this make sense to you? I don't know what's going to happen." By now I felt like I was breaking my own heart as well as his. "You know Billy and I spent every day of our childhood together. We knew what the other one was thinking, as if we were two halves of the same self. If one of us dies, I'm not sure the other would survive."

"Are you saying this is going to kill him? Then it will kill you?" Arthur asked. "Seriously, is that what you're saying?"

"No, I don't think so. That sounds absurd, and melodramatic. I'm not sure what I'm saying. I pray I'm exaggerating all this."

"I have no idea what to say to that," Arthur said. Before I could stop him, he turned away from me and walked swiftly back toward town. It was clear he wanted to get away from me. I stood there, remembering nights in Washington when he'd walked me back to my room in Georgetown, no matter how late the hour or how tired he was. Perhaps I was tasting my future, when I would have to make my way alone, in the dark.

I stood there, frozen, uncertain what to do. Eventually, a black figure came striding down the road toward me. "I'm sorry," Arthur said once he was in earshot, reaching out to take my hand. "I shouldn't have left you out here by yourself. We'll figure out a way through this. I couldn't think of anything but my own happiness. I know how much you love Billy. If you need to go home and get him settled, I can accept that. We'll see what happens. I think he'll pull out of this, but you're right—this could be worse than I understand."

"I promise I will come to Boston as soon as I can," I said, holding his hand until he pulled it away and let mine drop. We returned to town without speaking.

When we reached the stone stairs in front of the house where I was boarding, I tried to hug him, but his body felt stiff and wooden. With a quick "good night," the man who hated saying goodbye was gone.

In a few weeks my work was done. Billy still wasn't finished at the hospital, but he'd written me a perfectly lucid letter, promising to meet me in Paris as soon as he could, so I made my way there. I wished Arthur had been able to sail home with Billy and me—I would have felt so much safer—but Arthur's war would not be over until the treaty was signed. When the two of us said goodbye, we had no idea when we would see each other again. Ironically, the war had given us precious time together; now the peace was separating us.

CHAPTER 34

May 1919

Billy's and my trip home to California seemed never-ending. By the time the train reached Omaha, we were sitting separately most of the time. We'd fought over things as trivial as who would get an empty seat. I'd infuriated him by keeping him under close scrutiny, closer than he could tolerate. I could hardly wait for the trip to be over, and, no doubt, Billy felt the same. But then, as our train climbed down out of the Sierras, my feelings lurched in the opposite direction. I began to wish the journey would not end—because I dreaded the shock to Dora and Alice when they realized how hurt Billy was. I kept seeing them in my mind, waiting on the platform to greet the Billy they remembered, who protected them and made them laugh. Maybe he could hold it together for a few days, but once they began to see the truth, they were going to be broken-hearted. I had no idea how to cushion them.

To push this disturbing prospect out of my mind, I retreated into the past, thinking about home and my father, who was waiting for me every bit as eagerly as Dora was waiting for her Billy. Some of my happiest memories were of evenings when I was very young and Daddy and I had visited the station Billy and I were now hurtling toward. At the end of the day, after Daddy finished his work, he'd harness our old roan mare to the buggy. Looking back, I see how painful that effort must have been for a man who was forced to spend most of his day in a wheelchair. I'd scramble up beside him, intent on the favorite hour of my day. In winter he'd bundle me up in the fuzzy red-plaid blanket he kept under the seat just for me. He'd tuck the blanket in carefully around my legs until I was warm as toast, then hoist himself up onto the seat and pick up the reins, snapping them smartly.

While we sat waiting for the express to arrive, he'd tell me about the different trains and their engines, what they were made of and how they worked. When he was a boy, back home in Albany, he'd fallen in love with trains and spent all his spare time hanging around the railyard. As soon as he finished school, he'd left New York, working his way west on the railroad, rising to foreman, supervising the Chinamen who broke their backs doing the hard labor of breaking ground and laying track.

The two of us would talk, almost in whispers, while we waited. My eyes and ears perked up as soon as I heard first the long whistle, then the thrilling shriek of wheels grabbing the rails and gold sparks flying as the huge engine strained to stop.

As the train began to pull out of the station, we'd count the cars. Daddy loved to tease me, pointing out that the train looked like a giant, segmented metal worm. Why, he'd ask, was I scared of little earthworms in the garden when I loved this powerful mechanical worm? When I said earthworms were disgusting, he'd stroke my cheek, zigzagging a finger along the side of my face, and call me his "squirmy worm."

Once we started home, the closer we got to the house, the lower my spirits sank. My chest tightened. By the time I opened the screen door, I was bracing to fend off Mamma's criticisms, which rained down on me for even the smallest offense. Forgetting to put my napkin on my lap, failing to say thank you, reaching for the butter instead of asking for it to be passed—it didn't take much to set her off.

She'd light into me, and my throat would close up, which made it hard to choke down the food on my plate. But choke it down I did, because not cleaning my plate was the cardinal sin. If I didn't finish everything and Mamma was in a good humor, she'd take away my dessert. When she was in a bad mood, I'd get the bristles of her hairbrush on my backside.

As soon as we climbed down off the train in San Jose, Dora and Alice threw their arms around Billy, and he hugged them back. As I watched them cling to him, I hoped their love had the power to heal him.

My parents were on the platform waiting for me. Daddy looked scrawny, his hair almost white, peppered faintly with orange, a ghostly echo of its old carroty self. Had he caught the Spanish influenza that had killed millions? If so, why had nobody told me? Later, my mother admitted he had had the flu, but she had not written to tell me, having decided it would be thoughtless to add to my worries.

The change in my mother took me aback because she had always seemed so sturdy. When I left for Washington, there had been a few threads of gray in her dark brown hair; two years later, she was entirely gray. Thinner, stiffer, moving kind of slowly. She wasn't the robust middle-aged woman I'd left behind.

That night the six of us had dinner together. Mamma had prepared a celebratory meal starting with our favorite dish: short ribs, roasted until the fat crackled, resting on a bed of sauerkraut. We washed them down with a bottle of Riesling purchased especially for this occasion.

After Billy helped me clear the table, instead of reaching for a towel to dry the dishes, he said he needed to stretch his legs, and a moment later he was out the door. A current of uneasiness flowed through the house, but the rest of us chose to act as if nothing had happened.

After the dishwashing was done and the drainboard scoured, I joined Daddy on the porch, lowering myself down into the rocking chair next to his. Everyone else was still in the kitchen, putting away the dishes and making coffee, so we had a little time to ourselves. He said he wanted to hear everything about Washington and France, but first he had a question.

Dropping his voice so no one else could hear, he asked, "Is Billy all right?"

I couldn't lie to him. What's more, I was going to need his help. After I described Billy's withdrawal, his irritability and our angry clashes, he said, "I'm not surprised."

"How did you know?"

"Since he left, I've had years to sit here every evening, reading the casualty lists in the newspaper and brooding about what it was like for him to deal with mangled bodies day after day. His dad could have handled it, if anybody could. Such a strong fella, able to draw a boundary when he needed to protect himself. Doctors see so much suffering—they have to armor themselves. But Billy never learned to do that. He's gentle, which makes him vulnerable. Faced with the ghastly suffering caused by these new weapons, probably too vulnerable. I think he's in deep trouble."

"That's true," I said. "But why didn't I see that before it was too late?"

"Even if you had, what could you have done? Brains and boldness make him seem so strong, but Dora always protected him, especially since Doc died. Billy believed he had to fill his father's shoes, still does. That's why he took off as soon as the war started. He had something to prove."

"Over there he came as close to being a doctor as he could," I said. "I thought that was going to help him."

"At dinner I was watching his face," my father said. "If he'd been ten years older, he might have come through it. No boy should see what he's seen. We'll do our best to take care of him. It won't be easy. He's proud. If he feels dependent on us, he's going to hate it."

It felt strange to find myself in my old bed, the bed I'd slept in since I was a little girl. A memory of dancing with Billy in the dark in France floated into my mind. What had happened to that Billy? My sadness redoubled when I thought about Arthur, so far away, by my own choice. Would I be just one more person who had let him down? His mother had held him at arm's length since he was too young even to remember. His father had died and left him to cope. Isabel had died. Now I was thousands of miles away when I'd promised to love and marry him: Till death do us part. How much loss could he bear?

The moonlight shone on remnants of my childhood, old dolls and toys. The fact my mother had not thrown them out amazed me: Resting on the shelves, they spoke of an attachment she had never put into words. I'd traveled far from the place where I grew up, farther than she knew. I didn't want to be in this bed. I wanted to be lying in Arthur's arms, enjoying the peaceful languor that follows lovemaking.

I'd been too afraid to tell Billy about Arthur, and I knew how much it would hurt my father if I told him I was leaving for Boston. For now, I decided to keep Arthur a secret. One thing I could still do was to protect the family I loved from the specter of my abandoning them.

CHAPTER 35

Soon after I reached home, I received my first letter from Arthur. The peace conference wasn't over yet, and he was still driving with Andrew each day to the palace at Versailles. He had no idea when he would be able to return to Boston, but he hoped it would be soon. The treaty might be signed as early as the end of June, even though the French, the British, and the Americans were still fighting over how severely Germany should be punished. Arthur thought the Allies were behaving foolishly and would one day pay a price for their greed and harshness. He sent his love, and hoped Billy was growing stronger at home with his beloved family, far from the pain and misery he'd lived with every day at the hospital.

I wasn't sure what to say in reply. The more time I spent with Billy, the less sure I was he would mend. I didn't want to make promises I couldn't keep. But if I lost Arthur as well as Billy, I would be alone to a degree I had never imagined. My letter made clear how much I loved him, but said nothing about Billy's state of mind because I couldn't bear to.

To pass the time, I threw myself into housework. I saw how burdensome it had become to my mother, and I needed distraction. We gave the house a thorough turning-out. Mamma was ashamed of the state into which the house had fallen. While I was gone, she said, she hadn't attended to her spring-cleaning. The house was, of course, as always, spotless.

On an afternoon when we'd finally scrubbed every floor, washed every wall and rehung the curtains we'd laundered and ironed, the two of us celebrated with a pot of tea and slices of homemade apple pie. Once we'd finished, I decided to sit on the back porch and put my feet up. Across the yard, I saw Alice waving from her kitchen window, and I waved back, motioning for her to join me.

When I'd left for Washington, Alice was just a girl, only sixteen. In the time I'd been away, she'd become a young woman. I knew as little of what those years at home had been like for her as she knew of the life I'd led while I was gone. We'd never been close: Billy and I had cut her out pretty much every chance we got. We'd wanted only each other, and we had no need for a sidekick who couldn't keep up. Now she was on her own in that sad house with Dora and Billy, and it hit me how much she must need someone to talk to. I'd been so preoccupied with my own worries I hadn't given a thought to hers. Her unhappiness spilled out.

"I'm so mad at Billy. He barely talks. He has no interest in anything about my life. If I try to ask about France, I'm lucky to get even a flippant answer. If I call him on that, he leaves the room. Mamma acts like nothing's the matter. Is it as bad as it feels? Am I exaggerating?"

"No. I've been trying—and failing—to find out what he's going through ever since I met him in Paris. I know he's ashamed when he lashes out. All we can do is show him we will love him no matter what."

"It's so hard when he returns kindness with indifference," Alice said.

"It's not indifference. He's shut up inside himself. The horrors I saw at his hospital in just a couple of days are burned into my memory. He saw that torment every day and night for years. I doubt I could live with his memories, and I feel so sorry he isn't proud of what he did. His patients needed him—they lit up when they saw him coming—and that kept him going. He's lost that communion. Instead, he dwells on the men he failed to save. That's not just a guess on my part. He told me so, on the boat home."

"How can I get close enough to show him I love him when all he does is push me away?" Alice said. "Ever since Papa died, I've counted on Billy. He was always the sunshine we needed in our house. When he walked into the room, Mamma smiled, and suddenly everything was all right. I thought once he got home, the gloom would lift. Instead, it's worse. I can't talk to her—she doesn't want to know. It's not like her to pretend."

"Give her time," I said. "She had no preparation for this. None of us did."

CHAPTER 36

July 1919

When Arthur did not reply to my letter, I grew worried. Finally, I wrote again to ask if he was all right—had something happened? He should have been on his way home. The treaty had been signed on June 28; the headlines of every newspaper had trumpeted the fact in bold type. I felt compelled to tell him that Billy seemed if anything more anguished, that my father saw this even more clearly than I did. Billy hardly spoke to me. He left the house early in the morning. We had no idea where he went, and he'd lost so much weight he looked gaunt.

I didn't tell Arthur I hadn't told my family I was engaged, which made me feel ashamed, but I was caught between allegiances, to my family and to Arthur, with no idea how to be loyal to both. With trepidation, I sent the letter off, trusting he would understand. He'd always shown such faith in me and so great a willingness to stand by me that I told myself I was foolish to doubt him. I came to recognize the postman's step and made sure I was at the door every afternoon to take the letters from his hand. I didn't want my mother to see a letter from Arthur and ask nosy questions. Day after day, I sorted through the envelopes, mostly bills and circulars, not so much as a postcard from Arthur.

While I waited, I escaped into daydreams, imagining I was with him. Little memories would pop into my head, like how he would take his father's gold watch from his vest pocket and check it during the day. At first I'd assumed he was the kind of person who had to be on time for everything, but eventually I realized he did it because, for a moment, it brought him a little closer to his father.

To comfort myself I would take Arthur's precious ring out of the green leather box I kept hidden in my bureau and put it on my finger to wear it in the privacy of my bedroom. Just seeing it cheered me. Some days I wore it around my neck on a gold chain, tucked inside my blouse where no one could see it, so I could feel it against my skin. I still remembered what it felt like when I touched Arthur's cheek, when he put his arms around me, when he stroked my breasts, when he traced my hipbones with his fingers—the kind of sense memories that are pleasure and pain. Those memories were bound to fade, no matter how hard I tried to hang onto them.

I reminded myself how many letters got lost during the war: letters mailed to France and letters mailed from France, so I decided to write yet again because I couldn't stand being out of touch with him. After a long debate with myself, I asked him whether he could imagine moving to California if I couldn't go to him. I knew how much Harvard meant to him, and I knew he took his responsibilities at home every bit as seriously as I did mine. I examined my conscience: Could I ask him to leave Rose and Lily? I wasn't willing—or able—to leave Billy and my parents. How could I ask him? But I wanted him to come to me so badly that I did.

The war had caused an ungodly degree of inflation, and my parents were having trouble paying their bills. With me in the house, they had more expenses. I quickly saw there was no money for graduate school; that dream would have to be shelved, for now.

David Page wrote to tell me he wouldn't be returning to Stanford because he'd accepted a job at the Treasury

Department in Washington. Max Weiler, the chemist, had never left. He was stuck there, trying to solve the problem of what to do with one hundred and fifty tons of poison gas the United States had manufactured for use in 1919. Many had assumed the war would go into a fifth year.

I had to get work somehow, and it wasn't going to be easy because returning veterans were competing for every job that opened up. The only thing I knew how to do was teach. The only person I could think of who might be able to help me was my old tutor and teacher, Miss Koenig.

When I telephoned, she invited me to come over right away. Walking across town to her house, I thought about how, without her intervention, my world might have remained so insular. I would not have gone to Stanford, which meant I would never have worked in Washington or met Arthur or gone to France. But, despite all those extraordinary opportunities, I was back home and might not even be able to get the job my mother had always felt I was destined for: teaching high-school math. A job that would feel like a defeat, yet one I would be lucky to get. The irony was galling.

It felt funny to sit in an armchair drinking coffee in Miss Koenig's neatly ordered parlor. The walls were lined with shelves full of well-loved books that had been read and reread. An afghan she was crocheting waited on the couch. Cinnamon was in the air. To be honest, I'd never pictured her doing much beyond writing equations with a pencil, or a stick of chalk. I hadn't imagined her sitting alone in the evenings, with a ball of yarn in one hand and a crochet hook in the other. Why had she never married? She was an attractive, warm, intelligent woman who lived what looked to me like a lonely life. That this might well be my fate sent a shiver down my spine.

I still thought of her as my teacher, which made me feel awkward, like a schoolgirl. She teased me. "It's wonderful to have you home, Evelyn dear. But you went to France, you risked your life, and you're still calling me Miss Koenig. Isn't it time you called me Elsie like everybody else?" Despite her encouragement, I was unable to utter those two syllables. For the rest of the visit I avoided the problem by calling her nothing at all.

I finally got around to asking whether she knew a school in need of a teacher. "Right now, the answer is no. But as soon as there is one, they'll pick you, because you'll be the most qualified candidate by a factor of about a hundred. With your training and experience, however, it would be a shame for you to end up teaching in a high school."

A few weeks later Elsie called to tell me she was going into the hospital for an operation. She'd seemed so healthy and vigorous when I saw her I could hardly believe what I was hearing. A substitute was needed immediately, and she'd told Jim Spencer, her principal, to hire me.

I wanted to say how worried I was about her, but realized she needed me to address this crisis in the same brisk, businesslike manner she had adopted. Of course, I said, I would take on her classes.

Grabbing my hat, I glanced in the mirror to make sure it wasn't askew, and dashed out of the house to go see Jim Spencer before my mother had a chance to ask who'd telephoned. As I walked to the school, it struck me how life can turn itself upside down in a minute. My future, that had felt so undefined, seemed suddenly to be coming into focus. Unfortunately, though, Billy's future, was not. He felt like a time bomb, ticking away. He'd decided not to go back to college that fall. Maybe next year, he said. I should have been relieved, because I doubted he could tolerate the pressure, but I wasn't. He who had always rushed toward life was now pulling away from it.

CHAPTER 37

I took Elsie's job. I had little choice. Waiting for the school year to start, I felt the walls closing in. At Stanford, I'd pictured myself staying on for graduate school and teaching there one day. My professors had hinted as much. When I was in Washington, I'd met Arthur, who had awakened so much in me. In France, I had seen many horrible things, but I had also learned America was just one country among many, and not necessarily the best of all countries. The world had stretched out before me, just waiting for me to explore it. My heart was still open, but I did not know where it was leading me. While Billy and my parents resided there as fully as Arthur did, what they offered me was a life that felt diminished.

I didn't know how I was going to fit myself back into the small box of home, and I resented having to. Ashamed of feeling like a victim, I told myself it was my choice to climb back into this box, and I'd damned well better stop fighting the need to do it. But was it entirely my choice? I was compelled by forces that had shaped my character long before I was conscious they were at work. My mother had raised me to believe my first duty was to take care of my family—I hadn't accepted that obligation of my own free will.

Once David Page had settled into his job at the Treasury Department, he wrote asking if I would be interested in a job as his deputy. I would have given anything to be back in Washington, in the thick of things, close to Arthur. Instead, I thanked him for his faith in me but told him family responsibilities made it impossible for me to leave California.

He wrote that he'd read my letter with great regret. There was no one he'd rather work with than me and no one so well suited to the job. If my circumstances ever changed, I should let him know. For someone as gifted as I was, he could always find work.

Even so, I thought I heard an undercurrent of disappointment in his words. Eventually, I realized he wasn't disappointed in me: I was disappointed in myself. Perhaps I was unwilling to forge my own place in the world. Why didn't I seize the chance to go to Washington, where I would be near to Arthur? Was I afraid of marrying? I didn't think I was, but I had fooled myself before. How well does anyone know herself, in the hidden corners of the mind where such decisions are made, below the level of awareness? What drove me even closer to despair was that I couldn't tell if my staying home was helping Billy at all.

He avoided all of us, not just me. One night he didn't come home for dinner, and Dora grew frantic. When he came in the door, she asked where he'd been, and he could see how badly he'd scared her. He apologized and said it wouldn't happen again. But he sometimes walked in his sleep, and he couldn't control his dreams. She'd hear him screaming in the night, words like "blood" or "clamp" or "cold, cold, cold." She was afraid he might hurt himself—and I felt she was not wrong to be afraid.

I sometimes ate dinner at their house, and afterward I would ask him to sit out with me in the garden. He would beg off, saying he was tired, leaving Dora, Alice, and me behind at the table, not knowing what to say to each other. But I persisted, and finally one evening he agreed to sit with me while he smoked a cigarette. He lit up immediately, but I said nothing about the cigarette, grateful he'd finally consented. We talked a little about the news, especially the evident rage of the Germans who felt that the terms the peace treaty imposed were unfair. We were ambivalent. We'd lived through the destruction the Germans had wreaked. But we knew not all Germans were evil, for the simple reason we never forgot our mothers had been born there. Then we lapsed into silence. He looked haggard. I was willing to sit there indefinitely, relieved there was a small break in the wall that had grown up between us. After that, we often sat out together in the evenings, not talking much but keeping each other company.

CHAPTER 38

Once the school year started, I had no time to feel sorry for myself. I threw myself boldly into the job, but, before long, I grew wary of my classroom, packed with callow teenagers slouching at their beat-up desks, scarred with initials carved by earlier generations of equally bored students. At the staff school at Langres, I'd thought I was an excellent teacher. What I hadn't appreciated was how motivated those students were—they were on their way to the front where what they learned in my classroom might keep them alive.

Here, most of my students wanted to be anywhere but in a math class. When they weren't staring out the window, they were passing notes or poking the person next to them or falling asleep. I stood in the front of the room, feeling exposed, breathing the dry, chalky air, watching dust motes swirl before my eyes, trying everything I could think of to interest my students—and failing miserably.

I made the classic beginner's mistake: Because I wanted them to like me, I was too friendly. By the time I realized this approach had backfired, it was too late to shift gears and assert my authority. They'd smelled my insecurity, and the one lesson they had mastered in school was how to take advantage of a teacher who showed the slightest vulnerability.

Equally humbling was the discovery that using words to explain the behavior of numbers was harder than I'd imagined.

Suddenly I had to articulate concepts I understood intuitively. I'd counted on Elsie to teach me how to teach these classes, but the operation she'd made light of exposed a virulent cancer. She never made it home from the hospital. I visited her whenever I could, telling her about my travails in the classroom, in a vain attempt to make her laugh. Each time I saw her, she seemed smaller than the time before.

She died shortly after Thanksgiving. The next morning I told my students that Miss Koenig had passed away, that she had been my teacher, and I hoped someday to be as good a teacher as she had been. For a few days they stopped their endless ragging.

As the semester ground forward, I still heard nothing from Arthur. I blamed myself for making a ridiculous demand that he consider moving to California. At the same time, I grew angry. If he loved me so much, why wasn't he writing to me? But perhaps I had hurt him too deeply when I insisted I had to take Billy home. Looking back, I saw that I'd been so overwhelmed by the danger to Billy that, incapable of thinking, I'd been operating on blind instinct.

November 1919

My one true refuge during these difficult months was sitting with my father on our front porch after dinner, drinking a last cup of coffee before I went upstairs to prepare the next day's lessons. I entertained him with an account of my first visit to Chaumont, though I didn't mention Arthur had been there.

"In the evening we were invited for cocktails and dinner with General Pershing. The minute he walked in the room all eyes turned to him. He was an absolute ruler—and a hero with a capital H because we needed a hero. I have nothing to complain about; he went to every length to make sure I was well taken care of."

"I understand exactly what happened to Pershing," Daddy said. "You've been holding me in the palm of your hand since the day you were born."

He asked why I'd left my teaching job at Langres, something I'd never explained in my letters. I admitted I hadn't wanted to worry anyone at home, and, besides, the censors would have inked out what I wrote. It had all started when I was seated next to one of Pershing's aides at dinner, a major who'd realized a young woman fluent in German might have greater success convincing prisoners to talk to her than male intelligence officers did.

"Does this mean you were right at the front?"

"Not all the time."

"Thank God I didn't know that."

"I'm home now, so you can stop worrying," I said, reaching over and squeezing his hand.

"What were those men like, the ones you talked to?"

"Some bristled with hostility, but most of them were just scared. By that stage of the war, they'd lost heart."

"What did they tell you?"

"Not much. I promised no one was going to hurt them. But they didn't believe me, and feared compromising the safety of friends left behind in the trenches. There was one exception, a brave officer who broke ranks, to my astonishment. Last year, even at the end of October, only weeks before the armistice, we were still not certain who would be the victor. Our troops were being slaughtered in the ravines of the Argonne Forest.

"When a German major was led into my tent, my expectations were low. The higher the rank the less likely a prisoner was to reveal anything of military value. Most officers would choose a firing squad rather than betray their code of honor.

"As he marched stiffly into the room, I studied him closely, trying to assess how much of his stiffness was pride, how much training, how much age. Probably in his thirties, he looked twenty years older. Bloody scabs were oozing on the left side of his face. His hopelessness was hidden behind his sober, controlled demeanor, but I could feel it filling the room.

"We began by playing out the usual script. He stated name and rank: 'Herr Major Werner von Hebenstreit,' but then added defiantly, in German of course: 'I cannot answer any questions. That is my duty. You must know that.'

"I assured him that, even if he refused to answer my questions, I had to ask them—that was *my* duty. He wore me out, parrying every thrust I threw his way, and I expect I wore him out, too—he'd looked exhausted when he walked into the room. I got hungry, but tried to ignore my hunger. One scrap of information might be useful. But when I felt my concentration flagging, I asked an orderly to bring us plates from the mess. They arrived heaped with beef stew, boiled potatoes, and the usual gray string beans.

"The major tried to hide how famished he was, but his bites began disappearing more and more quickly. I asked for more food. The major insisted he'd had enough but dispatched the second helping as quickly as the first.

"Once he mopped up the last of the gravy, he said, in English, 'Thank you. I appreciate the meal that for me you have provided.'

"Startled, I said, 'English?'

" 'Four years at the high school and then at university.'

"I decided that, instead of hammering him with more questions about tactics and positions, I would ask about his past.

" 'Tell me something about yourself, please. Surely your childhood isn't a military secret. What did you do for fun?'

" 'That is an easy question. And I agree, *nicht verboten*. I loved to fish. We had a chalet by a lake in the Alps where we went to stay in the summers.'

"He turned inward, lost in memories of boyhood, long before he'd hardened himself to lead men into battle. 'I knew all the secret little streams,' he said, gazing into the distance. 'I leave the house before sunrise and come back at dark. When older I was, I sleep under the stars to be in the stream before the sun rises, hoping to surprise fish before they wake up.'

"I told him about Billy and me going after trout up at Boulder Creek. 'My cousin taught me to fish because he wanted company. Weren't you lonely fishing all by yourself?'

" 'Rarely.'

" 'Your mother didn't worry about you? Alone in the woods?'

"As he considered the possibility, he was almost smiling, and he shook his head. 'No, I don't think so. Our child raising is to make the child strong, brave, to build the good warrior.'

"He reached up to scratch the side of his face, unwittingly scraping off the scabs. When he pulled his fingertips away, they were covered with fresh blood. I took a handkerchief from my pocket and pressed it to the side of his face. That gesture, the bare minimum of kindness, touched something in him. His face softened. I could almost hear the internal debate: the officer arguing with the man. Then he asked, 'May I have pen and paper?'

"He wasn't the first prisoner who wanted to write a letter home, so I handed him my pen and some sheets of paper from the stack on my desk. But instead of a letter, he quickly drew a bunch of rough sketches. While I had no idea where this was going, my instincts told me to be quiet. I sat still, not moving so much as a hair. When he was done, he gathered all the sheets into a neat pile and handed them to me. His face was anguished, but his voice remained steady. These were maps, he said, of the ridges behind the one where he'd been captured. They marked machine gun emplacements, and identified obstacles intended to make the guns hard to detect: trees, bushes, camouflage. He'd included notes about troop strengths and positions.

"Before he could change his mind, I got up out of my chair, intending to hand the papers to the guard outside and tell him to rush them to the adjutant. But I couldn't believe what had just happened. I turned and asked, 'What made you do it?'

" '*My men!*' he cried out. 'They are not men. They are boys, sent to the slaughter. I know what is going to happen: Some will be killed because I draw these maps. For that I never forgive myself. But I am weighing consequences. Who am I to make such a choice? I cannot say, but I do make the choice. I hand you these drawings—soon a few hundred will die, but perhaps later thousands will not. Am I a traitor? My mother would say, 'Yes! a betrayal of the Fatherland.' It is good she is dead so she need not know. She died during the battle of the Somme. Men were dying all around. The first ten days we lost fifty thousand men. She was dying, but I could not return home to say the goodbye. I could not leave my men.'

"I handed his maps to the guard and told him to hurry. My inclination was to walk over to the major, to put my hand on his shoulder, to thank him. But I refrained. I feared that even so small a gesture might make him break down, and he would be ashamed. All I could leave him were the remnants of his self-possession."

Of course, I don't believe in ghosts, but even now, decades later, I sometimes feel as if the spirit of Werner von Hebenstreit is standing beside me, sustaining me in the life I have chosen. He wanted to be with his mother, but he stayed with his men. If we had not been born in warring countries, we might have been friends. I may be doing something as commonplace as washing the dishes when I hear his voice asking, "What was it all for?" When I look at the wreckage of Billy's life and mine, I whisper, "Less than nothing."

CHAPTER 39

December 1919

It felt like a thousand years until that first semester ended, but eventually it did. When Christmas passed with no word from Arthur, I decided to telephone. Long-distance calls were expensive in those days and not easy to place, but I had to do something, so I resolved to call Rose's house and ask for Arthur. The maid who answered said shortly, "Mr. Arthur is not here." When I asked her to take a message, she said crisply, "Why would I do that?" and hung up. I was flummoxed, wondering why she felt comfortable being so rude. Was Arthur truly not home yet? Or had he left word not to take a message from me? If he didn't want to delay our marriage, where was he?

Swallowing my pride, I wrote to Lily and asked her for help. I had put off writing to her because I couldn't bear thinking about how hurt she would be that I had hurt the person she loved most in the world. I explained where I was and why I was not in Boston. I explained Arthur had not replied to any of my letters, and I didn't even know if he was still in France.

Her reply explained that, after the peace conference, Arthur had been assigned to the Army of Occupation in Germany but that she had no idea why I had not heard from him. She offered to send him a letter inquiring, and, of course, I wrote asking her to get in touch with him as soon as possible.

On one of the first pleasant days of the year—in February when the quince were already in full bloom—I walked up the stairs to our front door, dragging a briefcase filled with tests to grade. My father was waiting on the porch to have tea with me, as we did whenever the weather was good enough.

After listening to an account of my day at school, he drew a letter from his pocket and handed it to me. This was odd. Generally, my mail was left on the hall table. He had intuited this was no ordinary letter. Instantly, I recognized Arthur's handwriting and the thick black ink he used. Instead of ripping it open, I put the letter in my bag and made myself drink my tea as if nothing untoward had happened. As soon as I could, I carried the tray into the house and forced myself not to run up the stairs.

Taking the letter opener from a drawer in my desk, I carefully slit the precious envelope. I couldn't bear to rip it. I took the pages out, but then shut my eyes for a moment, afraid of what I might read.

It began with his news: After the treaty was signed, he'd been asked to stay even longer in Europe, to work for the Army of Occupation in the Rhineland. He'd said yes because he hadn't wanted to return to Boston alone, without me. Lily's letter had reached him just as he was preparing to leave for a trip to Palestine; in fact, he was writing from Rome as he made his way to the Holy Land. From there, he would start his journey home to Boston.

He was happy I'd written to Lily, and he had no idea why I thought he hadn't written to me. He'd written several times. But when he received no reply, he'd been sad and worried but eventually decided I didn't want to hear from him, so he'd stopped writing to me. Now the whole thing seemed utterly mysterious to him. While he was away, he'd made certain his mother was forwarding mail to him, in the hope that I would write.

It hit me like a thunderclap that Rose had chosen not to send my letters on to him. She hadn't just withheld my letters; she'd probably destroyed them. I was lucky he'd just been hurt and not angered by my apparent silence. She'd come close to achieving her goal of separating us and killing off the possibility of our marriage.

Needless to say, that night I wrote a passionate letter to Lily telling her what I believed had happened and asking her to help me find a way to correspond with Arthur. Since he was already en route to Palestine, I wasn't sure how to reach him. I enclosed a sealed letter for him in the hope she might be able to pass it along. She sent my letter to Poste Restante in Jerusalem, which was where Arthur had instructed her to write to him, and it wasn't all that long before I received a letter from Arthur himself.

> *Jerusalem*
> *Palestine*
> *April 25, 1920*
>
> *Dearest,*
> *What a relief it was to see your handwriting on the letter Lily sent me. I truly cannot believe my mother would stoop so low. When I return home, I'll have it out with her.*
>
> *In the meantime, I will simply rejoice in knowing you still love me and in my hope we will be married soon. Please write, please tell me how you are and send me all your news.*
>
> *Much of Jerusalem is like a dream, as if one might actually be walking down a street two thousand years ago, just as Jesus did. In my next letter I will tell you much more, but I want to get this note off to you as quickly as possible.*
>
> *Never doubt my love.*
>
> *Arthur*

I sent him an exuberant letter celebrating our reunion. While I acknowledged Rose had tried to drive a wedge between us, I decided not to exult in the fact she had failed. Hammering that nail too deep would be graceless and might well alienate

Arthur, which was the last thing I wanted to do. I knew this was an argument he had to have with his mother. I hoped he would win, but I also knew she was a wily adversary.

A few weeks later the longer letter he had promised arrived, and I scooped it up off the hall table as soon as I reached home.

May 19, 1920

My dearest Evelyn,

Jerusalem is a busy city, but one can still feel it has long been a sacred place. When I visited the Mount of Olives, the tour guide took us to an old mosque to see what is reputed to be Jesus's last footprint on Earth. The idea of a 'last footprint' pierced my heart.

I went to the Western Wall by myself, without a guide. I wanted to leave a message, but, as a Christian, I felt like an intruder because it's a part of the Hebraic heritage. However, when I got there, I somehow knew God doesn't make such fine distinctions, even if we do. So I wrote a message on a scrap of paper and wedged it between two ancient stones. I asked Him to forgive me for making so little effort to help you, my darling, after you left France with Billy.

When I read those words, I put the letter down, needing to think before I read the rest. If anyone needed to ask God's forgiveness, it was me. I was the one who had left abruptly, who had chosen Billy, even if I had not felt I had a choice. I sat up late, framing a reply.

560 North Sixth Street
San Jose, California
June 8, 1920

Dearest Arthur,

I cannot believe how blind I've been. When you didn't write back, I thought you couldn't forgive me for choosing to go home with Billy. You've told me before that I have trouble trusting you. I thought you were wrong, but, as so often, you were wiser and saw more deeply into my heart than I could myself. You have never been unworthy of my trust.

When I read the account of your visit to see the "last footprint," I cried too, for different reasons. Because of the war, and living with Billy as he is now, I have lost faith in a God so cruel He could allow so much suffering and death. I envy you the comfort your faith brings you, not because I begrudge it to you but because I wish I still had faith myself.

Oh, my darling, how could you possibly think you were the one who needed God's forgiveness? I hurt you. I'm the one who should be asking God's forgiveness. But God has left me, and so I can only ask you to forgive.

To answer your questions about my life here—

Daddy had a bad case of the flu, and he never fully recovered. I had to take a job at my high school, teaching the classes my beloved Miss Koenig used to teach because she was ill—I'm sure you'll remember her. She believed I could be a mathematician long before I did. When she died, I remained in her job.

Billy—I hate to write these words—seems unchanged to me, worse if anything. He hasn't been able to go back to college or take a job. To the outside world, he seems like a quiet, serious young man who's lost his way. To those who live with him, he remains somber and remote. I haven't given up hope he will heal in time, but there's no way to know what the future holds for him—and so for me—and for us—that is, for you and me. I wish I could write that it's just a matter of time before I come to Boston. That doesn't mean I love you any less than I did the last time I held you in my arms.

With all my love,
Evelyn

CHAPTER 40

September 1920

A rthur and I exchanged many letters that summer, filled with happiness because we were once more in close communication. He was home in Boston soon enough to start teaching that fall.

When the school year started for me, I approached my students in a different spirit. All during the first year I'd told Billy tales of the little scoundrels in my classes, because their antics were one of few surefire ways to make him laugh. He'd given me many pep talks about the need to clamp down.

"Remember me wiggling out of homework and sassing teachers? You can never let them get the upper hand—it's fatal."

Seeing the wisdom of his advice, I spent the first weeks of the fall semester terrorizing my new crop of students. I discovered that, like the prospect of execution in the morning, the threat of a D or an F wonderfully concentrated their minds.

After that first year, I never made the mistake of wanting my students to be my friends. No doubt I was a bane to many. One day as I walked down the hall, I heard a boy behind me murmuring to himself, "Ah, yes, the wicked witch." I turned and stared him down. He shrank visibly, and I hurried down the hall to my office so I could shut the door before I started laughing. I had so much responsibility at home I needed my classroom to run smoothly.

The anxiety about Billy was unrelenting. Psychology was still in its infancy. There was no treatment for his condition, at least not where we lived. The term "shell shock" had just been invented—Billy was one of thousands of veterans who suffered from it. But there was little understanding of whether anything could be done about it, and many men hid their problems because they felt ashamed.

Billy kept putting off going back to school. I pushed him to return, eventually riding him so hard that one night he lost his temper.

"Do you think I don't want to go to medical school? That I don't want to be able to do everything my father did?

"When there was a baby on the way, I would hand him instruments and towels and hot water, watching while he promised a young woman the pain would stop, holding her hand, wiping the sweat off her forehead, helping her push that baby out into the world. Don't you know how much I looked forward to the day when I would be catching that baby? But I'll never do that."

"Why not?" I asked. "*Tell me.* I need to know."

"My God, why not just push the knife in a little deeper and twist it again?"

"That's not what I'm trying to do. I believe in you!"

"You believe in a me who doesn't exist anymore."

"You're *still* you, even if the war shook you. You're *still* Billy."

"I may look like Billy. But think about this. Last night I picked up Sherlock Holmes, to amuse myself. When Dr. Watson was serving in Afghanistan, he was shot through the shoulder, so his orderly loaded him onto a packhorse and lugged him back to the British lines. In my mind I saw Watson bleeding, and visions began pouring into my head, men at my hospital, blood gushing from their shoulders, necks, heads, chests. I couldn't breathe."

I couldn't breathe either. Billy's flood of words hadn't stopped. It hadn't even crested yet.

"I've tried to read Dad's books, on my own—I took down *Gray's Anatomy* from the shelf in his study. Looking at the drawings made me feel nauseous. When I looked at a dissection of the pectoral muscles, even though I knew I was just looking at a drawing of a healthy man's chest, it was obscured by gouts of blood I thought I saw pouring from it. I've tried to imagine picking up a scalpel and cutting into the dry, leathery flesh of a cadaver. To expose every muscle, tendon, blood vessel, nerve, bone, and organ would take hundreds of controlled, delicate cuts, and I don't think I could make a single one. One cut and I'd be back standing with my boots stuck in blood-soaked mud, bent over a patient who'd stopped breathing, praying to revive him, incoming shells roaring in my ears."

Exhausted, he stood up and walked back into the house. I'd forced him to talk about his humiliation. But I'd also made him say aloud what he feared. Perhaps there would be value, even relief, in naming it. Or maybe I was kidding myself and causing him greater pain.

While I put away my dream of Billy going to medical school, I never stopped worrying about how much time he had to brood. Dora and I talked about what we should do. I believed it would be good to encourage him to look for a job, but she disagreed, vehemently. I had no idea, she said, how hard his nights remained. He'd wake up screaming: "Just shoot! Finish it!" and his shouts would reverberate through the house, scaring her and Alice. The one time she tried going into his room to calm him, her presence had made him even more agitated, so she didn't know what to do except stay in bed and wait for the raging to subside.

As his mother, she had studied him more carefully than anyone else ever would. At the same time, I could see how embarrassed he was by his idleness when he saw other men going to work. Not that all veterans were employed. When the troopships docked, the country welcomed them with open arms, then quickly forgot them. After the war, every veteran received a sixty-dollar check called "separation pay" as a thank-you for serving his country, and that was it. Families that broke up when a husband couldn't fit back into life at home, veterans who committed suicide, those so desperate because they couldn't find jobs that they turned to crime—all that was swept under the rug. There were no veterans' benefits and no GI Bill. Those didn't come until after the Second World War.

I couldn't let go of the idea that a job would ground Billy in everyday life and maybe, in time, help him leave the past behind. I mentioned Mr. Wise needed a hand at the hardware store. I reminded Billy the cannery was always looking for workers. He nodded and did nothing.

If we sat out in the backyard in the evening, his hands shook so hard when he lit a cigarette I had to turn away. The tremor had never left him. Most of the time, we stuck to safe subjects like politics and old friends.

When I brought up the war and he said nothing in reply, I learned to sit quietly, holding his hand if he let me, until he chose to speak again.

The toll on me was enormous. One night, at the end of my tether, I refused to back down.

"I still need to talk about the war, and I believe you do, too. What you went through was more horrible than anything I experienced. I was safe in an office most of the time, but I still have bad dreams and you do, too. Dora told me."

He jumped up. "I hate you all talking behind my back. I'm fed up with being treated like spun glass!"

"That's exactly what I am *not* doing right now. We need to get it out in the open and deal with it, together."

"I've told you over and over I don't want to talk about it," he shouted. "It just makes it worse. Why is that so hard to understand?" He stalked into the house, slamming the screen door. The door was fragile—usually he shut it gently so as not to knock it off its hinges. But he no longer cared. One hinge buckled, and the door proceeded to fall, almost in slow motion, snapping the other hinge, and landing on the ground.

CHAPTER 41

March 1921

Just after Easter, Arthur thrilled me by asking if he could visit me in June as soon as the school year ended. His request threw me into a quandary—there was nothing I wanted more than to see him, but my family still didn't know about him. I suggested we meet at a hotel in San Francisco where we could spend time together in the privacy it would afford. Arthur booked his ticket and reserved a hotel room for us at the St. Francis. I lied flat-out to my parents, telling them I had to attend a teachers' conference in the city and would stay on afterward with friends to take a short vacation. Lying to them felt awful, but I couldn't see an alternative. Billy wasn't doing well, and I wasn't ready to tell them about Arthur—I think I'd hidden him for too long, and I know I feared the consequences of giving up my secret.

I packed all my favorite clothes, though I boarded the train wearing a prim charcoal-gray gabardine suit and a white cotton blouse tied with a neat white bow at the throat, the very picture of staid professionalism. I met Arthur in the lobby of the St. Francis where he had already checked us in as Mr. and Mrs. Arthur Bayard, and he instructed a bellhop to take my baggage to our room.

He asked if I would like to go for a walk or have tea, and I chose tea. At first, we were hesitant. It was so long since we'd seen each other that our conversation was halting. I poured out the tea; I inquired about his train trip, and he talked about crossing the plains, the Rockies, the Sierras, all familiar to me. But given our history, it felt odd to be listening to a travelogue. I could tell Arthur was uncomfortable, too, because he was dwelling on details that in the past would not have interested him all that much. I began to worry we would not be able to bridge the gap of years. But then, as I started to bite into a cucumber sandwich, Arthur took the sandwich from me and laid it on my plate. He took my hands and held them in both of his. That was all it took. He looked at me, I nodded, he paid the check, and moments later we were in the elevator. Once we reached our room, my nervousness began to fall away. Soon he was unbuttoning my jacket and untying the bow on my blouse. We spent the rest of the day and night in bed, stopping only to order dinner from room service when we were famished. We never turned off the lights: We just wanted to see each other.

The next morning, we set out to explore the city, walking up Telegraph Hill for the view, down to Fisherman's Wharf where we fed breadcrumbs to an aggressive pack of seagulls and back to Chinatown, where we peered into the doorways of cave-like dens where men reclined on couches, obscured by clouds of opium smoke.

Another morning Arthur went out early and came back to surprise me with a swimming suit he'd bought—I hadn't thought to bring one—and we took the streetcar out to the end of the line so we could swim in the saltwater pools at Sutro's Baths. I'd never seen Arthur swim, and I clung to the edge of the pool, watching his strong, fit body glide through the water, doing lap after lap with the greatest ease. Eventually, he joined me, swimming the length of the pool underwater and surfacing only when he was close enough to grab me around the waist, which made me laugh. Having almost forgotten his playful side, rediscovering it added to my pleasure.

Eventually, utterly relaxed, we dried off and dressed so we could have dinner at the Cliff House; then we splurged on a taxi back to the hotel for another night of lovemaking and sleeping wrapped in each other's arms. I needed to touch him constantly to reassure myself he was actually right there, within reach, after such an unbearably long separation. He played with my hair as he used to do and brushed it for me.

At the end of our first week, Arthur asked if I would take him to Stanford so he could see the school he'd heard so much about when we first met in Washington. That seemed like a good idea to me, so we caught a train and headed down to Palo Alto. It was somewhat unnerving for me to return to the place where I had developed my deepest hunger for mathematical investigation, a hunger so long thwarted by subsequent events. Being there reminded me of how much I had given up.

Seeing I was off balance, Arthur encouraged me to imagine myself there again. I asked him if he could picture himself there, teaching and continuing his research. He hesitated, then said, "Do you know what I want? Let's get back on the train and make the trip to San Jose. Introduce me to your family. Don't you think it's time?"

This question was what I had feared from the moment I'd read his letter proposing this trip.

"I want to meet your remarkable father, and your dragon of a mother. I've wanted to meet them for years. Don't you think I could charm them, make them love me, make them laugh? You know I can be pretty persuasive when I make an effort."

"Maybe next time," I said.

"Next time? I thought you wanted me here, in California."

"I do. I do. It's just they don't know about you yet."

"Are you serious?"

My silence made the answer to his question painfully clear. Of course, they could love him. But I had never opened that door. I was pierced by how heartless I had been by not telling them.

"Evelyn, we can't go on like this forever. I love you. I want to marry you. What's stopping you? Is it Billy?"

I nodded.

"Okay, you've made your choice clear."

"No, I haven't," I said. "I just need more time. This is too soon. He's still scaring me."

Quietly, Arthur said, "We're back where we were on that dark road in the woods in Souilly. As far as I can tell, nothing has changed." We returned to San Francisco, and that evening Arthur boarded the night train for Chicago, starting the long journey home to Cambridge, to Harvard, to Rose and Lily.

I stayed in the city by myself for a few days, unable to go home and tell a lie about my need to return early. I was upset Arthur had left, though I certainly understood why he had. Walking up and down those steep hills, I relived again and again all that had happened—our joy in each other and its abrupt end.

CHAPTER 42

To my surprise, Arthur did not give up on me entirely. Looking back I see how great was his generosity, also his patience and his willingness to trust what I had said: I just needed more time. He continued to write, trying to convince me to take a larger view of my life and its possibilities. The idea of my teaching in a high school, he argued, doomed to repeat the same simple lessons year after year, depressed him. It struck him, he wrote, "like Paderewski playing 'Chopsticks.'" Certain I should be forging ahead with my study of mathematics, he argued it was criminal for me to waste my gifts.

The tenderness in Arthur's letters told me I hadn't destroyed everything we'd once had. He still wanted to find a way we could marry. Not long after the war his brother Nathaniel had married his childhood sweetheart, and they'd had two children in quick succession. The family moved to Washington when Nat was hired by the Department of Labor, and Arthur never missed a chance to visit his niece and nephew. His detailed accounts of their exploits made it painfully clear how much he longed for children of his own.

At one point he proposed a plan, suggesting I hire servants to do the heaps of chores that ate up my time. If my family was well cared for, he wrote, wouldn't I be able to come to Boston? Tactfully, he conveyed he would be more than happy to pay all wages. His kind offer overwhelmed me. While I couldn't give him an immediate answer, I wrote back that I was thinking of little else. He replied: "There's nothing 'kind' about my offer—it's pure self-interest!"

I desperately wanted to say yes. But no matter how I argued it to myself, I believed his solution wouldn't work. Servants, no matter how excellent, could never fill the gaping hole I would leave behind. The longer I was home the more entirely my family depended on me.

March 21, 1923

My dearest Arthur,

I am so sorry. I'm sure you know it isn't just housework that keeps me here. This will sound self-aggrandizing, but I think I'm the essential glue that holds my family together.

Dora still grieves for the loss of her sweet Billy, and she always will. She needs someone to listen to her sorrows and keep faith with her that he will come back to us.

Alice needs a sister because she's lost her brother.

My mother needs me, though she hates the idea. I'd be lying if I didn't admit she is often a trial to me. The razor edge of her tongue has little dulled with age. But, I have a feeling she's sick and hiding the fact. Maybe she's just worn out because she's pushed herself too hard for too long. If I left, I'd place a burden on her shoulders she's no longer strong enough to carry.

You know that, as a child, I thrived on my father's love. Now the tables have turned, and he needs me.

My mother's commitment to his physical care is stead-fast, but he needs more. He needs to hear he is loved, and I am the one who never hesitates to say, "I love you."

Even so, if Billy had regained his strength and I knew they could depend on him, I believe I would be writing a very different letter—in fact, I believe we would long since have been married. That we are not breaks my heart.

Billy has not found a way to live with the demons that flay his nerves. He cannot talk about his agonies of mind, but I sometimes think my standing by him helps him endure them. He sees almost no one but us. With no job, no school, no wife, no children, he has little to cling to but me. I can't bear the idea he will spend the rest of his life suffering as he does. But that may be what happens.

I love you now, and I will love you always. Forgive me if you can.

Your Evelyn

After I sent that letter, Arthur went strangely silent. Perhaps it wasn't strange at all. He had to have been hurt by my refusal. It tortured me I didn't hear from him.

Finally, he wrote: "I am sorry to hear how difficult your life is now. I wish there were something I could do to change that." The remaining pages were friendly, relaying family news about Lily and Nathaniel and Nathaniel's children. I had expected him to write about my decision and my explanation—I wanted to know what he felt. I was hurt and confused that he said almost nothing, but I'd lost the right to ask why. And forfeited the right to be hurt.

CHAPTER 43

November 1924

Long after the war San Jose remained a small, provincial farm town. Psychotherapy, if anyone had even heard of it, was something that involved effete Europeans. Freud was dismissed as a complete nut whose ideas were absurd and salacious. On the other hand, when I met Arthur, he had encouraged me to read Freud and Jung: He'd helped me to see psychoanalysis as a promising treatment for disturbed minds. Desperate to find help for Billy, I read everything I could lay my hands on about the doctors in England and France who were treating shell shock victims, with some success.

One morning when I was drinking coffee in the teachers' lounge, a colleague mentioned a psychiatrist had come to town and opened an office on First Street. The friend who had told her about him had laughed, dismissing him as a sideshow freak. But to her such easy contempt seemed small-minded; she was reserving judgment on Dr. Humboldt. I didn't hesitate. Later that day I phoned and made an appointment.

Sitting with ragged nerves in his waiting room, I wondered if I was kidding myself. Perhaps I was chasing a will-o'-the-wisp—there was no help for Billy. On the hour, a man wearing a tweed suit opened the office door, introduced himself, and reached out to shake my hand. Neither old nor young, he was probably in his early forties.

I rushed to say, "I've never met a psychiatrist before. I really don't know what I'm doing."

His composure and the little wrinkles that formed around his eyes when he smiled were reassuring. "That's all right. There's no right or wrong here," he said, as he guided me toward his office. Once we settled in our chairs, he said, "You can say anything you want. I'm not in the business of making judgments. I just listen. Tell me what brought you to my office today, and we'll figure out where to go from there."

I explained I hadn't come for myself; I wanted to find out if he could help my cousin. I told him how Billy had bolted for France. I described his devotion to his patients. I jumped to our terrible meeting in Paris and the terrible trip home. By now, words were flying out of my mouth, revealing my despair and my fear Billy would never return from that remote place he'd gone to hide. He had no idea I was here, I added, and would be thoroughly annoyed if he found out.

"I won't be telling him," Dr. Humboldt said. "It will be up to you to decide whether you tell him about me or anything we say today."

"His hands shake like the hands of an old man. He tried to save a young soldier, during Château-Thierry, but the boy died, horribly. He dwells on how he made that boy suffer for no reason. Sometimes I see a light come into his eyes, and I'll think, he's back. A moment later the light dies out, and he's gone again, back to his own secret war."

I felt close to hysteria. Dr. Humboldt stood up and walked over to a cabinet by the door. He poured a glass of water from a pitcher and handed it to me, giving me time to collect myself. Sitting down behind his brand-new oak desk, he waited until I drank the water and set the glass down.

"I'm so sorry," he said. "This must be so lonely for you." That was all. My hands began to shake, and I clenched them into fists to make the shaking stop.

"Is there any . . . any . . . hope?" I stammered.

"I won't say there's always hope—I wouldn't insult your intelligence. But I've treated men with severe shell shock, and sometimes I've seen a good deal of improvement. Maybe I could encourage Billy to let himself off the hook. Maybe not. I doubt his nightmares will ever go away completely, but they might become less frequent, or less frightening." He paused, looking at me intently. "Are you all right? Do you want me to go on?"

I nodded.

"Think how helpless Billy felt when he sat with a man who was dying. Helplessness is hard to bear, and he must have felt helpless every day. The nights were worse. Patients often die at night. I'm not sure why. I think fear grows in the dark. People die when they have nothing left. All Billy could do was sit with them and wait for their dissolution.

"The doctors and nurses in those hospitals saw horrifying things all the time, but they had to repress them to keep going. The feelings they doggedly pushed down still haunt them in their sleep. Bad dreams make for poor sleep. Your Billy is worn out. I'm guessing he's so tired he can barely drag himself out of bed."

I nodded.

"Rest a little," the doctor said. "You're exhausted, too."

I covered my face with my hands. Billy had a right to pain. I didn't. Then I laid my hands in my lap, one cradling the other. When I tried to take a breath, my chest hurt, as if a huge weight were pressing on it.

"In France," he said, "Billy never had time to grieve. Everyone was always afraid because of the unending presence of violence. They pretended they were fine, but ultimately too much pretending hurt them.

"Blindness, stammering, loss of speech, deafness, even paralysis struck thousands of men. Many cursed them and called them cowards. But they were *not* faking. They lost their faculties because they were struck down by terror. Their suffering was as profound as the pain suffered by men riddled with shrapnel. Many were ordered to return to the front, which was often a death sentence. They were too fragmented to stay alert. And Billy was patching them up so he could send them back into that hell."

It dawned on me he was speaking from experience. "You were there, weren't you? In France?"

"Yes, but not at Billy's hospital. I was closer to Reims."

When I thanked him for talking with me, he said, "There's no need to thank me. This is my job. Please come again, if you want to. Bring Billy."

That evening I broached the idea to Billy of a meeting with Dr. Humboldt, but he refused, flat-out. Things deteriorated to the point that I found myself yelling at him.

"Why won't you help yourself? Do you want to spend the rest of your life shut up in the house?" Before he could answer, I left the room, afraid of what else I might say.

Too wrought up to sleep, I paced back and forth. Finally I'd found someone who might be able to help Billy, and he wouldn't spend one hour talking to the man.

My patience had run out. Why should I make all the sacrifices? Why should I give up everything for someone who didn't give a damn about himself, or me? Why not marry Arthur? So many times I had imagined playing with our children, cuddling and kissing them in a way my mother never did. Did my staying home help Billy? Maybe I was just letting him lean on me. If I left, would he have to learn to stand on his own? Why stay here and wither away? If I stayed, I would never be the mathematician I could be.

Grabbing the delicate, hand-blown turquoise vase Billy had given me for my birthday, I threw it against the wall, and it fell to the floor, smashing into a hundred thin fragments of glass. In frustration, I hit the wall with my fist, and pain shot through my hand. I didn't want to hit the wall—I wanted to hit Billy.

Hot and dizzy, I grabbed for the window frame to steady myself. But as I reached for it, I lost my balance and fell, hitting my head on the corner of the desk. When I came to, I was so woozy I just stayed on the floor, resting my cheek on the cold boards, and fell into a sleep so heavy I felt as if I had been drugged.

Sometime in the night I must have woken enough to crawl into my bed. Early the next morning, when the sun rose and shone through my window, I was startled awake, in the middle of a bad dream. My fingers felt a fat lump under my hair on the side of my head where I'd hit the desk.

Looking at the pieces of the vase on the floor, I wished I could pick them up and glue them all back together. When I climbed out of bed, pain shot through my foot. Once I saw blood on the sheets and shards of glass stuck in my heel, I realized I must have stepped on the glass when I was getting into my bed.

Walking gingerly down the hall, I slipped into the bathroom and locked the door. As I tweezed out the pieces of glass, I bit my lip to keep quiet. The last thing I needed was to rouse my mother. Pouring alcohol into the cuts, I bit my lip harder, and bandaged the foot.

Back in my room, I sat down to think. There was nothing here for me anymore. Throwing on a dress and coat, I left the house while my parents still slept. My foot hurt, but I gritted my teeth and started walking a slow, painful mile to the depot.

As I crept along the mostly empty streets, it became obvious to me I could hardly jump on the first cross-country train. My half-formed plan to bolt for Boston was heedless. I could barely walk. What's more, if I didn't show up at school or tell my parents I was leaving, I would scare everyone, which seemed heartless. But I also felt I needed to leave right away, before I lost my nerve.

It was Wednesday. I promised myself I'd be on the train Saturday morning. For a moment I was so happy I felt almost giddy—until I thought of Billy's gift, the vase broken beyond repair.

Before I left for school that morning, I swept up the fragments of the vase and soaked the sheets in lye to remove the blood stains. At breakfast I lied to my mother about why I was limping, telling her I'd cut my foot when I accidentally knocked the vase off the shelf in the dark.

I had trouble teaching that day, lost as I was in the dream of my new life with Arthur. I pictured the two of us sitting out on the back porch of his house in Cambridge on a summer day. Maybe we'd be sipping iced tea spiked with fresh mint I'd grown in my garden.

I was eager to see Lily, too. I wouldn't let Rose pierce my hide, which, by now, was plenty thick. If my students saw how distracted I was, I didn't care. I'd taught those classes so many times I could probably have written the equations on the blackboard in my sleep.

CHAPTER 44

Wednesday night at dinner I laid the groundwork for my departure on Saturday. When I launched into my tale, a complete fabrication, I felt despicable, especially when I heard how easily the details tripped off my tongue. But if my mother caught a whiff of my true intentions, I knew she'd call me disloyal and drown me in guilt. It disturbed me that I seemed to have grown so gifted at deception.

I claimed an old friend, from my college days, had invited me to spend the weekend at her house in San Francisco. She and her husband were giving a dinner on Saturday, and afterward a friend would sing some German *lieder*. I was looking forward to seeing my old classmate. While I spun this tale, I nervously began to wonder why I was so sure Arthur would welcome me if I showed up unannounced in Boston.

As soon as we finished eating, I lied again, claiming I had more papers than usual to grade. I couldn't sit with them any longer, conscious of my duplicity. I kissed my father goodnight. I didn't kiss my mother, but she wouldn't think there was anything odd about that. She didn't like me touching her, and I rarely did.

Two nights later I packed the suitcase I'd smuggled down from the attic. After brushing my traveling suit, I hung it at the front of the closet so I could put my hand on it quickly when I got up to dress.

Creeping out of the house the next morning, my need to escape outweighed my need to protect my family. I hadn't forgotten the night my mother tried to scare me into staying home from college by raising the specter of her death. In that case, she'd asked, who would take of your father? I didn't know what she would try now, but knew she would stop at nothing.

I planned to send Arthur a telegram from San Francisco. All week long I'd stopped myself from wiring him. I felt superstitiously that, if I told him I was coming, I'd never make it out of the house.

As the train chugged through the golden hills north of the city, the elation I'd felt at the moment of boarding began to fade. How could I have left my father without telling him where I was going and why? He would have understood, and he'd never betrayed any of my secrets.

I thought about what Dr. Humboldt had said about Billy: He hadn't chosen to fall apart. He didn't choose to hide in the house. And he couldn't escape the dead who visited him in dreams.

If I had suffered such terrible losses, would he have abandoned me? No.

If he hadn't been so much like a brother, what might have happened? Did I love him more than I should? I'd never told him about Arthur. I never wanted him to know he had a rival. I couldn't risk his loving me less than completely.

If I had told him about Arthur, he would have insisted I marry him. He couldn't have borne standing in the way of my happiness. I'd considered telling him about Arthur dozens of times. But in one of my dreams, I'd found him in the cellar where he'd hanged himself. Yet here I was, on the train, leaving him without so much as a word.

I wanted to go to Boston more than I had ever wanted anything, but I panicked, afraid that leaving my family might hurt them too much. When I got off the train in San Francisco, I didn't go straight to the Western Union window as I'd planned. Instead, I sat on an oak bench in the waiting room.

There was too much history, too much love, too much guilt, not enough resolution. The train left without me.

I stayed on that bench a long time, considering. Another cross-country train would leave that night. Finally, I went up to the window and bought a ticket to take me home to San Jose. The trip, one hour, felt like ten years. By the time I climbed off the train I was no longer the buoyant young woman who'd fallen in love with Arthur and chased him to France—far from it.

When I walked through the door, my mother demanded to know why I was home. I claimed that, after I'd reached my friend's house, I'd started to feel ill, too ill to attend the party. My mother offered no sympathy. In my room I carefully hung up my beautifully tailored suit and wondered if I'd ever have a reason to wear it again. Pulling on a shabby old dress, I went out to weed our vegetable garden. I needed time alone, to accept I'd backed away from my dreams, perhaps for the last time.

That night Billy knocked on the back door and asked if I could talk. I told him I'd join him on the porch as soon as I finished cleaning up the kitchen.

"Nope," he said. "Toss me a dish towel." The two of us slipped into our old roles: me scrubbing and rinsing while he dried every plate to my mother's standard—till it shone.

Afterward, when we were sitting in the dark, he said, "I know you have faith in that doctor. You believe he could help me. I tried to convince myself to talk to him, for your sake—I would do almost anything you asked—I just can't. But you don't have to put up with me being rude and hurting your feelings."

I sat there, looking at my hands folded in my lap, turning his words over in my mind. I was far too upset to say much.

"Don't be grateful for my little apology. What would I do without you? Your faith is my bedrock. Hell, who else would have trusted me enough to ride in a plane with me when I barely knew how to fly? I don't know if I'll ever fly again. But I want you to know how hard I am trying to help myself. My efforts don't look like much. In fact, they look pitiful. But you must always be sure I love you."

"There's nothing pitiful about you," I said. "Don't say it. Really. Nothing."

CHAPTER 45

I never told Arthur about my aborted trip. Knowing I had chickened out would have hurt him and done no one any good. We continued to write, but the intervals between his letters grew longer. I tried to tell myself he was just too busy. Over time this rationalization crumbled in my hands. In his earliest letters, he'd written "when you come to Boston," then "if you come to Boston," but finally he stopped mentioning the possibility at all. I noticed those changes because I read his letters over and over. I came to see that he couldn't wait forever. He was too lonely.

We were both so careful during those years. Letters are such a controlled way of communicating. You sit quietly by yourself with as much time as you need to decide what you want to say. If you write something you're afraid you'll regret, all you have to do is crumple the sheet of paper and start over. If only one of us had broken through the thin ice on which we skated during those years. If only one of us had written: "I miss you so much I can't go on." At least, that's what I would have written.

Spring 1925

After I returned home, I was never able to tell anyone about Arthur. I needed to bury my grief. It would have been harder to endure if I'd had to face anyone feeling sorry for me. Pity would have been intolerable. Self-pity was bad enough.

Nonetheless, Billy's sister Alice guessed my secret, though I refused to admit she had. While she was studying to be a teacher at the Normal School, she fell in love with George Wise, an earnest young fellow who worked in his father's hardware store, a business he would inherit one day. On a sunny afternoon when I was grading papers on the back porch, Alice ran across the yard to tell me her news—she was engaged to George. We all knew George thought she'd hung the moon. I was delighted for her. Nonetheless, watching them fall in love had made me wistful, because it made me think about all that Alice was going to have that I suspected I never would.

When she asked me to be her maid of honor, I couldn't help smiling. Maid was certainly not the right word for me. Misunderstanding the smile on my face, Alice said, "I'm pleased the idea makes you happy. I sometimes feel bad because . . . " She broke off, not sure how to complete the sentence. I almost changed the subject to spare us both the awkwardness. But as we'd tried to help Billy, she'd become my friend and ally, so I decided not to put up that barrier. "Go ahead," I said. "Tell me why you feel bad. It's okay."

"Is there a reason you hold yourself apart? You're beautiful, and you can be very charming. You're so smart I expect it scares off a lot of men, but surely not all of them."

I didn't want to tell her about Arthur, but I didn't feel good about lying to her. She broke the silence. "Mother and Billy and I are worried. We don't want you to end up alone in that house with your mother treating you like an insolent child."

"Goodness, it's not that bad," I said.

"It is, and you know it."

"My mother can be impossible, but I've grown accustomed to her cantankerousness."

"I don't believe you."

"No, it's true. Your mother once pointed out to me how my mother never bothered Billy. It took me a long time to understand what she meant—he just let her angry words flare up and die away, as if he knew burning wood turns to harmless ash. Now, when my mother starts in, I generally ignore her, which gives me a certain pleasure. There's something perverse in that, but it works. If I don't react, the drama splutters away."

"I'm sorry you came home to such a hard life. I admire you for choosing it, but I regret what you may have lost."

I wanted so badly to talk about Arthur. The night before I'd dreamed I was lying on a beach, warmed by the sun, lazily watching a family in the distance, a father tossing a child in the air while the mother read under an umbrella. When I heard the father call to one of the other children, he spoke in a language I couldn't understand, but there was no mistaking the voice: It belonged to Arthur.

I hesitated to tell Alice about Arthur because she might tell Billy. If he found out, he would feel guilty about the price I'd paid to protect him. If he knew, my sacrifice would have been worthless. So I stonewalled Alice. If I'd taken one more step toward the truth, the delicate web I'd woven to protect Billy might have been blown to pieces.

Soon after Alice and George married, they had three boys, one after the other. I could see Alice was worn out by her children's wild energy and the remarkable amount of work involved in running a household, so I babysat whenever I could. I adored those little imps.

But there were moments when I'd be giving them a bath or fixing dinner and I'd think, Oh, if only they were mine. Once I must have looked so unhappy that little George asked, "Auntie Evelyn, what's wrong? Can I kiss it and make it better?" Against my will, a couple of tears brimmed over and slid down my cheeks. I forced myself to smile and say, "I'm fine, darling. I was just a little sad. Give me a hug and I'll be fine. That's the best medicine for being sad, isn't it?" He looked at me gravely and nodded.

CHAPTER 46

Fall 1925

During those years Lily and I exchanged a good many letters. One afternoon when I walked in the front door, I was pleased to see a letter on the hall table addressed in her hand. Upstairs in my room, I cheerfully tore open the envelope, but, instead of the usual newsy bits, what I read snapped the last thin thread of hope that had tied Arthur to me and ripped it out of my hands altogether.

Arthur and Abigail Cranford had married. They were honeymooning in England and Ireland. Abigail? Oh my God, the woman in the gray silk gown and the rope of pearls who had sat next to Arthur at dinner that long-ago Christmas. I'd envied their animated conversation and her ease in that house. At the time, Arthur had dismissed my jealousy out of hand.

Arthur, Lily explained, had tried to write to me, but could not bring himself to do it. The day before the wedding he'd confessed his failure and asked Lily to do what he could not. "I am grieving for you every minute I am writing this letter. I love Arthur very much, but I am angry at him for sticking me with the painful task of being his messenger. I see pain for him in his decision to marry Abigail because he loses you. I would not write that if I did not believe it. It makes me worry for that dear girl. Think how dreadful it will be if Arthur hurts you both. I can't bear to think of it. I must trust that he knows his own heart. We must all hope they find happiness together, though I cannot imagine the cost to you, my dear Evelyn."

I pressed my face into my pillow so I could howl without my mother hearing me, keeping it there till I almost couldn't breathe anymore. Then I collapsed onto my side and looked out the window at the leaves turning on the chestnut tree in our backyard. The branch was so close to my window I could see the delicate shades of yellow and gold. Somehow their beauty made it all worse. Whatever beauty I had would now be wasted.

When I didn't come down for dinner, my mother came upstairs to ask why. She shook me awake, thinking I'd just needed a nap, but when I awoke, she looked at my face for a long time. She knew something had happened, but we'd learned the best way to coexist was to maintain a certain distance. She told me to tidy my hair and come to the table before the meal was stone cold.

The pot roast stuck in my throat. I was so upset I couldn't chew properly, and, for the first time since I was a little girl, I was in danger of gagging at the table. After we washed the dishes, I asked Mamma to go across and tell Billy I wasn't feeling well, so I wouldn't be able to visit with him as we'd planned. I needed to turn in early. She looked at me oddly but went out the back door to deliver my message without asking any questions. I was grateful. For once, she kept quiet.

For a long time I was a sleepwalker. I clung to the routines of daily life: teaching my classes, having tea with my father in the afternoon, sitting with Billy in the evening. I avoided my mother.

My only confidante was Lily, and her letters my only solace. How could I have expected Arthur to wait forever? I could no longer be the romantic lass, always lovelorn, waiting for a miracle. I had failed Arthur and failed myself. I had refused to choose my happiness. I had refused to see that he needed—and deserved—his.

Lily did her best to make sense for me of what had happened. In her eyes, Arthur had chosen to marry Abigail because he couldn't bear any more loss. He'd nearly been destroyed by the death of Isabel. When he'd come home from Europe, she'd seen that he had been crushed again because I had gone to California.

Reading this, I lamented the gentle, patient tone of so many of the letters Arthur had written to me. He'd left me with the illusion he could wait indefinitely for me to get to Boston. But how stupid could I have been? He had waited seven years for me to make my decision. He probably would have been willing to put my needs before his, but I had been afraid to risk asking him.

It seemed to Lily the two losses had been more than Arthur could sustain. "Perhaps I should have tried to tell you this sooner, in time, but I didn't, and now I have to live with my regret for not having spoken up."

Once the school year ended, the fact of Arthur's marriage became more intolerable because I had little to distract me. I decided to take a crack at proving the four-color map theorem. The premise of the theorem is that, given any division of a plane into regions that physically touch each other, producing a figure called a *map*, no more than four colors are required to color the regions of the map so that no two adjacent regions have the same color. It sounds simple enough, but mathematicians had tried and failed for decades to produce a convincing proof.

Some mornings when I buried myself in that challenge, I could forget for a short while what had happened. My failure to make progress, however, was also discouraging, even though I knew it wasn't realistic for me to think that I might. The problem was damnably difficult. But the effort reminded me of the hours I'd spent in Page's office, so long ago, hearing about the histories of the great mathematicians, secretly hoping that one day people would tell my story and talk about my discoveries.

In the afternoons, I wandered aimlessly around town, venturing into neighborhoods I didn't know well, trying to forget who I was. I had to avoid our back porch where Alice or Dora might join me because I knew they would sense something was wrong.

Like Billy, I needed to keep to myself. I was learning what it was like to live with wracking loss, to feel you've been gut-shot and, in my case, to know the wound was self-inflicted. Those months helped me to understand Billy: I began to forgive him for shutting us out. I watched myself do the same and learned that sometimes one has no other choice.

CHAPTER 47

While I was grieving for Arthur, Billy's misery finally began to ease, slowly. Edmund Howard, the same generous man who had paid my college fees, had found him a job working for the head gardener at a house that the Bloms, a wealthy family, were building out by Alum Rock. It was a long streetcar ride there and back, and it didn't pay a lot, but I think it was the saving of Billy. His boss was a veteran, who understood what he had been through. As far as I know, the two of them never discussed the war. I believe the older man knew talking was not what Billy needed. His tact allowed the younger man his pride, and Billy found he had a gift for the work.

August 1929

One sultry afternoon while I was ironing a pile of shirts, I heard a knock at the back door and saw Billy standing there. Since he'd gone to work for the Bloms, he'd begun to smile for the first time in years. He led me over to his garage to show me he'd cleaned and oiled our old bicycles and replaced the tires, long since rotted.

"Whaddya say? Go for a ride?"

"Give me two minutes. I have to take off this apron and turn off the iron so I don't burn the house down."

Once I got up on my bike, I teetered a bit—I hadn't ridden since before the war—but soon I got my balance, and we rode all the way out to the orchards. The trees were heavy with fruit, and Billy filled my basket with apricots and plums. When we reached our favorite spot, we washed a couple of apricots in the creek and ate them.

"Remember how we used to come here when we were little and tear off our clothes so we could jump in the water and cool off?" Billy said as he dipped his hands into the creek and scooped up water to wash the juice off his face.

"How could I forget?"

"Maybe I just wanted to remind you."

"I do remember," I said. "How happy we were. And innocent."

I would have given a great deal to be that young again and free, able to feel the kind of easy pleasure I felt when Billy towed me around the creek in his arms. I slipped off my shoes, and, as I reached over to untie Billy's shoelaces, he asked, "What're you doing, Squirt?"

"Let's dip our toes in the water."

He rolled up the legs of his trousers, and we sat on the creek bank, the cool water swirling blissfully around our legs. He put his arm around me, and I snuggled in closer, leaning my head on his shoulder.

Billy tore off a handful of grass and began sending it downstream, a couple of blades at a time. "That's progress," he said. "When we first got home, I couldn't have harmed a blade of grass."

On that sunny afternoon as we dabbled our toes in the creek, neither of us knew Black Thursday was almost upon us and the stock market was going to collapse.

The years of the Great Depression were not as hard for us as they were for many others. Daddy and I kept our jobs. Public school budgets were slashed but I didn't get fired, and, while the Southern Pacific lost millions, trains still had to be dispatched.

We shared what we had. The first hoboes who knocked on our back door, begging for food, frightened my mother. But she opened the screen door, and she told them to wait while she packed them a bag of sandwiches.

During those years I learned to appreciate the bedrock of my mother's generosity. She could have put an extra dollar in the collection plate and let it go at that. But when she went to church and saw men dressed shabbily, wearing greasy hats, and women with faces marked by sharp anxiety—people from our congregation—she couldn't sit idle. She and Dora volunteered many days at the church's soup kitchen.

One afternoon when I got home from school, I found my mother at the kitchen table in tears; I hadn't seen her cry since Billy's dad died. I sat down and reached for her hand, which, uncharacteristically, she allowed me to hold. She told me that at lunchtime the family that owned the grocery store where we shopped had come through the soup line. Father, mother, and six children had all trooped by her, heads down, as they accepted soup and bread from her hands.

When my first student, a fourteen-year-old boy, told me he was dropping out of school to go to work in the cannery, I had to steel myself to bear it. He needed my strength, not my pity. Eventually, so many of them had to leave I became almost numb to their going. Almost.

Lily still wrote to me, and eventually she asked whether it was too hard for me to hear Arthur's news. It was hard, but I couldn't bear not to know. Her next letter told me Arthur and Abigail had had their first child, a girl they named Elizabeth. Knowing Abigail was a fruitful wife for her husband did hurt. I knew it was ridiculous to begrudge them their happiness, but there were moments when I did. Three years later, in the depths of the Depression, a boy arrived, and they named him Philip, after Arthur's father. When I'd stayed with Lily that

Christmas, she'd shown me scrapbooks filled with photo-graphs of Arthur as a small boy in short pants, his hair still in thick, dark curls. In my mind I pictured Philip as a little Arthur. Four years later, Evangeline, their last child, was born. I had never forgotten the desolation on Arthur's face when he talked about the deaths of Isabel and little Lily. I knew he would never forget his first baby, and, when I remembered her, I was able to let my resentment go and be glad he had been blessed with three more children to love.

CHAPTER 48

September 4, 1939

On the first day of the new school year, we were all sick at heart. Hitler had invaded Poland four days earlier, so war seemed inevitable. Billy and I had spent the weekend listening to the radio and reading the newspapers to each other. If ever we knew that our war had been fought for nothing, that was the moment. Hitler's steamroller was crushing everything in its path. In the beginning he'd seemed like a two-bit Napoleon. But once we'd seen the newsreels in which he exhorted stadiums full of cheering, screaming Germans, eager to follow him to victory, he'd come to seem like a visitor from hell.

As I turned the corner onto our street, I saw Daddy wasn't where he should have been, waiting for me on the front porch. It was Indian summer, the sky was blue and cloudless, the air warm. I had expected to see his face, as familiar to me as my own, the wispy white hair, the light blue eyes half-hidden by gold-rimmed spectacles, the wrinkled cheeks. That empty porch scared me. But I dismissed my fear as foolishness, anticipating trouble, a bad habit.

When I found Mamma in the kitchen, she said, "It's just a chill," but the strain on her face suggested otherwise. "I had Dr. Rieger come by to see him. He says it's nothing to worry about."

Daddy's chest had always been his weak point. The chill deepened into pneumonia. We nursed him around the clock, following Dr. Rieger's directions to the letter, and we brought him through it, but afterward Rieger told us the strain on his lungs had weakened his heart. From now on he would have to be very careful: He wouldn't survive a second bout of pneumonia. This meant taking it easy. He had to give up the job he loved, which was a sore trial for him.

When spring came, some afternoons I'd find him on the porch waiting for me, but more often he'd be resting in the parlor on the couch, with pillows behind his head and a blanket tucked up around him.

After Christmas the following year, he took sick again. His chest filled with fluid and refused to clear; his breathing grew labored. The doctor said there was little we could do beyond keeping him comfortable. Friends in the math department taught my classes so I could be with him; they knew how close we were. Mamma sat up with him at night because he fretted and couldn't settle to sleep unless she was nearby. They'd been together more than forty years.

One afternoon when I was sitting with Daddy while he slept, the painful thought came to me that I wouldn't be the one nursing Arthur when death came for him. As I considered that loss, the never-endingness of it weighed on me. It's hard to live with one sorrow for so long. I was staring out the window at the bare branches of our chestnut tree when I felt a pat on my arm.

"What's wrong, darling?"

"Nothing, Daddy. I'm fine. How're you?"

"Something's bothering you. No need to protect me."

I felt myself teetering unexpectedly on a precipice, longing to reveal the secret I'd kept all these years. Then I thought better of it and pulled myself back from the edge. What good would it do to tell him about my unhappiness now? Knowing I would have to bear the weight of my sadness alone would make it harder for him to leave.

"I'm not your mother," he added. "I won't insist you tell me. But I am fairly observant. When I woke up just now, you didn't know I was watching. I could see pain, deep down. I've seen it before. Sometimes it helps to talk about it. Isn't that what you've always told Billy?"

"I wish you could stay."

"I know, sweetheart. You probably want it more than I do. It's time, and I'm ready. But I will be sorry to leave you. And your mother. If I could will it, I'd be the last to go. Except that I couldn't bear the pain of losing either of you."

January 1941

One bitterly cold night, Mamma woke me and told me the end was near. As we sat on either side of his bed, I felt ice cold, despite my thick woollen robe. I held one of his hands, and Mamma held the other so he would know we were there with him. Waking for a moment just before dawn, he looked at us and said, "Goodbye. I'm going to miss you." Then he gave a weak little wave, his hand barely flapping at the wrist. A few more shallow breaths, and he was gone. I whispered, "Goodbye, Daddy."

Mamma and I kept sitting with him, holding onto him, not wanting to leave him alone. She was the first to rise. Coming around to my side of the bed, she kissed the top of my head and whispered that she would go tell Dora. I tried to insist I should go, but she said, "No, please stay with him. I have to tell her." I sat and studied the empty husk, abandoned by his spirit.

Mamma told the minister she didn't want any "sentimental nonsense," for which I was grateful. I hated the idea of crying in front of mourners as much as she did. At the grave, Billy stood next to me, his arm cradling my shoulder, steadying me. Afterward, when we invited everyone back for cake and coffee, the house was packed. In his long life, my father had made many friends.

Once the guests had gone, Dora stayed behind to help with the washing up. After she left, it was just Mamma and me, faced with the sobering prospect of the life to come. The two of us were going to be alone in the house that had always been enlivened by Daddy. He could be as mischievous as a little boy. But when she and I ripped into each other, he'd been the grown-up who knew how to gentle us down. He'd known how to take our caterwauling in stride. How were we going to manage without him?

For the next couple of weeks his wheelchair sat in his office, a constant reminder he was gone. I tried shutting the office door, but that seemed a denial of what had happened, so I opened it again. Finally, I asked Billy if he would get rid of the chair. The next time Mamma was out of the house, he came over and wheeled it across the lawn to his garage. I didn't ask what he did with it, and he never said.

CHAPTER 49

I never saw my mother shed tears for my father, and she certainly never saw mine. We grieved alone, except for a single night when she talked to me, really talked, not long after he died. The parlor was chilly, so we'd drawn close to the fire. She was busy with the eternal mending, and I was reading. When a log broke up and shot two bright red pieces of burning wood onto the hearth, I got up to sweep them back where they belonged. After I put another log on the dying fire, I asked: "What was Daddy like before the accident?" I hadn't asked her about what had happened to him since I was very young when she'd given me to understand she didn't want to talk about it. I had no idea how she would react.

"Funny, I was just thinking about the day I met him . . . I left Uncle Bern's ranch the first chance I had. I had bigger dreams, and life on a ranch is hard. With my small savings, I bought a train ticket to San Francisco, found a room in a boarding house and a job as a salesgirl in a haberdashery downtown, near Market Street.

"When your father strode into the store, I noticed him right away—so tall and handsome. I helped him choose some new shirts and linen. The next day, on his lunch hour, he came again and asked if I would take a walk with him that evening. He was so polite, such a gentleman, I decided it couldn't do any harm.

"He said he'd felt my spirit immediately, just beneath the deference I'd had to show him because he was a customer.

Soon we were meeting every night after work, exploring the city, the wharves, Chinatown, Telegraph Hill, even out onto the Avenues when the days were long and the sunsets late."

The story of all that walking was so much like the early days with Arthur that it went through me like a hot knife.

"In those days, your father wasn't one to hide his light under a bushel basket. He let me know his star was rising at the Southern Pacific Railroad.

"When he asked me to marry him, of course I said yes. We were so happy until the accident.

"He was riding a cable car to work when the brakes failed. A nurse called from the hospital. Both legs were broken and his pelvis crushed, but they thought he would make it. When I was finally allowed in to see him, he was dazed from the anesthesia, but he gave me a faint half-smile.

"He spent months in a body cast. The doctors held out hope he'd walk again once they took it off, but they were wrong. The pain was unbearable. Eventually, we had to accept he was never going to be able to walk more than a few steps, leaning heavily on a cane. He hated that wheelchair with a passion.

"That chair wrecked a lot of our dreams. We'd never go climbing in Yosemite. We'd never even climb Russian Hill again."

I was shocked to hear my mother tell me all this. For the first time, I saw how much she, too, had lost. Not just her parents. She'd lost her sturdy, ambitious husband and their dream of a life lived leaping from peak to peak—we had more in common than I had let myself see. More loss than either of us could bear, but we'd had no choice other than to bear it. How sad we had both felt it necessary to bear our losses alone. I sat quietly so as not to break her concentration. As she got deeper into her story, I wasn't sure she even knew I was there.

"The railroad couldn't hold his job indefinitely. What a blow to his pride. After the accident, he became gentler, but less confident. That took some getting used to.

"Because he'd been a valued employee, the Southern Pacific offered him a job as a dispatcher. We were lucky. We would've had a tough time getting by on my little salary."

I thought about how Daddy had dressed for work every day. No one would have been the wiser if he'd tapped out those wires in his office wearing pajamas. Nonetheless, every morning Mamma had helped him put on a carefully pressed shirt, trousers, and neatly polished shoes. She sewed those shirts herself, embroidering his initials above the right cuff on every one. That ritual of dressing beautifully had been a way to preserve his dignity.

"The only dispatch job available at the time was in San Jose," Mamma continued. "That was a big step down from San Francisco—we had to reconcile ourselves. We told ourselves a little farm town would be a good place to raise children. You know the SP strung a telegraph wire from the station to the house so your father could work at home—that was generous of them. They didn't have to do it. We wanted a houseful of children, but, as the years went by and nothing happened, it seemed we might not have any.

"Finally, I got pregnant, and you were born, a little scrap of a thing bawling for all you were worth." I looked at my mother and saw her smiling at the thought of that little scrap. Until that moment I'd never been entirely sure she'd ever felt any deep love for me, no matter my father's assurances.

That night, despite our long history of discord, I harbored a hope the two of us might finally become friends. Instead, she turned more inward. Maybe she'd opened up in a way she'd never really wanted to, and it had made her recoil. I tried to show her in little ways that I wanted to be closer, but she didn't seem to notice.

To keep her mind off her grief, she cleaned the house more fanatically than ever; she volunteered at the hospital; she spent time with Dora. I seemed the one least able to comfort her. I'd lost my father, but I had never really had my mother—not in the way I wanted her. My father's death had made me sad. Death is in the natural order of things. A mother who can't embrace her daughter is not.

CHAPTER 50

O ne Sunday after the funeral Mamma went over to Dora's house to help her finish hemming a batch of new sheets, so I was alone when Edmund Howard came to pay a sympathy call. When I opened the door to his knock, I was relieved to see his face. I hadn't wanted to spend the next half-hour exchanging platitudes with someone I didn't even want to talk to.

"I'm really sorry about your dad," he said, giving me a hug. I invited him into the parlor, and we talked about many reasons we were going to miss him.

We talked, too, about the war, about how Hitler was moving into Russia and down through the Balkans on his way to devouring Yugoslavia. The Luftwaffe had been bombing England for more than a year; countless buildings in London had been leveled and thousands found dead in the rubble. For those of us who had lived through the first war, seeing newer, more powerful weapons reap greater destruction in this second war was beyond comprehension.

Unexpectedly, Edmund steered the conversation in another direction. "Evelyn, I hope I'm not presuming— it may be none of my business—but I've wanted to ask you something for a long time."

"Certainly."

"You came back to take care of them, didn't you? Billy and your dad."

In my lonely state, I wanted to cry out, "Yes, yes, I did," but instead I sat still, trying to make my face a mask. I'd schooled myself to deny that truth to everyone. All lives are shaped by time and place. I'd been born into a world where duty was a sacred word. Later, the world changed, and duty became a term of derision, but I never cottoned to that new world. Wanting no pity, I said as calmly as I could, "What makes you think that?"

"I've watched your dedication to this family, but you deserve something for yourself. You're a lovely woman. You must have had opportunities. If I'd been thirty years younger, I'd have been tempted."

I'm pretty sure I blushed, and I know I beat a retreat, snatching at a platitude: "Every woman should dedicate herself to her family."

"Yes, but at the expense of her own happiness? You came home, put your head down, and went to work. You let your mother maintain the illusion she was running things while you took care of them all. The only reason Billy held himself together was because you were always at his side. I think you were both casualties of the war."

"There's something to what you say," I said, "but, just think, if I hadn't stayed home, my mother would have grown more bitter. That would've poisoned my father's life. Dora would have broken under the strain of caring for Billy. Even with my help, she's had a hard time.

"No one at home had seen what I saw. At Billy's hospital men arrived soaked in blood, the life running out of them. He gave until he had nothing left.

"Besides, I owe him so much. He might as well be my brother. So how, when he needed me, could I turn my back? He would've done the same for me. You see that, don't you?"

"But more is asked of women," Edmund said. "If Billy had come home and gone to medical school, married, and had children, nobody would have thought a thing about it. Women are expected to put their parents first without a murmur about the sacrifice that entails."

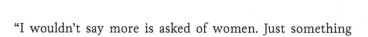

"I wouldn't say more is asked of women. Just something different."

"My dear Evelyn, I respect your conviction, but . . . "

"Don't," I said. "I don't. That would make my life even harder than it is. There's more happiness in caring for them than you know."

"I'm glad if that's true," he said.

After he left, I sat and thought about why I'd lied to him, insisting I was accepting of my lot. It was a necessary lie, but one that left me walled up with my memories.

Later, in bed, I gave way to tears. I was sad I'd lost my father; I was angry about losing Arthur. I had no idea if my sacrifice had helped Billy. Usually, I suppressed the rage that poured out that dark night, because I knew it could turn me into a harridan. But sometimes, it broke through and washed over me in huge, cresting waves. Afterward, I felt as if I'd been rolled by those waves and tossed up on the beach, my mouth full of sand.

CHAPTER 51

On the afternoon of December 7, 1941, Billy came over so we could listen to our favorite serial, a silly family saga we looked forward to every Sunday because it never failed to make us laugh. When he turned on the radio, we thought the station was broadcasting a different show, a drama about a war raging in the Pacific. All too quickly we realized that what we were hearing wasn't fiction: The Japanese had decimated the U.S. Navy at Pearl Harbor, and the battle wasn't over. For the rest of the day we sat by the radio, waiting for more bulletins, ill with dread. Mamma went over to get Dora, and the four of us had dinner together. There was little conversation—we were all straining to hear the radio.

After we finished eating Billy lit a fire in the fireplace. Leaving the dirty dishes on the table, a first in our household, we stayed up listening far into the night. None of us were going to sleep much anyway.

The next day President Roosevelt asked Congress to declare war on Japan. My memory of the succeeding days is somewhat confused. We learned that American ships sailing in the Pacific had been torpedoed by the Japanese in addition to the attack on Pearl Harbor. No one knew if invasion was imminent. There was as yet no system to deliver air raid warnings, so one night police drove through neighborhoods telling people Japanese planes had been sighted from the coast, which created panic. Fortunately, there was no attack, and we were never sure if there truly had been planes just offshore. The authorities were tight-lipped.

Every cuckoo came out of the woodwork. One sighting of submarines turned out to be whales surfacing for air.

A couple of weeks later, I was teaching a geometry class when the school secretary came in to tell me I was needed in the teachers' lounge. Jim Spencer, the principal, told the assembled teachers he'd had a phone call from the mayor's office. A Japanese aircraft carrier had been detected off the coast. Oakland was closing its schools. After a good deal of discussion, we decided to keep the children with us at school rather than send them home, possibly to empty houses where they'd be alone and scared.

After the last bell had rung and the halls had emptied, I sat down in my classroom, relieved we'd made it through the day. I knew how helpless America would be, since we'd made no preparations for this war, just as we had failed to last time. Once again, while war raged in Europe, we'd assumed we were protected by oceans until Pearl Harbor incinerated that illusion.

My students were the closest thing I had to children. I'd long since stopped holding them at such a distance. I'd grown fond of many of them, and wanted to keep them all safe, even the ones who were lazy as pigs. None of them deserved what was coming. There would be another draft. Many boys in the senior class were already eighteen; they would be the first to go. I rarely prayed anymore—after the war I'd come to believe only actions had meaning. I'd rejected the idea of a mythological realm ruled by a God who wanted men to suffer as they had in France. Nonetheless, that afternoon I begged God to stop this war, to spare my students who would be sent to die. But my prayer was too late. We were already at war, and there would be no turning back.

I worried Arthur might try to enlist, despite his age—it was the sort of thing he would feel compelled to do. I had no idea what to expect from Billy. His ghosts would be pursuing him in ways I didn't want to think about. Whatever happened, millions were going to die again.

After Christmas vacation, Jim Spencer called me in to tell me he'd enlisted. I wasn't surprised, but what he said next caught me unaware. He was about to leave for MacDill Field, an Army Air Corps base in Florida, and wanted me to take over in his absence. We had an assistant principal, Timothy Hunter, the logical choice for the job.

When I suggested Hunter, Jim burst out laughing. "You're wrong there, Evelyn. The teachers respect you. Hunter's too young, too inexperienced, and, let's be honest here, he'll never be up to the job. Do not ever tell anyone I said that, but you know it's true. You'll be excellent. Your first job is going to be hard: finding someone to take your classes who's half as good a teacher as you are."

I left his office hoping it would all go as smoothly as he believed. He was right about one thing—I'd never thought much of Hunter. Strutting around the halls like a banty rooster, he looked pathetic to everyone but himself.

Billy scared me by volunteering. Mercifully, the draft board rejected his application. But he had another trick up his sleeve. A couple of weeks later, he announced at dinner that he'd spent the day at Moffett Field. After he'd demonstrated his knowledge of planes and engines, the Army had hired him on the spot as a mechanic.

Being part of the war effort was good for Billy. Having to sit on the sidelines would have eaten away at him. Most of the planes he repaired were used for reconnaissance, to protect the coast of California. I was grateful he hadn't been sent to the Philippines to repair bombers that rained death on Japan.

November 14, 1942

The first student from our school to be killed in action was Paul MacKinnon. After Paul's father called to tell me his son had died at Guadalcanal, I sat in my office hoping no one would come in to talk to me. The moment I had dreaded had finally arrived. I wanted the students to know that, no matter what happened, I would be calm and reliable, though I felt anything but calm. The first thing I did was to arrange for a teacher to find Paul's younger brother, Peter, and take him home.

I called an assembly in the middle of the day, which was unheard of; unease rippled through the auditorium while everyone took their seats. I wasn't sure how long I'd be able to talk before my voice broke, so I'd written a short speech to tell them Paul had been killed when a Japanese plane crashed onto the deck of his ship at Guadalcanal. I registered the fear on those very young faces and wished there was anything I could say to make the news less frightening, but there wasn't.

Back in my office I sank into my chair, utterly drained. Many students had brothers or fathers overseas, and they all knew a Western Union man might knock on their door any day to deliver the same devastating telegram that had just arrived at the MacKinnon house.

Though the prospect filled me with anxiety, I knew I had to call on the MacKinnons after school. As I approached their house, I had no idea what to say to Maggie, Paul's mother. When the door opened and she saw me standing there, her face crumpled.

While she put the kettle on for tea, I surveyed the dining room table covered with cakes and pies brought by neighbors eager to show how sorry they were. As far as I could see, none of these offerings had been touched.

When I apologized to Maggie for putting her to the trouble of making tea, she said it was a relief to have something to do. She'd been longing to talk about Paul. For her, the worst was sitting alone, imagining his death.

She had only one child left. In three months, Peter would be eighteen and eligible for the draft. She'd heard the army had a policy of not taking the last son and hoped it was true. Her hand trembled every time she tried to lift her teacup, and her tea kept spilling. Finally, she put the cup down in its saucer and left it on the coffee table. Peter had shut himself up in his room, she said. He would have to go back to school, but she didn't have the heart to make him. Would I talk to him? I had no right to intrude on her child's grief, but I couldn't refuse her.

When I knocked on Peter's bedroom door, there was no answer. I knocked a little harder and thought I heard a faint "come in." He was sitting in a high-backed wooden chair, turned away from me, looking out the window. A rusty old swing set sat in the backyard, the ghosts of two little boys pumping hard and flying through the air.

"Peter, it's Miss Havilland. May I come in?"

He was silent, which I took for a grudging consent.

Finally, I ventured, "I'm very sorry about your brother. I know there's nothing I can say that would make you feel better."

He said nothing.

"I know it won't be easy to come back to school."

Still he said nothing.

"What do you think Paul would do, if he were you?"

"He would go back. He always knew what to do. And he could always do it. I'm not like him."

"I doubt it was always as easy for him as it looked. Some people are just better at hiding their fears. He wouldn't want you to give up, would he?"

"No."

I felt cruel, using his dead brother to pressure him, but I didn't know how else to fulfill his mother's request.

In 1944 Jim Spencer's plane was shot down on a bombing raid over Tokyo, and I had to break that news to the school. Did any of us ever entirely get over the loss of Jim? I didn't. Becoming principal of the high school because of his death was the last thing I wanted.

CHAPTER 52

Our family was lucky. Alice's George had enlisted in the navy right after Pearl Harbor, but he came home in one piece. Alice drove up to San Francisco to meet his ship when it docked, and I stayed home to watch the children. They spent the afternoon in the living room, peeking out the front window every few minutes. As soon as they saw the family car drive up the street, they raced out of the house with me trailing behind them. When George got out of the car, the littlest one climbed his leg as if it were a tree and clung to him like a monkey.

With George home, Alice had a bit of freedom for the first time in a long time, so the two of us celebrated by having breakfast at a coffee shop on the weekend whenever we had the chance. One Saturday morning when she arrived at my house, my mother and I were arguing, and she could hear our raised voices from the front porch.

I finally disengaged myself and grabbed my hat and purse. As soon as we reached the sidewalk, Alice asked what we were fighting about.

"Nothing that amounted to a hill of beans."

"Why do you put up with it? I hate the ugly way she lights into you."

"She can't force me to do anything anymore," I said. "She's brittle. Think of her as a lump of burning coal that needs to remain whole. There are fault lines running all through the red-hot rock she is now. If she ever gave in, she'd crack and fly apart into a million cinders."

"She must dislike herself so much," Alice said.

"I've spent a lot of time pondering my mother's behavior. She's certain her severity is justified. When I was young, she thought her job was to prepare me for a world she'd found utterly unforgiving. She didn't choose to be mean. But when I was little, it felt like she did, so I could not like her. Imagine how terrible it would be to know you had only one child and that child hated you. She had to know. I didn't hide it.

"My father protected me. He showered love on me. He wanted to shower it on her, too. He would have done anything to make her happy—*anything*—but she rarely let him. So he turned to me, the little girl who adored him. She had to feel shut out, and she punished me for it."

"There must have been times the three of you were happy together."

"I think the closest we ever came was when she gave in and let me go to college. I tried to let her know how grateful I was, to find a way into her heart. But there wasn't time. Life took me far away from her. And I was always trying so hard to get away. Escaping was essential for me and hurtful to her. She thought I was leaving because I hated her, not because I had to save myself."

"I couldn't have stood the strain," Alice said. "It sounds exhausting."

"It was. But none of us had any choice. We were who we were. My mother was scarred irrevocably when her parents died."

"I can't forgive her," Alice said. "I've seen her hurt you too often."

"Billy helped me to understand all this."

"I'm not surprised," his sister said. "He understands people so well."

"That's not what I meant. Like my mother, he changed profoundly, after the war, because the damage was so deep. I spent years waiting for him to get better. There were times

I was furious he wouldn't help himself. But over the years I realized he did not choose to become who he is any more than she did."

"How strange," Alice said. "I would have said there aren't two more different people in the world. But I certainly had a hard time forgiving him, and he didn't cause half the pain your mother did—and does."

Patting her hand, I said, "I love you for defending me. But I had to forgive my mother, or I would have become unbearable to myself and everyone else. I was bitter, but then I saw that my bitterness was flowing up and out and over everything. That doesn't mean I never lose patience with her. I'm not a saint, you know."

"Really," she said and winked.

CHAPTER 53

1947

L ily wrote to tell me Rose had died, after a series of strokes. Arthur was taking it hard.

I didn't know what to feel. I'd assumed Rose would live forever. She was too mean to die. But I still felt for Arthur because she was his mother, and he had loved her, as impossible as that might be for me to comprehend. For anyone else who had lost a parent, I would have picked up pen and paper immediately to write a letter of sympathy. But in this case I vacillated. On the one hand, not writing to Arthur seemed graceless. On the other, I worried I was seizing on the convention as an excuse to get in touch with him. In the end, I decided I was being ridiculous. There was no way to construe a letter of condolence as anything but a wish to acknowledge loss.

Still, after mailing the letter, I worried I might have been thoughtless, stirring up painful memories when he was already burdened by sadness. Then I decided I was flattering myself. By now I had to be little more than a memory for Arthur. He had Abigail and the children to comfort him.

He replied, thanking me for my kind letter and hoping I was well and happy. I thought that would be the last time I would ever hear from him.

Rose's death caused me to take stock of myself. The rest of my life stretching out ahead of me, like a desert. Until I retired, I would be principal of the high school. I was proud of my work: The school was stronger since I'd taken it in hand. I'd hired and trained good teachers, and more students were headed for college. But when I looked in the mirror, I saw a woman whose iron will had taken a toll. I was gaunt. My high forehead and chiseled cheekbones reminded me of Nina Chapman. When I met her in Washington, she'd been in her fifties, just as I was now, and the similarity of our lives was distressing. If I'd married Arthur, I would have been spared the sense of scarcity that plagued both Nina and me.

One good thing was that Billy seemed steadier to me, no longer thin as paper, and quicker to laugh. But he had never entirely lost that haunted look.

My mother kept up her relentless routine. Her posture remained ramrod straight, though back pain plagued her. When she bent down to wring out the mop, I could see how she pressed a hand on her back to ease the strain. I volunteered to wash the floors, but she wouldn't hear of it.

Dora was slowing down, too. Her house was no longer spick-and-span, and she didn't seem to care. Like my mother, she'd been a devoted housekeeper. Now dishes piled up in the sink. Billy mentioned he'd come across a few past due notices in the mail, so he'd quietly started paying the bills for her. I dropped by on Saturday to help with chores like washing windows.

Our households became more closely intertwined, and I saw how much I was needed in both of them. Yet when I thought about how little my life was ever likely to change, my spirits sometimes sank. But no one else in the family was having an easy time. The last thing they needed was to feel I begrudged them my help.

November 1950

I never had much patience for the petty squabbles that sometimes dominated faculty meetings. If need be, I'd cut the meeting short, but one day I'd grown so fed up with their whining about problems as trivial as rowdiness at morning assembly I'd just stared out the window and let them ramble on. I wanted to say: "Why didn't you just tell them to shut up?" but I didn't. Never one to suffer fools gladly, I wondered if I didn't care as much as I used to.

As I brooded about my indifference, Arthur was far from my mind until I saw an envelope on the hall table addressed in his distinctive hand. I instantly felt that only truly bad news would have brought him to write after such a long time. Had Lily died? I steeled myself to open the envelope. Instead, I was delighted to read that Arthur was attending a linguistics symposium at Stanford in January and wondered if I would be willing to see him. Willing? My rib cage rocked with silent laughter.

I was thrilled until I tried to picture the meeting. What would he look like? Would I recognize him? Would he recognize me? Would he be repulsed by my gray hair and the age spots on the back of my hands? In my mind he hadn't aged at all, but of course he had. I couldn't imagine an Arthur who looked old. I treasured my memories of the handsome, vital young man I'd loved to distraction. Would it make me sad to see him frail or round-shouldered?

Of course, there was no way I was passing up a chance to see him. I had to force myself not to write back the same night. I didn't want to seem like an impetuous girl, though that's pretty much what I felt like.

Over dinner Mamma asked, "Who is Mr. Bayard, from Cambridge?"

I bridled at her nosiness—my father would never have asked such an intrusive question—but stifled the impulse to tell her it was none of her business. I knew it would be wise not to get into an argument. As casually as I could, I said, "An old friend who lives in Boston. A professor I worked with during the war. He's making a trip to the West Coast, and wrote to ask if we could get together."

"He must have been a very good friend," she said archly. "Strange you haven't heard from him all this time. Or perhaps you have?"

CHAPTER 54

For the next two months I thought of little else but seeing Arthur. I fretted about what to wear, a question that hadn't crossed my mind in a long time. Apparently, my vanity wasn't dead. After careful consideration, I chose a dark navy challis suit my mother had made, exquisitely tailored with a fitted jacket and a slightly full skirt, very Dior. It made me feel beautiful, despite the ravages of age that were plain on my face.

Finally, the day arrived. Though I wasn't meeting Arthur until noon, I took a train that got to Palo Alto at ten. I hadn't seen the campus in a long time and wanted to walk around and remember. It all came flooding back—my anxiety about Page's class, Billy's encouragement, his departure, then my burst of confidence once Page invited me into his inner circle and—so hard to revisit—starting my own work in number theory, just before I had to leave for Washington.

I couldn't help but remember the night Billy told me he was going to France when I'd run off, leaving him alone with his momentous and possibly fatal decision, indulging myself in a fury that was just a cover for fear. I'd been unable to see beyond what his going would mean to me. While I'd been shocked then, in retrospect, his decision fit with everything else about him: his sense of honor, his daring, the need to prove he was as brave as his father.

That wasn't the only black memory I had to recall. I had brought Arthur here to see my beloved school. Then I had refused, right here, to introduce him to my family, which may have been the worst choice I ever made in my life.

At noon I met Arthur. I knew him instantly. The same sweet smile and dark blue eyes, more prominent now because of the contrast with his silver hair. Surrounded by all the baggy corduroy jackets on the quad, his hand-tailored cashmere overcoat made him stand out: a swan among pigeons.

His face lit up when he saw me.

"My dear Evelyn, thank you so much for meeting me. I hesitated to write, but I wanted so much to see you. I hope you don't mind."

"Mind?" I had a hard time not laughing. "How could you think such a thing?"

"Well, that's good to hear. I wouldn't have dared to ask if you hadn't written when Mother died. I knew then that you still thought about me. I decided I could let myself see you, just this once. But I didn't want to cause you pain."

I didn't trust myself to speak. This conversation was quickly taking us into waters that might prove treacherous for me to navigate. Taking my arm, he asked if I was hungry for lunch and led the way to a French restaurant in town, recommended by a friend at the conference. The food was good, but we agreed it didn't compare to the delicious meals we'd eaten in France.

He told me about his time in Washington during the recent war, where he'd headed up a division of the cryptography service. The War Department had learned a hard lesson from the lack of expertise that had hamstrung their efforts in the first war, so they'd formed the Office of Strategic Services, an intelligence agency with a broad mandate. The OSS had asked him to take charge of researching analytic methods used in other countries, which led to a stint at a country house in England, a secret installation where they raced to break the German codes every day.

At first the Brits teased him relentlessly, imitating his Boston accent and sending up his Yankee mannerisms. But once they realized he knew enough to advance their efforts, he became part of the team. Living conditions had been spartan. "They were unwilling to waste a handful of coal that might be better used in the boiler of a troop train or a destroyer. I literally heard my teeth chatter." Lily and Abigail had knitted him sweater after sweater, but no matter how many layers he donned he was never warm.

We talked about Lily. It was a short walk from his house to hers, and she had spoiled his children as thoroughly as she'd spoiled him. He wouldn't have made it through his mother's final illness without her. She'd moved into the house on Beacon Hill for seven months to keep Rose company and care for her so he could keep on teaching.

Finally, he broached the most difficult topic, Billy. How ironic that Arthur was the one person to whom I could truly talk about Billy. "For years, I hoped he would get better. I prayed the nightmares would stop and the tremors subside, that time, and love, would do the work of bringing him back to himself.

"He has had too much time alone, to brood about the past. I pressured him to go back to work; I even suggested he apply for a job as an orderly at the hospital. I thought taking care of people in that setting might lead him back to the world where he'd helped so many others to survive. But seeing people in pain just brought it all back. When he had to quit, he felt ashamed, and it was all my fault. During the Depression he got a job working in a garden, and he found peace there."

"Why do you blame yourself?" Arthur asked. "The war wasn't your fault."

"Why didn't I see that asking him to work in a hospital was like asking him to walk back into the fire? What a stupid, benighted idea. I still regret not talking him out of going to France in the first place."

"How could you possibly have done that? I'm sure he felt just as Nathaniel and I did. We had to go."

"Maybe if he hadn't been there the whole time . . . "

Arthur cut me off. "That was his choice. You couldn't have stopped him. That's why I love you. Once you take responsibility, you never let go. You're not hearing a word I'm saying, are you? Stop punishing yourself for something you could not possibly have changed."

"Maybe," I said. "But I wrecked all our lives."

"Have you been living with that crazy notion all this time?"

I nodded.

After a moment, he said, "You broke my heart—you know that. And hearts badly broken never mend completely. I clung to the hope you would decide to come to me. In that, I was supremely selfish. I wanted you to leave Billy. That I put myself ahead of a man so damaged, damaged in the very act of trying to save lives destroyed by the war I despised. Next to his sacrifices, mine were insignificant.

"I failed you, utterly, that night in Souilly. Why didn't I listen? Why couldn't I hear what you were telling me? Instead, I closed myself off, like a razor clam slamming shut. I'm ashamed to admit it, but I didn't really hear a word about what Billy needed. You needed me to understand how impossible your position was. You needed me to see there was only one decision you could make. That didn't mean you were turning away from me, but that was how it felt.

"All I could think was that I had lost Isabel, and now I was losing you. I was just a welter of pain, and I had to get away. All I felt was rejection—you turning your back on me—when what you needed was my help.

"It took me years to see that. By the time I did, it was too late. Unfortunately for us, it was only after I had a family that loved and protected me did I grow strong enough to understand what I couldn't see in Souilly—that I, too, was damaged, earlier, in a more hidden, more commonplace way, nothing to do with the war. A sense of abandonment dogged me after my father died, and I was left alone, with my mother. All that had obscured my vision. I was always protecting myself, without knowing I did.

"In the years when you were still reaching out for me, I told myself you wanted me to leave you alone, to respect your decision—to go home, to care for Billy—a decision made instinctively, that spoke for the best in you.

"I knew you were sacrificing your happiness to care for those who needed you, and I didn't know what to do about that. If you'd come to Boston and left them to fend for themselves, I believed you would never have forgiven yourself. Guilt would have dogged you. I know you haven't been carefree here, but I think your conscience rested easier."

"I feel so guilty about the pain I caused you, and the sadness," I said. Reaching into my handbag, I took out the small green leather box and handed it to him. He looked uncertain, so I said: "Open it."

Inside the box was the ring, the oval sapphire encircled by little gold leaves, he'd given me when he asked me to marry him. I heard a sharp intake of breath.

"It doesn't really belong to me," I said. "Because I left you. I wanted you to fight to keep me. You tried, then you gave up, but I shouldn't blame you." I hadn't meant to be so direct. The words just slipped out. They sounded accusatory.

"No, no, Evelyn, please keep it. It does belong to you." He reached over and took my hand in his. I returned the pressure.

"You made the sacrifices. I had Abigail. I had the children you and I dreamed about. I hate that you ended up in that high school. That you lost the chance to become a mathematician. You would have done work no one else has done. That's an incalculable loss."

"Perhaps. When I was younger, it galled me that I'd had to let go of my theoretical work. But as time went by, I made at least a partial peace with it, as I grew to see value in my teaching. Until I met you, I'd lived too much in my mind, discounting people and their needs. You showed me people are more important than numbers."

"You're giving me too much credit. Your father taught you everything you needed to know about love, long before I met you." A smile spread across his face. "However, I would agree that when I first met you, you were a little lost in the world of the abstract. But it wasn't hard to lure you out of there. Mathematicians can have hearts, too—though there are quite a few who don't." He laughed and I joined in. "But that would never have been you."

"When I first got home, I thought I would go to graduate school," I said. "But my parents could barely pay their bills. They needed me to bring in an income. Such commonplace concerns govern more lives than you think, Arthur."

The chagrin on his face shut me up. I apologized. The last thing I wanted was to make him feel guilty, especially for something that was not his fault.

"My darling," he said, "this is our one chance to talk. I don't want to spoil it by arguing. I came because I wanted to know about you. May I ask a question?"

"Of course."

"Are you happy?"

"Sometimes," I said. "And you?"

"Yes, I am. Abigail is wonderful to me. But you and I know there are different kinds of happiness, don't we?"

CHAPTER 55

June 3, 1951

Five months later, Lily phoned me to tell me Arthur had died in the night. Once I understood what she had said, I dropped the phone and stood there, unable to move.

Eventually, I picked up the receiver and asked the operator to place a call for me to Lily. When she answered, I apologized, and she said, "No need, darling."

"But I just saw him in January," I said to her. "He was in the prime of life. Too young to die."

"It was his heart," Lily said.

"But I just saw him—I don't believe it."

"None of us do yet, dear. This morning the doctor told me he'd had angina for years, like his father, but he never mentioned it. He didn't want to worry us."

"So you didn't have a chance to say goodbye."

"That's what he wanted. You know how he hated saying goodbye."

She asked if I would come for the funeral. I told her I would let her know soon, but I needed a little time to think.

I stood there in the hall, by the phone, after we hung up, held captive by the childlike idea that as long as I didn't move, it wouldn't be true. Arthur wouldn't be dead.

That night, when I lay down in bed, I could no longer pretend. I was grieving, but I couldn't cry. Some things are too deep for tears. When I woke up the next morning, my body ached as if I'd been beaten.

I wasn't sure about the funeral. Like Arthur, I hated saying goodbye, but I needed to.

CHAPTER 56

Cambridge, Massachusetts
June 11, 1951

The church, built before the Revolution, was spare and white, no stained glass or ornaments of any kind, just what you'd expect in New England. The austerity of the building made the scarlet cross embroidered on the white damask pall shine like a jewel. I'd finally made my trip to Boston, much too late.

Nathaniel, Arthur's brother, delivered the eulogy. A good deal taller and thinner than Arthur, he was nearly as angular as Jedidiah had been. He began by talking about what a shock it had been to see his little brother transformed from a pest into one of the most illustrious linguists of the twentieth century, which made everyone laugh.

I couldn't stop thinking I'd missed my chance, in that restaurant, when we were together. If only I had told him I loved him more now than I did then. If only.

Nathaniel ended with a story. A few weeks earlier, the two of them had sat up late, by the fire in Arthur's library, reminiscing about the war.

Suddenly Arthur had said, "I still feel badly—you were at the front, fighting, and I wasn't."

"Of course, I argued that he was looking at it all wrong," Nathaniel said. "I pointed out that successful code-breakers, savers of lives, had been scarce as hen's teeth. For every talented cryptographer like him, there'd been a thousand lieutenants like me who could blow a whistle and go over the top."

Gazing at the dying embers, Arthur had said, "You're not hearing what I need to tell you. This is about my personal accounting to myself. I was never tested as you were. I will never know if I could have faced my fears. I think about the man who took my place in the line. Did he die? Was his body wounded? His mind damaged? Why him and not me?"

Nathaniel had captured the essence of his brother, the man who could never rest easy, who always asked too much of himself. When Arthur and I had talked a few months earlier, he'd argued that this same quality had been a liability for me, causing me to sacrifice my happiness. The pot had called the kettle black.

After the last psalm was read, we all went to the graveside and watched as the coffin was lowered into the ground. Abigail, Lily, and the children dropped white roses into the grave. I saw the grief on their faces and wondered if anyone saw mine. I hoped not. If they saw how profound it was, that might lead to questions about who I was, and I didn't want that.

Afterward, back at the house, the hardest moment for me was being introduced to Philip, Arthur's son. As I'd imagined, he looked a lot like his father. I'd always hoped he resembled his father, but at that moment it would have been easier if he had not. I felt a strange sense of dislocation: An old woman now, it was as if I were talking to the double of the man I'd fallen in love with when I was only twenty-three.

When the silence became awkward, I found myself falling back on the obvious. "You look so much like your father. We worked together during the First World War."

Philip answered pleasantly, "Yes, everyone says I look like him. Even Dad thought so." Then he turned to the couple next to me, cousins, and welcomed them to the house. I wanted to grab his arm and say something outrageous like, "I loved your father. And he loved me."

Being in Arthur's house was torture: the beautifully framed photographs on the piano, the sofa where he must have sat with his family in the evenings, an oil portrait of Abigail and her children above the mantel. Perhaps I should have stayed home to mourn Arthur by myself. Then I heard Jedidiah's voice as clearly as if he were standing beside me. "Warned you the first time you were here, during the war. Told you straight off. Bunch of self-congratulatory skunks. Except for Arthur and Lily of course, and that Abigail—she's the genuine article. Couldn't abide most of them when I was alive, don't like 'em anymore now I'm dead."

I smiled to myself. I was glad to see a familiar face approach through the crowd. David Page held out his hand but then, thinking better of it, reached out to hug me. We'd corresponded, but I hadn't seen him for thirty years, a lifetime ago. He'd stayed in Washington at the Treasury Department, rising steadily in the civil service as an economic policy analyst, excellent for the country but a loss for him—he'd given up his chance to be a pioneer in mathematics. I wondered if he regretted passing that up, but I would never have asked.

"It's lovely to see you, dear Evelyn, though I wish it weren't for such a sad reason. Arthur was so young. I never thought he'd go before I did. One of my closest friends. One of those rare folks who cared to listen—and knew how. If the war hadn't brought us together, I would never have had the privilege of knowing him. You must feel that, too."

Page's feelings, so close to my own, might have caused me to unravel, so I just smiled, carefully.

"I often think about you," he continued. "You should have lived the life of a mathematician. You were destined for it. I've asked myself if that didn't happen because you were a woman. Would I have been quicker to see that a male student had his chance? God help me, but I think it's possible."

"I see it differently. I chose to care for my family. For my sake, forgive yourself."

"You're too kind, my dear. Funerals are days of reckoning, when we should face last things. I know you were very close to Arthur. His death must be a huge loss."

Fortunately, Lily appeared. She was tinier even than I remembered but every bit as warm and enthusiastic. Slipping her arm through mine, she pulled me down to where she could kiss my cheek. "I'm so glad you're here. It means a great deal to me you came all this way."

She eased us forward. "Maybe a nice cup of tea would be good. I know you use lemon. Let's get a cup, and I'll introduce you to Abigail. She'll want to meet you."

I considered fleeing the house, but, standing next to Lily, I remembered she had never been anything but kind to me. It would have been thoughtless of me to hurt her and rude to ignore Abigail. This was Abigail's home, and I was her guest. But I whispered to Lily, "I don't know if I can. I'm afraid." I'd watched Abigail as she stood by the grave. In her face and elegant bearing were echoes of the luminous, self-possessed young woman who'd shone at Rose's dinner party so many Christmases ago.

"Afraid?" Lily said. "Now there's no reason for that. It will be fine. I'll be with you. Abigail's a lady, but she's also a straight shooter. Jed was crazy about her, loved that she never took any crap from Rose. You'll feel better if you talk to her. Don't you think?"

After we drank our tea, Lily led me over to Abigail. Kissing her on the cheek, she said, "Dear, I want you to meet someone."

Abigail took my hand and said, "Haven't we met before? A long time ago, during the first war?" I could hardly speak.

"Yes. One Christmas."

"You were Arthur's friend, the one from California."

When I explained that I'd worked with Arthur as a cryptographer in Washington, her face lit up. She asked me to tell her more, because that was the period in his life about which she knew least. He'd never wanted to talk about it. She asked question after question and listened intently to every answer. By the time we were done, I was wrung out, but I also knew how much she'd loved him. All these years I'd cherished the fantasy I would have been the better wife for Arthur. Talking to Abigail, I saw how self-serving that notion had been.

CHAPTER 57

I decided to take the train home instead of flying. I wanted time to be alone and contemplate Arthur's death, to prepare for a life where I would never again see, hear, or touch the man I had most loved. For me, the world had been diminished in a final, irreversible way: A grayness was descending.

As we crossed the plains, I spent hours looking out the window, studying all the little towns that had sprung up. When I'd taken the same train to Washington before I'd even met Arthur, I'd seen little but unbroken prairie. My life had been opening out before me. I was young; anything seemed possible. I was a mathematician who might do great things.

After the war I'd ridden this same train again, home to California, watching Billy break apart, leaving Arthur behind, unsure of how much heartache lay ahead. But still I had had a measure of hope.

Now I was making this journey for the third time, knowing I would never again see Arthur in this life. The engine strained as the train climbed laboriously up into the Sierras, but, after reaching the summit, it raced down the other side of the mountains. I felt precarious, as if the whole train might slide off the tracks into eternity. Without Arthur I had no true anchor in the world.

I was grateful I'd been able to see him one last time. I went over and over that day in January, thinking about something he'd said to me that I hadn't understood at the time: "I decided I could let myself see you, just this once." A message I'd missed then suddenly made sense to me: He'd known death was coming for him. He'd come to say goodbye, and to let me know he'd never stopped loving me. One last gift, carefully hidden— or had I just been too wrapped up in myself to see it? Now it leapt out at me, and I felt his generosity. Arthur owed me less than nothing, but he hadn't seen it that way. I wouldn't have to die wondering if he'd forgiven me.

I began shedding a burden of guilt I'd borne for a long time. For this and for so many other things, I had Arthur to thank. I wished he knew that.

Meeting Abigail had forced me to let go of the egotistical notion that I'd ruined Arthur's life. He had loved her and been loved by her. It was painful to face how badly I'd needed to deceive myself. Our love had been my one great romance, not his.

CHAPTER 58

When I'd been home for a few days, Billy invited me to sit with him in the garden after dinner. Lighting a cigarette and taking a long drag, he said, "Tell me about your trip, dear. I think it was hard."

"Funerals are always hard. Losing an old friend is never easy."

"Old friend?" he asked, gently shaking his head. "I think Arthur was the one. The one from France."

I'd spent so many years guarding my secret. The illusion I'd succeeded had kept me going. But if anyone knew, it would be Billy.

What did it mean to him that I'd never told him about Arthur?

What did it mean to me?

I'd wanted so much to hide what I'd given up in order to protect Billy. Even in this, I had failed.

"You loved him, didn't you?"

I nodded.

"You're the one who always tells me how important it is to talk," he said. "You don't have to, but maybe it would help."

"How did you know?"

"You were so different in France. Radiant. The first time I saw you, at that bombed-out house where you were living, as soon as I looked at your face, I could see something had happened. You were so happy. I'd never seen you like that.

"After we got home, I watched you put the straitjacket on and tie the strings tight. Your face turned gray—you lost heart.

I could see it, but I was so lost in my own sorrow I had nothing left to give.

"You must have felt so alone when I wouldn't talk. It makes me sad—thinking about all the evenings you sat here and kept me company, no matter how silent or moody I was. The truth is I needed you here, so I shut my eyes to anything that might take you away. I stole your happiness."

Billy was answering the questions that had plagued me all these years. Had it helped him that I was there beside him? Yes, he had known I was there, and that had made a difference. Had giving up Arthur been for naught? No. Though I would never stop grieving for the loss of Arthur, my sacrifice had not been pointless. I had helped Billy to get through, to survive.

But I didn't want Billy to pay any more for what I had given up. "That's not how it was," I said. "You know I promised my parents I would come home as soon as the war was over. I couldn't break that promise."

"Maybe you were that crazy. But I don't think so. Let's tell the truth about this before it's too late. The truth can set you free, kiddo. I was the one who ran from it. I think you came home because you thought it was your job to take care of *me*."

I'd never wanted him to know any of this. Now when all I wanted was to be alone with my sorrow, he was dragging me out of the shadows where I'd hidden so long. But it had taken courage for him to say what he'd said. I couldn't lie to him anymore than I could have lied to Arthur.

"I missed him, always."

"Of course you did, honey. Think about all you missed. The husband you wanted. Children. The chance to be a mathematician. We asked too much of you. We just took and took and you gave and gave. It kills me, because it's too late to do anything about it. But that's easy to say now. I got what I wanted."

"No, I made the right choice for me. If I'd left you and gone to Boston, I couldn't have lived with myself, any more than you would have been able to live with yourself if you hadn't gone to France."

"Maybe. But I was just a headstrong kid who needed to prove something to himself."

"God knows we were both headstrong," I said. "But there are moments in life when you have to make a choice, even if the cost is high."

"Will you tell me about him?" Billy said. "Who he was, and what he was like? I'm sure he was a hell of a guy."

Would Billy have asked me these questions if Arthur hadn't died? I would never know. But better, certainly, to have one of them to love than no one at all. I would get something back from all I had lost, perhaps because of all I had lost. I would have the companion I needed on the final leg of my journey.

I looked at Billy's eyes and saw love there. The deadness was gone. I would always miss Arthur, but at least I had the comfort of knowing he'd forgiven me. Billy was right. It would be easier to live with my grief if I could talk about Arthur sometimes. There was so much to tell. Where to begin?

"Arthur believed in me, just as you did, and that meant everything to me."

AFTERWORD

Miss Havilland is a work of fiction, but, in order to write it, I drew on a handful of facts and family legends about my grandmother's cousin Evelyn. I still wear the gold-and-pearl bracelet she gave me for Christmas the year I was thirteen. The last time I saw her, she was in her eighties, and when she stretched her wrinkled hand out to reach for mine, I saw for the first time that she, too, had an identical bracelet.

Cousin Evelyn, as she was always called by my family, earned her master's degree in mathematics at Stanford University in the spring of 1917, soon after the United States made its late entrance into WWI. She was only twenty-two at a time when few women were admitted to the closely guarded preserve of science: Men were happy to slam its gate shut in their faces. But one of Evelyn's professors, for reasons unknown, asked her to accompany him to Washington to do military intelligence. She worked in one of the temporary offices that had been thrown up quickly on the Mall near the Lincoln Memorial. I know nothing about the actual work she did. My grandmother once told me she thought Evelyn had studied the decomposition of German war materiel as part of the effort to determine whether the German army was close to collapse.

My grandmother told my mother that, while Evelyn was in Washington, she had fallen in love with one of her colleagues, who may have been a professor at a college on the Eastern seaboard. She believed that this man had asked Evelyn to marry him and that she had said yes.

But Evelyn's mother—widely regarded by my family as a great witch—insisted that Evelyn return home to care for her father, who was wheelchair-bound. After the war ended, she returned to California, foregoing the marriage and her chance to become a mathematician. Many women of her generation were raised with an iron sense of filial duty. Evelyn chose to do what was expected of her. As far as I know, she never talked about the pain of the sacrifices she made. She was a tough-minded woman who wanted no one's pity.

After Evelyn took the train home from Washington, she was offered two jobs: one teaching math at a private school for girls in San Francisco, the other at a public high school close to home that would have paid a higher salary. My grandmother said Evelyn's mother forced her to take the job in San Francisco. But, as an adult, I noticed that Evelyn was sometimes a bit snobbish. Perhaps she, not her mother, made the decision to teach at the more prestigious school. From 1919 until 1965, when she retired, she taught mathematics, commuting fifty miles by train from San Jose to San Francisco five days a week.

At ninety-four, when Evelyn knew she was dying, she said to my Aunt Vivian, the person in our family closest to her: "Dear, I want you to go to my safe deposit box. There's a ring there, and I want to make sure *you* have that ring."

When Vivian went to the bank, she found a jeweler's box, and, inside it, an old-fashioned solitaire diamond ring. Vivian never dared to ask Evelyn the significance of the ring, and Evelyn never volunteered it.

At six feet tall, Evelyn towered over me when I was a girl. She had the loud voice and commanding presence of a teacher accustomed to ruling her classroom, and she had no trouble holding her own in a political argument with my father, no easy thing.

In those years, my ear was always out on a stalk, especially when it came to Cousin Evelyn. I loved to sit in a corner of my grandmother's living room listening to the women talk. When Evelyn was not there, she was often a subject of conversation, always sympathetic. They were certain Evelyn's mother's selfishness was unforgivable; they talked about how sad it was she had never married and had no children to love.

What made Evelyn riveting to me was the fact that she was the only woman in my family who held a job with intellectual challenge. (Evelyn lived long enough to know that the four color map theorem was finally proved in 1976 by Kenneth Appel and Wolfgang Haken—with the help of a computer.)

It's no coincidence I dreamed about going to Stanford or that I wanted to be a mathematician. I always loved math and still do, but once I saw I wouldn't be traveling beyond calculus, I turned to my greater strength—a love of words. Unlike Evelyn, I have had a good husband, two inspiring daughters, and the chance to become a writer.

I learned many things from Evelyn:

That a woman can stand alone.

That giving up the man you love may be a terrible mistake.

That keeping heartbreak a private matter might be a good choice.

That there can be a value to sacrifice even when it comes at great cost.

In my closet, I keep Evelyn's tattered blue lace dress, handed down to me by my mother. Once in a while I take it out of the box to look at it and imagine the brilliant, charming, surprising young woman who wore it. I hope that when she did, sometimes, she was floating around a dance floor, in the arms of the man she loved.

ACKNOWLEDGMENTS

This book wouldn't exist if I hadn't been lucky enough to marry the gifted editor Jay Lovinger. The year I was sixty, he said, "You've always wanted to write a novel, and you're not getting any younger. One other thing: stop comparing everything you write to Virginia Woolf and Henry James. Just write it."

I did write it, but it would have been a much lesser book without his encouragement and painstaking edits. He read *Miss Havilland* in many incarnations; he even read it out loud to me because he believed that was the best way to spot a saggy sentence or to find out if the voice of a character sounds true.

My great regret is that Jay did not live to see the finished book and hold it in his hand.

Wendy Lucero and Shelly Robelotto, my sisters, were my first readers. I figured they probably wouldn't trash it, bad for family relations. Instead, their enthusiasm for what I had written gave me the courage I needed to keep going. For this I will always be grateful.

Miss Havilland might never have seen the light of day if it weren't for my daring, kind and hilarious publisher Mike Sager. He founded his company, The Sager Group, with the intention of harnessing the means of production: for the sake of the writer but also with an appreciation for every person involved in the actual making of a book. If there were more publishers like Mike, fewer writers would be hanging off a ledge considering a jump.

My dear friend Gerri Hirshey introduced me to Mike Sager, for which I thank her. She also connected me with her superb agent, Flip Brophy. Flip and her invaluable assistant, Nell Pierce, never lost faith in my book, and I appreciate their willingness to take a risk on a writer who showed up with a first novel in hand.

So many friends have stood by me I could not list them all. They include Peter Carlson, Ingfei and Eefei Chen, Candace Cohen, John Crew, Joseph D'Agnese, my brother John Daly, the late Brad Darrach, Bruce Duffy, Brian Fallon, Robert Fleder and Marilyn Johnson, Stuart Gardiner and Mary Frances Burns, the late Bart Giamatti, Geoffrey and Annabel Hemstedt, Elisabeth Herz, Rebecca High, Diane and Esme Howard, Deborah Hudson and Robert Cox, Linda Hutton, Brenda Hyde, Heidi Jerome, the late Jay Leyda, Robert Lipsyte, Rachel Lovinger, James McBride, Steven Mays, Jack and Lila Nields, Jenifer Nields, Laura and Mark Page, Jay Reddersen, Vassa Shevel, James, Rob and Sandy Swinehart, Michael Small and Cindy Ruskin, John and Ellen Walsh, Michael Walsh, and Phyllis Wender.

Because they have taught me so much about courage and about love, I thank my daughters Woo and Wendy Lovinger.

GUIDE FOR BOOK CLUB DISCUSSION

Evelyn:

In the last months of the war, Evelyn comes to see that the idealism, which led her and Arthur to dedicate themselves to the war effort, has started to wither and die. During the final battle of the Meuse-Argonne, she calls herself no better than a sniper, just one of "thousands of cogs in a giant machine that ground forward, destroying everything in its path." Do you think her experience of herself as a destroyer may have increased the responsibility she felt to become Billy's protector?

When Evelyn visits Billy at his hospital after the armistice, she quickly decides she will have to take him home to California instead of traveling to Boston to marry Arthur. How did you feel when she changed her plans?

Did Evelyn's long experience of seeing the constant care her father needed influence her sense of personal responsibility to care for Billy?

Once Evelyn and Billy return home, she is never able to leave Billy or go to Boston, even though she wants to. Why do you feel she couldn't?

If Evelyn had been a man, do you think she would have made the same decisions?

Arthur:

Why do you think Arthur could not leave his family and go to California to marry Evelyn?

He tells her, early in their courtship, that he is still heavily influenced by the Boston Brahmin culture in which he was raised, even though he has long fought to resist the limitations and absurdities of that culture. Do you believe his heritage held him back?

Did you feel his inability to find a way to bring about their marriage was a failure of emotional strength? To what extent did his sense of responsibility to care for Rose and for Lily stop him from leaving Boston?

In his final conversation with Evelyn, he holds himself to account and explains that he believes he failed her. How did you feel about his choices as you read the book?

Were you sympathetic to him because he felt rejected by Evelyn?

Or did you feel that, living in a time and place where men had far greater power to make decisions about their lives than women did, he was right—he did fail Evelyn?

Or did you feel sorry for them because in the end they were both victims of their circumstances, daunted by challenges and misunderstandings so complicated they could not overcome them to be together?

Billy:

One could argue that Billy pays the highest price in human suffering of any character in the book because of the degree to which he is hurt by what he lived through during the war. His willingness to help the Allies, even when his own country was not willing to engage, speaks of courage and selflessness. On the other hand, his withdrawal from Evelyn and his irritation with—as he sees it—her meddling and pressuring him to do what she wants exacts a great price from her, and it might be easy to lose patience with Billy. At moments, even Evelyn, who loves him deeply, gets angry with him.

Did you ever feel angry with Billy, and, if you did, why do you think that you were?

Will:

Evelyn's father is her teacher and her protector. She is grateful to him and depends upon his support, especially when she is young, for her intellectual growth and emotional safety. But he also demands a great deal of her, sometimes in subtle ways.

Do you think she realizes that he does? Does he stand in the way of her living a life she would have chosen?

Did your view of Will change after his death when Hannah finally tells Evelyn about their courtship, his accident and the early years of their marriage?

Hannah:

Does Evelyn's relationship with her mother change over the course of the book? Are there moments when you feel Hannah does love Evelyn or that she is at least trying to show Evelyn she loves her? How does Hannah express her feelings?

What is missing in their relationship, and why do you think it is missing?

Does Evelyn feel guilty about her inability to love her mother?

Is it possible that by sacrificing herself to care for Billy Evelyn is, without realizing it, trying to prove to her mother she is not proud or selfish?

Does your view of Hannah change while she is telling the story of falling in love with Will and the accident that changed the course of their life together?

What part do clothes play in the book, with regard not only to how Evelyn sees herself but especially with regard to Hannah and Evelyn's relationship?

Rose:

One could dismiss Rose Bayard in her effort to secure Abigail Cranford as a wife for Arthur as just one more in the long tradition of fictional mothers who wish to secure for their child a suitable mate from the right sort of family and possessed of a substantial inheritance.

Do you see anything in Rose's demeanor or behavior that suggests there may have been deeper layers of genuine feeling and concern hidden beneath her hard social persona? Perhaps in her reaction to her husband's death? Or in Nathaniel's teasing his brother when he says Rose would happily move to New Haven if Arthur chooses Yale over Harvard?

Lily:
Arthur's Aunt Lily is perhaps the only character in the book who loves Evelyn unconditionally. Unlike Rose, she feels no competition with Evelyn for Arthur's love and attention. What sets Lily apart from the other women in the book?

Like Evelyn, she never marries, but she seems to have made peace with that fact. Does she strike you in this way? If she doesn't seem at peace to you, why not?

Mentors:
Evelyn's mother is often—though not always—harsh, demanding and short-tempered. In the course of the story, Evelyn builds relationships with several older women: Elsie Koenig, Nina Chapman, and Arthur's Aunt Lily, who serve as mentors and offer Evelyn a good deal of the approval and affection she would have liked to receive from her mother.

What does Evelyn learn from her mentors? Does she change in light of what she has learned?

Women in mathematics:
The Afterword mentions that my grandmother's cousin, the woman who inspired me to write this novel, received her master's degree in mathematics in 1917 "when few women were admitted to the closely guarded preserve of science." It

may be easier today for women to become mathematicians, but that does *not* mean it is anything resembling easy.

In 2016, in the United States, women in academia held 15 percent of tenure-track positions in math, 18 percent in computer science and 14 percent in engineering.

Growing up, did you find mathematics interesting? Did you feel comfortable in math classes? Did you persist even if you were not always comfortable?

If you have daughters—or sons since math can be difficult for anyone—have you tried to encourage them to explore mathematics?

World War I and shell shock:
World War I marked the beginning of modern warfare. Developments in weapon technology: machine guns, barbed wire, poison gas and airplanes, turned war into slaughter on a scale the world had never seen. At the start of the war, the effects of these fresh horrors were not known. The term shell shock was invented on the battlefields by soldiers and doctors who saw it happening before their eyes.

The term did not appear in the medical literature until a psychiatrist published an article in the British journal *Lancet* in February 1915, six months after the Germans swept into neutral Belgium and sparked the start of the war.

Shell shock was often dismissed as cowardice, and men suffering from it were sometimes shot for treason. The phenomenon of shell shock was confounding to the military and to the doctors trying to treat it because it manifested in such a wide array of symptoms, including tremor, nightmares, insomnia, impaired sight or hearing, stammering, muteness and paralysis. As the war progressed, many strategies were tried, from electroshock to ether or chloroform to extended periods of rest, rest being usually offered to officers rather than to enlisted men.

In 1942, 58 percent of patients in Veterans Administration hospitals were still being treated for shell shock from WWI. So Billy would not have been alone.

Vietnam and the wars in Iraq and Afghanistan, fought with even more vicious weapons, have added PTSD (post-traumatic stress disorder) and TBI (traumatic brain injury) to our medical lexicon. While they are no longer ignored, and treatment has advanced, there is still a refusal to fund the care these veterans need and to make sure the VA provides the highest standard of care.

Why do you think that we, as a nation, cannot commit to meeting the physical and psychological needs of the men and women who have protected our freedoms at such great cost to themselves?

Evelyn and Billy:
As children, Evelyn and Billy experience each other almost as twins. They often know what the other one is thinking. That closeness grows and grows until the emotional damage that Billy suffered during the war creates tension between them.

However, Evelyn's love for Billy is deep enough that she tolerates the tension and fights to save Billy, no matter how stoutly he resists. Only once does she make an overt bid to escape Billy when she sets out to take the train to Boston.

As she sits on bench in the waiting room of the station in San Francisco, she asks herself questions about her relationship with Billy that may also have occurred to the reader: "If [Billy] hadn't been so much like a brother, what might have happened? Did I love him more than I should? I'd never told him about Arthur. I never wanted him to know he had a rival. I couldn't risk his loving me less than completely."

Evelyn doesn't answer those questions directly. As a reader who has observed her closely, how would you answer them?

A Different Time:
Inevitably, we look at books we read through the lens of our own moment in history, which can make it hard to assess the strains and difficulties Evelyn and Arthur face, despite the fact that they loved each other deeply.

Some readers may wonder why Evelyn didn't insist her own happiness was important. But perhaps others won't find that so difficult to imagine—many women today who hold down demanding jobs also struggle to run a household, find child-care and take care of their parents or their spouse's parents—so they may have more in common with Evelyn than one might guess.

Where do you see yourself on this spectrum? Do you feel confident you would have gone to Boston? Or uncertain?

Do you feel Evelyn was trapped by her moment in history? Or that she should have fought more fiercely for her own happiness?

Can you imagine why she felt such a binding responsibility to stay home to take care of Billy as well as her parents and Dora? Or do you feel she failed herself by not getting on the train and making the journey to Boston?

Have you thought about the experiences of your grandmothers or great-grandmothers, who grew up in the same years as Evelyn and may have faced equally hard choices?

FOR FURTHER READING

If you want to learn more about the context and texture of Evelyn Havilland's life during the war, here are a few suggestions for books to read. There are also film clips of battles, the trenches and field hospitals available online.

An excellent account of WWI:
Gilbert, Martin. *The First World War: a complete history*. New York, Henry Holt, 1994.

For more about the experience of soldiers who endured shell shock during WWI and in the years afterward:
Shephard, Ben. *A War of Nerves: soldiers and psychiatrists in the 20ᵗʰ Century*. Cambridge, Harvard University Press, 2001.

To learn about the nurses who cared for the wounded and dying:
Brittain, Vera. *The Testament of Youth*. New York, Penguin Books, 1994.

Extraordinary poetry was written by soldiers, sailors and pilots:
Egremont, Max. *Some Desperate Glory: the First World War the poets knew*. New York, Farrar, Straus & Giroux, 2014.

For more about the history of cryptography:
Kahn, David. *The Codebreakers: the history of secret writing*. New York, Macmillan, 1967.

The character Herbert Yardley, fictional leader of the cryptographic department in which Evelyn works, is based on the life of Herbert O. Yardley, who headed that department during the war:

Kahn, David. *The Reader of Gentlemen's Mail: Herbert O. Yardley and the birth of American codebreaking*. New Haven, Yale University Press, 2004.

Yardley, Herbert O. *The American Black Chamber*. Indianapolis, Indiana, Bobbs-Merrill, 1931.

To learn more about the American expatriates who cared for refugees in Paris and built an ambulance corps, read this extraordinary memoir:

Wood, Eric Fisher. *The Note Book of an Attaché: Seven Months in the War Zone*. New York, A. L. Burt Company, 1915.

You can easily find film clips of the war on the Internet. To watch an eleven-minute montage of combat footage uploaded by the Marine Corps Film Archive:

https://www.youtube.com/watch?v=Lgfi-udrLne

There is a wealth of still photographs and unpublished memoirs on the Internet. During the war, soldiers and battles were documented by painters and illustrators hired by the U.S. Army to create a visual history:

Cornebise, Alfred E. *War Diary of a Combat Artist: Captain Harry Everett Townsend*. Niwot, Colorado, University Press of Colorado, 1991.

ABOUT THE AUTHOR

Gay Daly attended Sarah Lawrence College for two years, then transferred into the first class of women undergraduates at Yale, graduating summa cum laude in 1971. She stayed at Yale for graduate school, where she wrote *Foundresses of Nothing*, a dissertation about George Eliot's ambivalence toward her heroines.

After teaching at Memphis State University, St. Lawrence University, and Antioch College, Daly left academics to pursue a career as a writer. In New York she worked as a fact-checker and reporter at *People* while she wrote the book *Preraphaelites in Love*, a history of seven women who modeled for Victorian painters and then married them.

Later, Daly worked as a senior editor at *Discover*, where she covered medicine, archaeology, and the politics of science. Annually she edited the year-end issue: 100 Stories of the Year in Science. Since returning to freelancing, Daly has specialized in medical and environmental journalism. *Miss Havilland* is her first novel.

ABOUT THE PUBLISHER

The Sager Group was founded in 1984. In 2012, it was chartered as a multimedia content brand, with the intent of empowering those who create art—an umbrella beneath which makers can pursue, and profit from, their craft directly, without gatekeepers. TSG publishes books; ministers to artists and provides modest grants; designs logos, products and packaging, and produces documentary, feature, and commercial films. By harnessing the means of production, The Sager Group helps artists help themselves. To read more from The Sager Group, visit www.TheSagerGroup.net

Artifex Te Adiuva